D1055549

THE EDGE OF FOREVER

THE EDGE OF FOREVER

NANCY KELLEY

FIVE STAR

An imprint of Thomson Gale, a part of The Thomson Corporation

Detroit • New York • San Francisco • New Haven, Conn. • Waterville, Maine • London

THOMSON
GALE

LIBRARY OF CONGRESS CATALOGING-IN-PUBLICATION DATA

Kelley, Nancy.
    The edge of forever / Nancy Kelley. — 1st ed.
      p. cm.
    ISBN-13: 978-1-59414-578-0 (alk. paper)
    ISBN-10: 1-59414-578-4 (alk. paper)
    1. Drug traffic—Fiction. 2. Kidnapping victims—Fiction. 3. Washington (D.C.)—Fiction. I. Title.
PS3611.E4434E34 2007
813'.6—dc22
                                    2006038266

First Edition. First Printing: July 2007.

Published in 2007 in conjunction with Tekno Books.

Printed in the United States of America on permanent paper
10 9 8 7 6 5 4 3 2 1

I dedicate this book to my grandmother, whose love of story telling was my first inspiration for writing, and to my mother, in recognition of her unwavering support and constant encouragement for me to pursue my dreams.

CHAPTER ONE

" 'To the vultures assembled to feed on my carcass, I leave to each one of them the sum of one hundred dollars.' "

The lawyer's statement caused a choked, communal gasp among the Wilsons. They stared back at him in stunned silence as though some noxious substance had been released into the air of the drawing room, robbing them of speech and movement.

Jennifer Denton hitched her shoulder away from the furnace heat of the over-sized fireplace and looked toward the closely herded family group. Their facial expressions ranged from young Phil's amused contempt to his mother's stunned disbelief.

And who could blame them?

Jennifer's gaze moved around the room. Well-polished, antique furniture, sitting on priceless rugs, showcased the kind of wealth most people could only imagine. Paintings by well-known artists hung on every wall. She studied the contents of the glass-fronted cabinets. The crisply burning logs cast a mellow glow on a collection of porcelain figurines and shelf after shelf of silver and gold objects.

The contents of this room must represent only the tip of the iceberg in the value of Belinda Wilson's estate. No wonder her family members were so upset. Some of them had traveled several thousand miles to the Washington, D.C. area for the reading of the will. They expected to leave with a sizeable inheritance.

Instead, they each had one hundred dollars.

A log on the fireplace burst with a gigantic pop that ricocheted around the room like a controlled explosion. Closer to the sound than the others, Jennifer jumped forward in the high-backed chair before she realized what caused the noise. She smiled and then settled back against the plush velvet.

The noise apparently freed the tongues of the family members. Strident voices overlapped each other as they jumped to their feet and surged toward the lawyer's table.

Jennifer wrinkled her nose when Phil's sister Barbara crossed in front of the fireplace. The woman's perfume left a musty layer of scent in her wake that threatened to suffocate the pleasant aromas of the Christmas tree and the other evergreens.

"This is ridiculous!"

Jennifer had heard that shrill, female voice every day for the past six months. The tone never varied. She would have bet every dollar in her meager bank account that Amelia, the new matriarch of the family, would be the first to recover her senses and her outrage.

"There must be some mistake, Mr. Banning." Amelia shook an accusing finger at the lawyer. "I saw the will. The assets of the estate are divided equally among all of us."

Barbara pushed to her mother's side. "That's right." Tall and fashionably thin, she bore little resemblance to her dumpy brother Phil who stood behind her. "And Aunt Belinda promised to give me half of her jewelry."

"Pay no attention to my sister." Phil's lips curved into a mocking smile. "She gets greedy at Christmas time."

"Shut up, Phil," Barbara shot back. "You're the greedy one."

"Stop it, both of you." Amelia's wrinkled features twisted with anger. "We have to find the original will."

"Ten days ago, Mrs. Wilson drew up a new one."

The lawyer had stunned them for the second time. They

exchanged glances and murmured among themselves until Amelia shrugged and said, "She must have gone senile."

"At her request, a team of psychiatrists examined Mrs. Wilson when she was in the hospital last month," Banning replied. "They pronounced her sane and competent."

Amelia's husband Harold stood several inches taller than the others. He cleared his throat and said, over the tops of their heads, "My attorney will contact you, Mr. Banning. You can expect a visit from him when he returns to Washington after Christmas."

"We'll discuss that later." Amelia swung around and pointed a bony finger in Jennifer's direction. "After she leaves."

The Wilsons turned to stare at Jennifer. The open hostility on their faces contrasted sharply with the cheerful Christmas decorations and the glow of the crackling flames.

Amelia's thin shoulders lifted with an incensed breath. "I want that woman out of my house."

"*Your* house, Mrs. Wilson?"

Spots of color bloomed in the woman's sallow cheeks in response to the lawyer's question. "We've lived here for ten years. I've been the mistress of this house since poor Aunt Belinda had her stroke. Who else would look after the place as I've done?"

He held up the paper in his hand. "You only heard the first sentence of this document. I am instructed to read the contents to everyone concerned."

"Then tell that woman to leave."

"My client requested that Miss Denton be present. She will therefore remain." Banning looked toward Jennifer. "Mrs. Wilson included some final remarks to you."

"Tough luck, Jen," Phil murmured.

The comment evoked a few laughs, but they died out when Banning said, "This is hardly the time for levity."

Phil shrugged. "I only meant that if Jen expected something more than gratitude from her patient, she has our sympathy."

The family laughed their appreciation of the remark but fell silent when Banning's narrowed gaze moved among them. With his stocky build, sparse, gray hair, and bushy eyebrows, he reminded Jennifer of a formidable teacher from her high school years. One look from that man's dark eyes could quiet a noisy classroom in two seconds flat. Apparently, Banning wielded the same influence.

Amelia's narrowed glance stabbed at Jennifer. "Look at her. Sitting there as if she owned the place."

"Don't distress yourself, madam," Banning cautioned.

"Instead of dealing with her like the ill-trained servant that she is, you're treating her like one of the family." Amelia gave a disgusted snort. "Next, you'll tell me that this insulting woman is a long lost relative."

"I assure you, madam. Miss Denton is not related to you."

"Of course not." Amelia's thin lips pushed into a sneer. "No Wilson ever had hair like that."

She gave Jennifer another contemptuous glance and then turned away amid chuckles from her family.

Carrot head, carrot head, nobody likes a carrot head.

No one had said those words to Jennifer for a long time, but the childhood taunt still carried a sting. For six months, she'd put up with the family's interfering, their thinly veiled insults about her and her capabilities as a nurse, and their pointed avoidance of Mrs. Wilson.

After today, she'd never have to see any of them again.

"If you must read the document, get on with it. This has been an upsetting day." Amelia heaved a sigh. "We need to be alone, to deal with our grief."

Banning looked toward Jennifer. She dismissed the twinkle in his eyes as a reflection caused by the burning logs until the corners of his mouth lifted. What was there in any of this business that the lawyer found amusing?

He lifted the sheet of paper and read, " 'My great-niece Martha was the only member of the family who showed me kindness and love. Had she lived, she would have been my heiress.' "

"Is this some sort of a joke?" Amelia screeched.

Banning continued reading. " 'Martha's husband is missing and presumed dead. Since her will leaves custody of her son to me, in the event her husband is also deceased, I leave all of the money and properties in my possession to Martha's son, John Stuart Kendall.' "

"It . . . it can't be true."

" 'Upon his arrival in my home, I direct that John be placed in Jennifer Denton's care.' "

The Wilsons turned as one to look in her direction.

She dug her fingernails into the rich fabric covering the arm of the chair and said, in a voice that only wobbled a bit, "Why does John need my care?"

"Because he's only six years old."

"I knew that nurse was up to no good," Amelia scoffed. "I never trusted her."

Other family members echoed the words.

Jennifer's mouth had gone dry. She focused on the lawyer's face. "The boy's father is dead?"

"Presumably." Before she could fashion the obvious question, he added, "Two weeks ago, Mrs. Wilson received a letter from the American Embassy in Panama concerning John's father, Stuart Kendall, a member of the diplomatic corps. His car had been found nearly a month previous in a nearby river." He paused. "They didn't find Kendall. They think that he drowned. The local authorities are, however, continuing the search for another few weeks."

Jennifer whispered, "Poor little boy."

"Since that time, John has been under the care of the embassy nurse." Banning turned to speak to the Wilsons. "As is the custom, both Martha and her husband filed wills at the embassy. Each document contains the provision that should John's parents be unable to provide for him, his custody shall revert to Belinda Wilson. As per those instructions, the embassy letter to Mrs. Wilson stated that the boy would be delivered to this house within two weeks." Banning paused for emphasis. "It was after receipt of the letter that Mrs. Wilson changed her will."

"But Aunt Belinda's gone," Amelia protested. "One of us should have been named the child's guardian."

Harold held up a hand to quiet his wife. "All in good time, my dear."

Banning bent over the document again. " 'If Jennifer accepts the responsibility, her guardianship of John shall be for a six-month period, during which time American authorities will launch an all-out search for Stuart Kendall. At the end of that time, the situation with Jennifer and the boy will be reviewed and a decision made about a more permanent arrangement.' "

"Maybe Jen doesn't want to play mother to Martha's brat," Barbara suggested.

"Mrs. Wilson considered that." Banning began reading again. " 'If Jennifer chooses not to accept the proposed offer, she shall be paid fifty thousand dollars for her services to me. The responsibility for John will then be addressed in another letter in the possession of Mr. Banning.' "

Phil moved forward. "What does the other letter say?"

"That doesn't concern you."

"It concerns all of us," Phil countered.

"Be quiet, son," Harold commanded. "Let him finish."

The lawyer adjusted the glasses on his nose and bent over the document again. " 'Walter Banning has been my advisor and my friend for more than twenty years. The management of

John's estate is hereby entrusted to Mr. Banning with the stipulation that all moneys, stipends, or monthly payments previously allotted to the Wilson family be immediately stopped.' "

"It isn't legal." Amelia's complexion grew alarmingly pale. "It can't be."

" 'If Jennifer assumes the guardianship for John, she will live in my home and function as its mistress. At her discretion, Amelia's family may retain their current living quarters within the house.' "

"A common nurse, mistress of this home?" Amelia's chin jutted at the lawyer. "Aunt Belinda wouldn't do that to me."

" 'Should Jennifer decide at any time to relinquish her duties toward John or should John's father return to claim his son, her tenure as John's guardian will cease. She will then be tendered a lump sum payment of fifty thousand dollars.' " Banning refolded the sheet of paper. "The remainder of the letter is to be read privately to Miss Denton." He looked in her direction. "Will you accompany me to the library?"

"That won't be necessary," Harold commented. "We'll go upstairs."

Jennifer had only had a moment to wonder about the pleased look on the lawyer's face before Barbara stalked closer.

"You can't lose either way, Jen." Her lips curved into a humorless smile. "You did your work well, didn't you? Poisoning Aunt Belinda against us, telling her lies to win her trust."

Phil's eyes chilled to chips of blue ice as his gaze focused on Jennifer's face. "Martha was adopted. She wasn't a Wilson by blood. Neither is her son."

Barbara's fingers flexed as though she meant to claw Jennifer's face with her long nails. "You won't get away with this, Jen. I'll see you dead first!"

"Easy, Barb." Phil leaped forward and grabbed his sister's

13

arms. "We'll get what we deserve." His malevolent gaze raked Jennifer's face. "And so will you."

"You look a bit shaken, Miss Denton."

She pushed off the chair and walked over to the desk. "It isn't every day that someone threatens to kill me."

"Empty words." Banning turned away toward a serving cart. "How about some coffee?"

"Thank you."

She sat down on the nearest seat, a beautiful and irreplaceable French Provincial chair that belonged in a museum. Ordinarily, she wouldn't sit on the delicately embroidered surface, but these weren't ordinary circumstances.

"Miss Denton?"

She jumped. "Hmmnn?"

"Do you like cream?" At her nod, Banning poured a generous dollop into one of the cups and walked back to her chair. "This will fix you up."

She cradled the cup in her hands, willing the hot liquid to warm her fingers. "Please call me Jennifer."

"It will be my pleasure."

He lowered his bulk gingerly into the chair matching hers, heard an ominous squeak, and quickly rose to his feet and retrieved another chair. "Are you ready to hear the portion of the document addressed to you?"

She nodded.

He stretched across the table and scooped it up. " 'I chose you, Jennifer, because you have sense and good character. I also like and trust you. It is my fervent wish that you accept this responsibility. Forgive me if I exert an old lady's privilege and beg you, in remembrance of our friendship, to accept the guardianship of John.' "

"She has made it difficult for me to refuse."

Banning chuckled. "That's exactly what she meant to do."

"John must be feeling lost. He needs friendship and understanding."

Banning's narrowed gaze studied her for a moment. "That sounds like you've had first-hand experience in child welfare."

The delicious brew turned bitter in Jennifer's mouth. "I acquired that first-hand experience, as you put it, by losing my mother when I was only a little older than John. A social worker delivered me to my one living relative, an elderly aunt whom I'd never seen before. She didn't want me, but she couldn't refuse to take care of me. It would have damaged her social standing."

"A bad situation for you."

"I lived in a small room on the top floor of her house except when she had visitors. She liked to exhibit me before her friends, to show them what an honorable thing she was doing in taking care of an ungrateful child."

"Is that what you were?"

"Of course not. I was grateful that she took me in and gave me a place to live, but how would you feel toward someone who didn't like you and constantly told you how worthless you were?"

He nodded. "I understand."

Memories flooded over the barriers Jennifer had erected against them. "She locked me in a closet once. Instead of breaking my spirit, as she intended, that incident made me determined to survive." Jennifer paused. "She always told me that I was ugly."

Banning murmured, "Your hair in particular?"

That surprised her. "How did you know?"

"I saw your reaction when Mrs. Wilson made that unfortunate remark." His gaze fastened on Jennifer's face. "You have the kind of low, soft voice that anyone, particularly a child, would find soothing. You also have pretty, red hair, even if you *do* keep it in a bun."

15

Her hand lifted defensively to the back of her neck.

"You're tall and slender, and your green eyes twinkle when you smile." Banning reached out to pat her hand. "You have a great deal of beauty, Jennifer Denton."

"Thank you."

The chime of his cell phone prompted a whispered, "Excuse me."

She took a calming breath and released it in a long sigh. An understanding teacher had helped her through those first, traumatic months in her aunt's house. Warm memories set a smile on Jennifer's lips. Ada Perkins had kept in touch with her through the years and had encouraged her to pursue nurse's training. By helping John to find his way at this difficult time of his life, she could repay at least a part of the debt she owed to that wonderful lady.

Jennifer's gaze focused upon the rosewood grand piano, sitting on a raised platform at the end of the room. On her patient's last trip downstairs, the old lady had hobbled over to sit on the padded seat and lovingly run her swollen fingers over the keys.

"My husband gave me . . . this piano for . . . a wedding present. He used to serenade me. This was his . . . favorite song."

Though short of breath and obviously in pain, she had sung an off-key version of "Let Me Call You Sweetheart."

That same night, Mrs. Wilson had talked about her life with her husband and her sorrow at their inability to have children. She had asked if Jennifer liked children. When she said yes, the old lady asked if she would do her a favor but fell asleep without revealing what the favor might be.

Jennifer didn't have to wonder about it any longer.

When Banning lowered his voice and moved to the other side of the room, she turned toward the fireplace. Flames curled around the large chunks of wood in a sinister embrace that destroyed the very matter feeding its life. It was the same with some people. They entwined their lives around yours, sapping your strength to bolster theirs.

She frowned at a lick of flame with a peculiar, greenish tinge around the edges. It was almost the same green as that man's eyes.

Why did she remember them so clearly?

She had seen him for the first time a week ago, when she drove her car through the open gates leading to the Wilson estate. He was there again today, a tall, bearded man with ink-dark hair and a scar at the corner of his right eye. As before, he leaned against a mud-spattered pickup truck.

When she slowed to pass between the open halves of the gates, he had straightened and moved a few paces closer to her. Eyes the color of green bottle glass had studied her face with an intensity that made her shiver with uneasiness.

Who could he be?

The gates opened, and she'd tromped hard on the accelerator. In the rear view mirror, she had seen him looking after her car, but he didn't enter the grounds. Perhaps he liked to frighten females.

He looked scruffy enough to frighten anybody.

Maybe she should tell Banning about him. But what could she say? That a tall, bearded man with muddy boots watched the house? Besides, she couldn't cite anything particularly memorable about him.

Except for those eyes.

". . . about six months ago."

The soft words jerked her back to the present. "What?"

"I said that Martha died about six months ago."

Jennifer nodded. "The doctor believed the news caused Mrs. Wilson's stroke."

"Very probably."

"She liked Martha's husband very much."

For the first time, Banning's eyes held an evasive look. Jennifer said, "Poor John, losing his father so soon after his mother," and watched to see Banning's reaction.

"Yes . . . a terrible thing."

His words lacked the depth of feeling a genuine expression of regret should contain. The secretive look in his eyes whetted her curiosity. Perhaps the lawyer didn't share Mrs. Wilson's opinion of Stuart Kendall.

Banning took a drink of his coffee. "You grew up in bad surroundings, but you didn't allow that experience to make you bitter. That says a lot about you as a person." He studied her for a moment. "Do you want children of your own, Jennifer?"

"Why are you asking me that?"

He chuckled. "Don't pretend to be dumb. You finished at the top of your nursing class."

"What else do you know about me?"

He began to count on his fingers. "You're twenty-four years old. You just gave a man named Frank the heave-ho. Your bank balance is pitifully small. You have no near relatives. And your building is about to become a condo. You have to leave within two months."

She said, "You've been busy," and heard his hearty laugh.

"You didn't answer my question."

"Yes. I want children, and I'll do my best for John."

Banning nodded his approval. "I'm sure of that." A frown wrinkled his forehead. "You heard Phil say that Martha wasn't a true Wilson." He drained his cup and set it down. "As you also observed, the family has transferred their resentment from her to her son."

The blunt statement made Jennifer remember Phil's chilling comment. "Why did they hate her so much?"

"Mrs. Wilson's nephew adopted Martha when she was four years old. She was a shy, introverted child who somehow bonded with her great-aunt. After her father's death, Martha moved into this house and spent most of her time with Mrs. Wilson. The old lady loved her very much, which was enough to make the rest of the family resent the girl."

Jennifer nodded. "And now Martha's son stands between them and their inheritance."

"He isn't alone, Jennifer. He has you." Banning stood up. "By the way, he's here."

The cup dropped from her fingers and rattled in the saucer.

"John and his nurse Maria arrived while we were at the funeral."

Jennifer paused with her hand on the door knob leading to the nursery. With children, first meetings were critical. She had to assure the young boy that she wanted to be his friend. She couldn't pressure him, even though sad circumstances had uprooted him from the only familiar surroundings he knew. He must be feeling lost and alone. She had to go slow.

When Jennifer pushed the door open, a short, thin woman in a nondescript, dark dress moved forward. She wore her black hair bundled onto the back of her head. The large roll looked too heavy for her small neck to support, but she stood straight and proud.

"Are you Maria?"

"Yes, miss."

She wasn't young, not with that liberal sprinkling of gray through her hair, but her face showed no lines. She had the seemingly ageless complexion of some Asian women whom Jennifer knew.

A small boy came through the doorway of the room behind Maria and moved to her side. He stood straight with his shoulders back, an unusually challenging posture for such a young child. His pink cheeks and dark, tousled hair gave him an adorable appeal. He reminded Jennifer of the son of a friend of hers who always greeted her with a kiss and a throttling hug.

That wasn't going to happen with this child.

She smiled. "Hello, John."

"My name is Johnny. Who are you?"

"Jennifer Denton. I'm a nurse."

The greenish-blue eyes surveying her held no approval in their depths. "I'm not sick."

"Of course you're not."

"I don't need a nurse. Maria takes care of me."

"I'm sure she does a wonderful job," Jennifer commented. This wasn't the right time to tell him about his great-aunt's arrangement for his future. "How old are you, Johnny?"

"How old are you?"

"A gentleman never asks a lady her age."

"Why not?"

"It isn't polite," she explained.

Satisfaction spread across his small features. "Then I won't tell you my age." His steady gaze, unsettling in one so young, didn't waver from her face. "Are you a witch?"

She couldn't prevent a start. "No."

"They have red hair."

"Who told you that?"

"One of my story books has a witch in it. She has red hair. So you must be one."

"An artist drew that picture, Johnny."

His eyes brightened with interest. "I can draw."

Jennifer said, "I'd like very much to see you draw something." Her darting gaze noted a scarred wooden duck in the top shelf of the toy cabinet. "How about that bird?"

Johnny's gaze followed her pointing figure. "That's a mallard."

"How do you know?"

"My daddy told me. He's coming here soon."

The older woman said something to him. He leaned close to say something to her and then went back into the room behind her.

Jennifer whispered, "It's cruel to allow him to believe that his father may return at any moment."

"It would hurt him more to take away his hope."

Hours later, Jennifer sat at a dressing table and twisted her hair into a long plait. The meeting with Johnny hadn't gone well. For the first time since she had become a nurse, she doubted her ability to do the job set before her. He wasn't like any other child she had met. He didn't have childish mannerisms. And, with Maria hovering about, it would be difficult to get to know him.

Jennifer put her brush down and then reached out to smooth her fingers across the dresser's cool, pink marble top. She looked at each of her reflections in the triple mirrors before she slid off the padded seat to survey the sumptuous room behind her.

A sea of pale green carpet stretched across to the French doors leading to a large balcony. Delicate furniture upholstered in peach colored silk provided comfortable places to relax. A chaise lounge, covered in plum velvet, coaxed her to enjoy the warmth of the fireplace. On the other side of the room, lush satin, in a rich apricot tone, formed the canopy over the double bed and draped the padded headboard. An ornate bathroom with a sunken tub lay behind a door beyond the bed.

Belinda Wilson shared this master suite with her husband until his death. Afterward, she moved down the hall. As instructed by Mr. Banning, the housekeeper had cleaned and aired the suite for the new mistress of the house.

Jennifer let out her breath in a long sigh. Amelia coveted these rooms and often spoke of residing in them. Though it hadn't been intentional, Jennifer's occupancy gave the woman another reason to resent her.

The soft carpeting cushioned Jennifer's feet as she walked to the bedside table and bent to sniff the delicate perfume of red and white roses standing in a crystal vase. She fingered a soft, velvety petal while she studied the inviting bed turned down and ready for her occupancy.

It was well past midnight. It had been a long day. She should be sleepy, but she wasn't. She turned and walked to the double doors leading to the hall. She'd often told her patients about the benefits of warm milk as a sleep inducer. Maybe it was time that she tried it.

Maria had used all of the milk in the upstairs refrigerator for Johnny. Jennifer heaved another sigh and turned toward the stairs.

Nightlights burned at intervals along the hallway. Her trip to the main kitchen wouldn't be the classical walk through a dark house. She smiled at her thoughts and moved to the top of the circular staircase. With a hand slipping along the smooth, wood banister, she descended the stairs. The servants would all be asleep, but she knew her way around the kitchen.

Her slippers made no sound when she crossed the polished tiles of the entry hall and headed toward the kitchen. She flicked the light switch and surveyed the pristine surface of the counters as she headed toward the large, double-door refrigerator. She nodded approval and resolved to leave everything as clean as she'd found it.

She whipped around when she heard a click from somewhere behind her. The kitchen door swung open to admit the tall, bearded man she'd seen outside the fence.

He closed the heavy door behind him but didn't advance any closer toward her. "Don't be afraid. I won't hurt you."

Jennifer shivered, not entirely from the blast of cold air that accompanied his entry. No matter what he said, he had an illegal key to this house. That made him dangerous.

She gathered her breath to call for help.

He held his gloved hands up as though to assure her. "Don't scream. I'm Stuart Kendall."

CHAPTER TWO

"Everyone thinks you're dead!"

"To paraphrase Mark Twain, the reports of my death were grossly exaggerated."

"Can you prove it?" When his lips curved into a smile, Jennifer snapped, "That isn't what I meant. How do I know you're Stuart Kendall?"

He reached into a jacket pocket and produced a long, thin wallet. Stepping closer, he flipped it open. "Here's my passport."

Passport pictures were always bad, and the male face in the picture had no beard, but the likeness couldn't be anyone other than the man standing before her. The printed name identified him as Stuart R. Kendall. Her gaze flicked to the other side of the wallet. She had time for only a quick glimpse of some very official looking sentences before he closed the wallet and returned it to his jacket pocket.

"Satisfied?"

"It's a picture of you," she conceded, "but it doesn't prove you're Johnny's father."

"As much as I'd enjoy exchanging barbs with you, I'm short of time." He headed toward the door to the hall. "I want to see my son."

Jennifer darted over and whirled around with her arms outstretched. "You can't go into the house."

Stuart halted a yard or so away from her. Though she stood five feet eight in her stocking feet, she had to tilt her chin up to see his face. He had to be six feet four inches tall, with a heavily muscled upper body. Also, he outweighed her by at least a hundred pounds.

He didn't laugh at her, but she couldn't blame him if he did. She must look silly trying to bar his way. All he had to do was to step forward, pick her up, and set her aside. When he reached out a hand toward her, she sucked in a breath.

"I'm sorry. I didn't mean to scare you."

"Well, you did." She glared at him. "How did you get a key to this house?"

"The key belonged to my wife." Reaching into another pocket, he pulled out an envelope and handed it to her.

"What's in this?" she asked.

"Johnny's birth certificate and a picture of me and his mother."

The dog-eared piece of stationery had a dark red stain on one corner. Avoiding that spot, she slid her fingers under the flap and pulled out a folded piece of paper and a photograph.

The birth certificate looked genuine. She refolded the document and examined the small picture. Two people stared back at her. One of them was the man standing in front of her, the other a fragile, blonde girl of about her own age. Jennifer recognized Martha from a framed portrait in her former patient's bedroom.

"People believe you died in that river, Mr. Kendall."

"For the time being, I intend to stay dead."

There might be several good reasons for a man to want others to think he was dead, but she could only think of one. "The lawyer said you were attached to the American Embassy in Panama," she commented. "Are you on a special mission or something?"

"You've seen too many movies."

Maybe he meant to be funny, but she didn't find anything

amusing in this situation. She opened her mouth to say so but jerked around when she heard the lock on the kitchen door click.

He whipped the papers away from her. His hand dived into his jacket and brought out a wicked looking revolver. Moving in front of her, he called, "Come in where I can see you."

Jennifer shifted to peep around his broad shoulder and saw a familiar weaving figure step through the doorway. She let out a sigh of relief. "That's Philip Wilson. He lives here."

"Well now . . ." Phil closed the door behind him. "I wondered what our angel of mercy did at night when Aunt Belinda was asleep. Who's your friend, Jen?" Phil's lips formed a knowing smile. "He must be a good friend. You're wearing a robe."

"He's drunk," she whispered.

The smile froze on Phil's lips when his gaze shifted to the gun. He stumbled backward. "Please don't shoot . . . didn't mean anything."

Jennifer took a step, but Stuart put out an arm to prevent her from moving in front of him. "Why did you pull a gun on him?" She pointed toward Phil. "I told you. He lives here. He isn't dangerous."

Phil lifted a protective hand in front of his face. He blinked several times and tried to focus his eyes. "Don't shoot." He slumped down. "Tell him, Jen . . . tell him."

"Don't hurt him," she urged the tall man.

Turning toward Stuart, she watched him flip the pistol back into its holster with a smooth movement that made her blink in admiration.

He moved forward and knelt down. In one, fluid motion, he hauled Phil up off the floor and slung the limp body over his shoulder. "I'll carry him upstairs."

Jennifer led the way. When she stepped onto the second floor landing, she turned to watch Stuart's progress. He was right behind her, and he didn't appear to be breathing any harder from the effort of carrying his unconscious burden.

She pointed toward the Wilson's wing of the house and reached toward a closed door at one end of the hallway. Stuart headed that way, opened the door, and bent down to step through. A few feet inside, he put Phil down and sat him up against the wall.

Stuart returned to her side. "He may not remember seeing me." He stared at her for a moment and then said, in a very different voice, "Is Jen short for Jennifer?"

"Yes."

"Jennifer what?"

"Denton."

He murmured, "I thought it might be Rapunzel."

She felt her cheeks growing warm and put a self-conscious hand on the long plait. "I'll take you to Johnny."

Stuart's eyebrows arched. "No more questions?"

"Not right now."

He walked close beside her, near enough for the sleeve of his jacket to touch her arm. Twice he turned and looked behind him. What sort of a life did he lead to make him so cautious? She felt sure that Banning knew the answers. Did he know Stuart was alive? If so, he was part of whatever was going on. That's why he had looked so strange yesterday when she mentioned Johnny's father. Whatever was going on with Stuart, Banning knew all about it.

The next time she saw him, she meant to have some straight answers.

She opened a door on the right side of the hallway. The dim light of a shaded figure of Mother Goose revealed Maria sitting in a chair by the child's bed. Stuart spoke to her in a Spanish-sounding language but with added, guttural phrases. Maria answered him. He looked at Jennifer and said something else.

Maria also looked at Jennifer before she stood up, went into the back room, and closed the door.

"What language were you speaking?" Jennifer asked.

"A dialect common to a certain region in South America."

"But aren't you part of the embassy staff in Panama?"

"Yes."

A gentle snub, but she got the message. He didn't want to answer any questions. That was too bad, because she wanted some information.

Stuart leaned over the bed. The same hand that earlier had held the revolver now gently caressed the top of his son's head.

"Mr. Kendall . . ."

"My name is Stuart."

"Very well . . . Stuart." She hesitated. "Since you're alive and able to take care of Johnny, why did you let Maria bring him to the United States?"

Stuart made no answer.

"I'm entitled to know."

"You're entitled to know nothing."

The point-blank answer surprised her.

"Why are you in this house, Jen?"

"Oh, you're allowed to ask questions, but I can't?"

He ignored that. "What are you doing here?"

Annoyance pushed her to pursue the topic, but he had a right to know about the boy's care. "I'm a nurse. I took care of Mrs. Wilson during her last illness. Since everyone thought you were dead, she assumed custody of your son by the instructions in your will. She asked me to move into the house to take care of Johnny."

"Was that to be a permanent arrangement?"

"Initially it would be for six months with a review at the end of that time."

"What do you get out of it?"

The direct question brought a blush to her cheeks, but she didn't look away. "Fifty thousand dollars."

"Not a bad salary for a few months work."

She resented that. "I didn't do it for the money."

"Why else would a woman give up her career and her own life to take care of another woman's child?"

"Mrs. Wilson asked me to accept the job as a personal favor to her."

"Fifty thousand dollars buys a lot of favors."

She tried again. "I admired her very much. She liked and trusted me enough to ask me to take care of Johnny, the most precious person on earth to her. I take that responsibility seriously. Every child has the right to experience happiness and security."

"Tall, slender, and pretty," he noted. "Also compassionate. A woman like you should have a full life going for herself. Are you hiding from something, Jen?" His gaze narrowed. "Or perhaps from someone?"

"I'm not hiding from anything."

She interpreted his silence to mean he didn't believe her, but what difference did it make? Stuart was back. Johnny didn't need her. Not that it mattered. He didn't like her anyway. A feeling of emptiness swept over her, as strong as it was unexpected. How had one small, hostile boy affected her so deeply?

"For what it's worth, Jen, I believe you."

"Thank you." She said, after a moment, "The lawyer said that your job puts you into harm's way."

"That's a fair statement." He put a gentle hand on Johnny's cheek. "I have to leave now."

He couldn't be serious. "You can't leave. Johnny needs someone to look after him."

"That's your job."

29

Anger stiffened her shoulders. "If you didn't intend to stay, why did you come here at all?"

"To see Johnny." Stuart added, after a moment, "And you."

"You came here to look me over?"

A moment later, she wished she could take the words back. His gaze traveled leisurely from her head to the toes of her slippers and back again.

"I'm satisfied, Jen."

The soft words sent a rush of heat into her cheeks. She followed him out into the hall. "Wait a minute. You can't just leave. Johnny expects to see you. What am I supposed to tell him?"

"Tell him nothing." Stuart checked the hallway in both directions and then looked back at her. "A man will come to see you within the next two days. His name is Julio." Stuart gave the word a Spanish-sounding pronunciation. "Offer him a job, any job. You can trust him completely."

"Is he a friend of yours?"

"Yes. He'll watch over you and Johnny."

A shiver ran up her arms. "Why do we need watching?"

"I can't explain now. You'll have to trust me."

"Where will you be?"

"It's better if you don't know."

"Are you . . ." Glancing down the hallway, she lowered her voice. "Are the authorities after you?"

"Funny you should say that."

She whispered, "You're running from the law?"

"Not in the way you mean, but I am a sort of fugitive." He studied her for a moment. "Take care of my son, Jen."

She moved to the railing and watched him descend the staircase. Seconds later, he opened the front door and closed it behind him.

★　★　★　★　★

A few running steps took Stuart to the edge of the lighted porch. Placing one hand on the railing, he vaulted into the dense shadows by the side of the house. He hit the ground with only a slight scraping noise and then slithered under a large shrub before sprinting across the grass. Moments later, he darted into the darkness beneath the trees.

Stuart bent low to avoid the snow-laden branches and squirmed deeper into the shadows. He dropped to one knee and whistled a combination of musical notes a few seconds before a hand touched his shoulder. Twisting around, he studied the faint blur of a man's face, only a little lighter than the surrounding darkness. "You have to stop doing that, Julio. My nerves aren't what they used to be."

"I have looked around, Stuart. All is clear."

"Where did you learn to move so quietly?"

"In the jungle, animals that make noise are quickly eaten."

Stuart nodded. "Ask a foolish question."

"You talk to the lady?"

"Yes. She's a nurse. She took care of Mrs. Wilson for several months. I think she's okay."

The other man said nothing.

"I know, Julio. We stay alive by not trusting our feelings, but there's something about her, something I can't put into words."

"You like her?"

Stuart gave a snort of laughter. "I sometimes forget that you operate on a very basic level." He pushed to his feet. "I told Miss Denton to expect you tomorrow. She'll offer you some sort of work, but you're really going to be a bodyguard for her and my son."

"But I also watch her?"

"You also watch her."

★　★　★　★　★

Stuart checked his watch. Five o'clock. At least another hour and a half before daylight. He looked into his truck's rear view mirror again. The black sedan had moved a little closer behind him. He adjusted the side mirror and checked the car's hood and front end. The bumper of the car he'd seen earlier carried a clump of icy slush with a brightly colored, candy bar wrapper stuck in it. As the bumper of the dark sedan came into view, he saw the red wrapper still frozen into position.

The bad guys had found him.

Stuart hurried through a light about to turn red, but the sedan didn't make it in time. He had one minute, maybe two, before they found him again.

Opening a specially built compartment in the dashboard, he pulled out a small device the size of the palm of his hand. A green light glowed on a dial. He pressed a button. When the light turned red, he tossed the device onto the passenger seat.

Counting the seconds, he swerved into an alley and then saw a brick wall looming in the distance. Still counting, he set the wheel straight and jumped.

His forehead hit a sharp projection on the wall. He dodged to protect his eyes, and his ribcage collided with some loose bricks producing an instant, dull throbbing in his right side. Pulling the gun from its holster, he staggered to a nearby door and tried the knob. It turned.

He lurched through the entranceway into a small room and immediately dropped into a crouch. A quick glance around the walls showed boxes and broken crates. Nothing big enough to conceal someone his size.

What was that burning sensation in his left eye? He reached up a hand to his forehead. His fingers touched a warm, sticky liquid. He dug in a back pocket and brought out a dark cloth. Wrapping it tightly around his head, he ran on tiptoes across the floor and twisted the knob on the inner door.

It didn't open.

Still counting, he closed the outside door to within an inch or so of the sill, leaving a space big enough to allow him to observe the alley. He heard an explosion just before the black car whispered past the door. Stuart dropped to the floor and wormed his way toward the opening. Despite the cold blast of air, sweat ran down his face. He eased forward, inch by careful inch, until he could see down the alley.

No one shot at him.

He stretched out farther and saw the black car. The alley stood dark at this early hour of the morning, but he saw the car doors standing open. Three men moved toward the burning truck. Stepping out into the alley, Stuart closed the door and headed in the opposite direction.

Every step sent a jab of pain through his side as he moved out of the alley and joined a queue of people waiting at a bus stop. He stood behind two women engaged in an animated conversation, punctuated by frequent laughter. He didn't mind the smaller woman's soft laugh, but the tall one's high-pitched cackle made his head hurt worse.

His gaze swept both sides of the street. No cover. Not even a mailbox. Hiding behind a parked car would be suicidal. He stretched to look over the heads of the people, saw the bus approaching, and stepped ahead of a man in torn jeans standing at the front of the line.

"What do you think you're . . ."

His voice petered out when Stuart looked back over his shoulder.

He boarded the bus and headed for the back seats. Several people stared at him, but his narrow-eyed look didn't encourage their attention. They squirmed under his direct gaze and looked away. Stuart didn't blame them. In his mud-smeared clothes, he probably looked like some ill-tempered derelict.

He sat down by a window but couldn't shift to any position to ease the pain in his side. The peculiar sensation of lightheadedness made his situation worse. Maybe if he sat still, it would go away. He squeezed his eyelids shut, but a strange kaleidoscope of colors danced behind his lids. What was going on? This wasn't the time to pass out. He opened his eyes and turned toward the window as the three men ran out of the alley.

Making the motion normal and unhurried, Stuart turned away from the window. He watched from the corners of his eyes and saw the men studying the windows as the bus pulled away from the curb. Stuart fought the natural impulse to duck down out of sight as their gazes sweep the length of the bus and paused on him.

He blew out his breath in a long gush when they turned away. His ribs, protesting the sudden deflation, gave him another jab. He needed treatment and a place to hide for a while. There was only one place he could go.

"Get ready, Jen. You're going to have a patient."

Jennifer lay in bed in the early morning hours staring at the stars visible in the gap between the opened curtains. She couldn't forget Stuart's cryptic remark about his friend Julio.

He'll watch over you and Johnny.

Stuart must be in some sort of trouble that he feared might threaten his son . . . and his son's nurse. But, if that were true, why didn't he notify the American authorities for police protection? Unless, of course, it was those same authorities whom Stuart feared.

Her thoughts went around and around and came back to the same place. Stuart wouldn't answer her questions. The only person who might was the lawyer. She'd question Banning the next time she saw him.

What could she tell Johnny if he mentioned his father? She couldn't tell the boy that she'd seen Stuart. He had said that he'd try to return today. If he didn't make it back, she didn't want to excite Johnny's hopes for nothing.

Her bedside clock read six-thirty. She wasn't going to get any more sleep.

Pushing the covers aside, rising, she slid her feet into her slippers and tugged on her robe. Maybe some coffee would clear her head. She could go to the small upstairs kitchen and fix some.

Jennifer opened her door and stepped outside, closing the door behind her. She took a step and then another. Then she stopped. The corridor lights weren't burning. Why would they all go out at the same time?

She didn't have an abnormal fear of the dark, but something about that stretch of unlighted hallway made her uneasy. A whisper of sound spun her around, but she couldn't see anything. She took a step back toward her room. Her foot contacted something soft and wriggly. The next instant, an outraged squall made her fall back against the wall. She gave a nervous laugh. The cook's pet cat Charles roamed the house at night. Jennifer often gave him a saucer of milk. No doubt he was looking for one now.

Fear exploded in her stomach when a hand clamped over her mouth. At the same time, an arm slid around her waist from behind, yanked her away from the wall, and squeezed her body against a man's broad chest.

Panic stabbed through her. Drawing her right arm forward, she drove her elbow against the man's rib cage. He grunted as though in pain and immediately reached across to immobilize her arm. Opening her mouth farther, she got her teeth into his hand at the base of his thumb and bit down hard. She heard a muttered oath. The hand on her mouth tightened to a vise.

Something warm and faintly salty ran across her lips. She must have bitten hard enough to draw blood.

A strong arm lifted her off her feet. She kicked backward with her heels and made contact with one of his shins.

He muttered something she didn't understand, and then a door opened behind her. She tried to grasp hold of the sill as he carried her backward, but her fingers slid off the smooth wood. Prepared to fight for her life, she gasped in surprise when the man dropped her onto her feet and pushed her away. Bright light flooded the area around them.

She blinked a few times and saw Stuart leaning back against the closed door. He held up his hand, allowing her to see the thin line of blood running down his wrist.

"Always a pleasure to see you, Jen."

CHAPTER THREE

Relief mingled with guilt as Jennifer said, "Why didn't you speak to me?" Her gaze shifted to the reddish stain on the cloth tied across his forehead. "What happened to your head?"

"It stopped bleeding some time ago." Stuart held up his hand. "But this needs attention."

"You shouldn't have scared me. In all the movies I ever saw, the man who surprises a woman like that is always the bad guy."

"I assure you, Jen, I'm not the bad guy."

She stepped closer, took hold of his hand, and gently pressed her finger on the area of the puncture wounds. When he winced, she murmured, "I'm sorry," and pointed to his forehead. "I'd better treat that injury first."

He whipped the covering off before she could stop him. A gouge just above his left eyebrow began to seep.

"I thought it might be stuck. I was going to use some water." Jennifer studied the wound. "It's deep. You need a few stitches." She moved around him and headed for the door. When Stuart grabbed her arm, she turned to look at him.

"Be careful."

"There's no one out there."

"I waited for you at the top of the stairs, and you didn't know I was there. Remember?" He gave her a long look and then pointed toward the door. "Open it and look outside."

"What should I do if someone's out there?"

"Tell them goodnight."

She took a moment to arrange her features into what she hoped looked like a casual expression and then opened the door and stepped outside. Light spilled out into the corridor from the room behind her. She looked both ways. "As you would say, the coast is clear."

He followed her out into the hall. "Believe it or not, Jen, I've never said those words." He frowned. "Where did you ever hear that expression?"

"From my grandmother."

When she reached down to turn on one of the nightlights, he said, "Not yet." He gave her a gentle push and then reached back to close the door.

"There's nobody here but us," she whispered.

"It doesn't pay to take chances."

"Someday I hope you'll tell me what it is you do for a living that makes you so distrustful of people."

"You don't want to know."

"I'm beginning to feel like I'm watching a bad movie."

"Better to watch it than to be in it."

Jennifer had no answer for that one. She swept out a hand to find the wall. "My medical equipment is in Mrs. Wilson's suite. At the end of this hall, turn right."

He stepped past her. "Take my hand, Jen."

She groped for his hand and heard him grunt.

"The other one, please."

"Sorry."

Sweeping her palm lightly across his back, she found the hand he extended toward her. She could hear the sound of her own breathing, but she couldn't hear anything from him. Apparently he'd learned to breathe quietly. She wondered how she acquired that particular skill and could almost hear him saying she didn't want to know.

He exerted a slight pressure on her hand, making her understand he was about to stop. Jennifer heard a door open. After they passed through, light flooded the area around them.

It took a few seconds to focus her eyes. As she led the way across the rose-pink carpet, she looked up and smiled in appreciation of the décor. A clever artist had created an arbor of pink and white roses across the domed ceiling. Blossoms, vines, and leaves spilled down each of the walls, furthering the illusion of standing in a rose garden.

"Mrs. Wilson moved into this suite after her husband died," Jennifer commented. "Beautiful, isn't it?"

"Yes."

Jennifer led him to an inside hallway and into a small but complete kitchen. It took her less than a minute to collect what she needed from the refrigerator. Placing two small vials on the table, she went to a cabinet over the sink and lifted down a metal box the size and shape of a small suitcase.

"Have you had a tetanus shot recently, Stuart?"

"Yes."

From behind the refrigerator, she took out a small, wrapped package.

"Bad cheese?" he suggested.

Jennifer broke open the package and held up a key. "I have drugs in the box, so I keep it locked."

She opened the case and took out dressings, scissors, and tape. Rinsing her hands in alcohol over a small basin contained in the case, she wiped them on some of the dressing material. From a smaller case, she took out a sterile hypodermic pack.

Jennifer looked up to find him studying the hypodermic. "Stuart?"

He continued to stare at the needle.

"Is something wrong?"

His lips thinned to a narrow line.

39

She saw his nostrils distend upon a long inhalation. "What is it?"

His eyes held a dull, glazed look. He didn't respond.

Jennifer took hold of his good hand. He didn't return the pressure of her fingers.

"Stuart!"

He jumped like a man who'd had an electric shock.

"What's wrong? Are you ill?" She moved closer. "Can I do anything to help you?"

He took a deep breath and then another. His searching gaze locked with hers.

She felt her pulse lurch and then resume at a faster pace. Deep in his eyes, she saw something that wrapped around her like a warm blanket.

He made a smothered exclamation. One long arm swept around her waist, catching her close. He tightened his grip to press the soft lines of her body against the hard muscle of his. His green eyes glowed like precious jewels as his other arm slid around her shoulders.

When his lips came down on hers, a shock wave traveled over her, leaving her trembling in its wake. Jennifer pushed against a heavily muscled shoulder, but she might as well try to uproot one of the huge oak trees in the yard. A moment later, something stirred to life inside her, replacing her fear with an eagerness to press closer to him.

His lips lifted from hers to press feathery kisses on her eyes, her cheeks, and along her jaw. He murmured strange words in her ear. She only had time to wince at the scrape of his beard before his mouth settled over hers again. A shiver swept over her. She marveled at her sense of completeness as she stood within the circle of his arms.

What was happening to her?

Mustering all of her willpower, she pulled her head back and pushed against his chest. The warmth in his eyes tore the air out of her lungs. She felt as though she was falling from a great height, but she had no dread of the final hit at the bottom.

Seconds passed before she noted the muscle jerking in his cheek. She pushed against his chest again. This time, he released her and stepped back.

"I didn't intend to do that, Jen. It won't happen again."

She managed a smile. "You're not yourself. You've had a shock."

"And you feel sorry for me."

The banked fire in his eyes made her take a couple of steps backward.

"Ah . . . now you begin to understand. You're a little scared of me, aren't you, Jen?" His shoulders slumped like a man who was unbearably weary. "Don't be so quick to offer comfort and sympathy to strangers. You're young, pretty, and have a soft heart—three things that men prey upon."

Jennifer stared back at him but said nothing.

He said, quietly, "Sew up my forehead. I don't need a shot."

"As you wish."

A short time later, she put down the needle. Stitching his wound must have been painful. Beyond an occasional grimace, Stuart showed no reaction. She put a bandage on his palm and turned away to pack up the dressings.

"Don't put everything away yet, Jen." He began tugging his shirt out of his waistband. "I may have a cracked rib."

She felt a stab of guilt. Her thrashing around when he grabbed her earlier in the hallway must have hurt him. "You've had a full day."

"It hasn't been dull."

He began undoing the buttons. When she stepped forward to help push the shirt off his shoulders, he grabbed her hands.

"I have to examine your ribs, Stuart."

He looked at her for a few seconds and then shrugged and released her.

She eased the shirt off his left arm and moved around behind him to do the same with the right sleeve. When the shirt dropped away, she gasped in alarm. The muscles of his back carried purple bruises and deep cuts, none of which had completely healed. Lower down, she saw damaged skin that looked like it had been burned.

She said, between trembling lips, "What happened?"

"As I said before, you don't want to know."

"You mean . . . someone did this to you?"

"It looks worse than it is."

She heard a faint buzzing sound.

Stuart took a small, cylindrical device from his pocket and clicked a switch on the top. A red light began to flicker. He thrust his arms through the sleeves of his shirt and turned away. "I'll be back."

Using his pocket flashlight, Stuart located the switch for the hall lights and turned it on. He stepped into a room, flipped the light switch, and looked around. Then he retrieved his cellular phone. Punching in some numbers, he waited for two rings and then ended the call and immediately dialed again.

"You have a disconnected number," a voice said.

"I'll pay the bill," Stuart replied.

"Heads up, *Sombra*. Old acquaintances are looking for you."

"They found me a while ago."

"Are you safe where you are?"

Stuart hesitated and then said, "Probably."

"Do you want transport to another location?"

"No. I'll stay here. Any instructions?"

"Not at this time."

"Right."

Stuart turned off the phone and stepped back into the hall.

Jennifer shivered and wrapped her arms around her body. She'd seen wounds before but nothing like those on Stuart's back. The burns were a peculiar size and shape, as if someone had held the end of a burning cigarette to his skin.

"I'm back."

She jerked around. He stood a couple of feet behind her. "Could you please make a little noise when you come up behind me?"

"Sorry." He opened his shirt and held the fabric away to expose his ribs.

The skin looked swollen. She reached out to touch it and felt him flinch. The area was probably sore, but her cold fingers against his much warmer skin provided a more likely reason for his quick intake of breath.

"You should have an x-ray."

"After that, what would a doctor do?"

"Wrap your ribs."

"Can't you do it?"

"Yes, but you could have other injuries."

"I don't think so. I ran into a wall."

Jennifer twisted around and scooped the bandage out of a compartment in one end of the case. "I worry about you."

Something in his silence drew her head around.

"It's been a while since anyone worried about me."

Why did she have to say something to remind him about Martha? "I didn't mean to stir up painful memories about your wife, Stuart." She paused and said, "Do you want to talk about her?"

"No."

"I'm sorry. I shouldn't have mentioned her."

He reached out and cupped Jennifer's cheek in his bandaged

43

hand. "I'm sorry, too. You offered me comfort, and I refused it."

"It's okay."

His hand dropped away from her face. "No, it isn't okay."

Deprived of the warmth of his hand, her cheek felt cold.

She dredged up her best, professional manner, unrolled the bandage, and began wrapping it around his ribs. Her fingers didn't have their usual dexterity, but she blamed it on the rough skin her fingertips brushed each time she reached around his waist. Knowing he was watching her face made her efforts more difficult.

At last, she hooked the barbed teeth of the catch into the fabric and stepped back. "If your side continues to bother you, you should see a doctor."

"How old are you, Jen?"

"Twenty-four."

Stuart turned away to pick up his jacket. "I'm thirty-five. In experience, I'm a lot more than eleven years older than you are."

He grunted in pain when he thrust his right arm through the sleeve. The sound prodded Jennifer forward to help him draw the jacket over his bandaged left hand.

"You asked about my wife."

"I'm sorry, Stuart. It's none of my business."

"I didn't want to talk about her because I killed her."

Jennifer couldn't prevent an involuntary step backward.

"Did I shock you, Jen?"

Not trusting her voice, she said nothing.

"You might have said I didn't, to protect my feelings." He gave a soft laugh. "Although, at this moment, you're probably wondering if I have any feelings worth protecting."

She whispered, "No."

"Of course, you are." Stuart grabbed his jacket. "I didn't put a gun to Martha's head and pull the trigger, but I might as well have done that." His mouth thinned to a harsh line. "Are you still going to worry about me?"

Her head lifted. "People have to care about one another, or we're no better than animals."

"What makes you think we *are* any better?"

"We have to be."

After a moment, he said, "My wife believed as you do."

"Would you have wanted her to be different?"

"If she hadn't been so worried about me, she'd still be alive."

"What do you mean?"

His lips twisted into a humorless smile. "I shocked you again, didn't I?"

"What happened to her?"

"I'll bet you bring home stray cats and dogs, too." He stared at Jennifer for a few seconds and then shrugged. "I met Martha when I rescued her from a couple of punks who had dragged her into an alley. I heard her screaming."

"Oh, Stuart."

"They'd cut her with knives and were ripping off her clothes. As soon as they saw my gun, they ran away. I picked her up, but she froze like she was in some sort of a trance. I flagged a taxi and took her to the emergency area of a hospital. She got hysterical and wouldn't go inside, so I took her to a friend of mine, a retired doctor."

"He treated her?"

"He patched her up. She wouldn't tell me where she lived, and I couldn't just put her into a cab, so I took her to my apartment. She woke up screaming that night and for several nights thereafter."

"Female victims of attacks often behave in strange ways."

"I tried to get her to contact her family," Stuart continued, "but she said they hated her. She also said she loved me and if I didn't want her she might as well kill herself."

45

"And you believed her?"

"A buddy of mine lost his kid sister that way. She told her boyfriend the same thing, but the guy didn't believe her." Stuart paused. "I felt responsible for Martha, so I married her." He paused again. "That shocks you most of all, I suppose."

She wasn't sure to what he referred, but she made the most logical reply. "People often marry for reasons that seem good to them at the time."

"Would you do that, Jen?"

"I'd have to be deeply in love to marry anyone."

"Martha was kind, gentle, and desperately lonely." He gave Jennifer another, longer look. "You remind me of her."

That went a little too deep for comfort. "You think I look desperately lonely?"

"You have her kindness. I don't know you well enough to comment on the lonely part."

Recalling Martha's unsmiling face in the photograph, Jennifer understood what he meant. Emotional scars healed the slowest. Sometimes, they didn't heal at all.

"Your thoughts show on your face, Jen. Don't ever play poker for money."

She had no answer for that.

He moved back to the table. Reaching down, he scooped up the small bottle of numbing agent. "Years later, when I went to Panama, I took her with me, but I didn't know I'd be captured or that she'd have to be alone for several days. When I finally escaped and got home, I found her cringing in a corner of the bathroom." A muscle kicked in his jaw. "I was in no shape to help her." His fingers closed convulsively around the small bottle. "My captors left me with a few problems of my own."

Jennifer darted forward. Grabbing his hand, she pried at his fingers to get the vial before he crushed it. She heard him take a long breath. When his fingers relaxed their grip, she whipped the bottle away.

"Because of me, Martha lost her life."

"That isn't true. You *gave* her life."

"Thank you for that." He studied her face for a moment. "I'm grateful to you, Jen, for everything."

He turned away and left the kitchen.

Stuart closed the door to the suite and stood for a moment, leaning back against the smooth panels. A chemist friend had once told him that the phenomenon of chemical attraction between people was an accepted fact. Stuart had always believed the statement was his friend's hopeful theory to explain his attraction to his wife. Robert, a vegetarian as well as a dedicated scientist, had a scatter-brained, meat-loving, extroverted wife. On the surface, they had nothing in common, but the marriage was the happiest Stuart had ever encountered.

Scientific or not, something about Jen affected him. Some women were adept at projecting whatever emotion they wanted to display. The soreness in his back served as a constant reminder that he'd trusted a woman and gotten captured because of it. The sister of a fellow agent had looked innocent and trustworthy, but she sold him out for five thousand dollars.

The candid gaze of Jen's beautiful eyes might be calculated to attract the interest of the nearest man, but Stuart doubted it. Not many women would put their own life on hold to attend to the needs of another woman's child. Jen was much too pretty not to have men trailing after her. She must be looking for something she hadn't yet found.

Wasn't everyone?

Stuart pushed away from the door and headed for his son's room. He'd soon find out whether Jen was trustworthy and honest or treacherous and conniving. Either way, he'd started something he would probably regret.

The weekend passed and the first few days of the following week. Stuart continued his visits to the house by using a back staircase in the nursery wing. Jennifer began offering him coffee, which he accepted with apparent pleasure. Though they talked about many things, he gave her no more information about himself.

On Thursday morning she had an appointment with Banning. At twenty minutes before ten, she sat in a lobby coffee shop of the building where the lawyer had an office suite and rehearsed the questions she wanted to ask about Stuart. She had to do this in the right way to make Banning understand that she had to have some answers.

She felt instinctively that she could trust Stuart, but she had been wrong before. Jennifer's jaws tightened over her clenched teeth. Frank knew how to flatter a woman and make the kind of promises she wanted to hear, but he had proved to be false. She had believed him when he said he loved her and wanted a future for them, until he dumped her for his boss's daughter.

But Jennifer couldn't blame Frank for everything. He wasn't her real problem. She wore her memories like a suit of armor that no one could penetrate. She kept reliving her unhappy years, refusing to put them away and let them die.

"Hello, Jen."

Annoyance tightened the corners of her mouth. She took a drink of her coffee before she looked up. "Hello, Frank."

"May I join you?"

"No. I have an appointment at ten."

He pulled out the chair across from her and sat down. "That gives us plenty of time."

The same engaging smile and twinkling, blue eyes, but they'd lost their impact. She looked around the coffee shop and saw more than one woman staring in Frank's direction. Most women considered him handsome. So had she, once.

Infatuation clouds a woman's good sense and allows her to see what she wants to see.

The bright lights highlighted his features. What she once considered flattering crinkles at the corners of his eyes and mouth had deepened into definite lines, no doubt the effect of a temper too often given full rein.

"You're more beautiful than ever, Jen." He gave her a charming smile. His teeth were very nice, the result of a complete set of caps. Leaning across the table, he reached for her hand. "It's wonderful to see you again. I've missed you, darling."

She kept both hands on her cup. "Where's Barbara?"

"You're mad at me." His rueful smile said he understood and forgave her. "I don't blame you, darling. I acted badly. My only excuse is that I had an important client on my mind, and Barbara knew his wife quite well." A smug expression tilted his lips. "I landed the account."

"Congratulations."

"Afterwards, Barbara and I went our separate ways."

The potent scent of his shaving lotion made her wrinkle her nostrils. "What do you want, Frank?"

His eyebrows formed two innocent arcs. "What do you mean?"

"You didn't come over here just to say hello."

He gave her a warm smile. "You never stay angry with me for very long."

Jennifer's gaze lifted to the large clock on the far wall. Ten minutes to ten. She set the cup down.

Frank's hand darted out and grabbed her left hand. "I have something for you, darling."

He plunged his other hand into an inside pocket of his topcoat and brought out a small, velvet box. Flipping the lid open, he turned the box around to show her a diamond solitaire nestling on a bed of dark blue velvet.

"It's pretty."

Judging by his quick frown, this wasn't the reply he expected. "Is that all you can say, Jen?"

"It's very pretty."

"Most women have more of a reaction when they see their engagement ring." The charming smile reappeared. "I know you haven't completely forgiven me, but I'll make it up to you."

"No, Frank."

The corners of his mouth pinched together. He obviously hadn't expected any resistance.

"It's over," she said.

"How can it be over, Jen? We're going to be married."

"No."

She gave her hand a tug, but his fingers tightened.

"Now, darling . . ." He smiled at some nearby diners and shrugged as though admitting he was totally at fault and seeking their approval. "I know you're mad at me, Jen. I'm sorry we had that misunderstanding, and I'm going to make it up to you. I promise."

"I don't want anything more to do with you, Frank. If you don't let go of my hand, I'll pour this hot coffee where it'll do the most good."

His eyes narrowed as though he was trying to decide whether she meant it or not.

Jennifer stretched out her hand holding the cup and held it over his lap. "You have five seconds."

The smile flashed again.

"Four."

"Now, Jen . . ."

"Three."

He released his hold on her fingers. "It's the ring you admired

50

in that jewelry store. Remember?"

"I remember lots of things."

The lines around his mouth deepened. "I made mistakes, Jen, but I never stopped loving you."

He looked and sounded sincere. She almost believed him. "I remember what you called me."

A dull red climbed into his cheeks. "You made me angry."

"I'm about to make you angry again."

He leaned closer to her. "Don't make a hasty decision."

"I don't need you in my life, Frank. The truth is that I never did."

His lips twisted into a sneer. "Too good for me now?"

"I think I was always too good for you."

"I see." The flush in his cheeks deepened. "You're living in the Wilson mansion now."

"I wouldn't want you, Frank, if I were living in a cave."

Malice glittered in his eyes. "You and I have unfinished business, my dear."

"Don't be silly." She gathered up her coat and purse and slid off the seat. "You'll find another woman."

"Not one who can provide me with the style of living that you can."

"Goodbye, Frank."

Jennifer walked to the front of the coffee shop. She placed the bill and some change on the counter, smiled at the waitress, and went out into the lobby without looking back.

"Not so fast, Jen."

She turned to see Frank behind her.

"I'll be over to see you soon."

"Don't bother."

"You and I have a lot to talk about."

"We have nothing to talk about. Leave me alone."

"Got another man so soon?" He grasped her arm in a vise-like grip. "I'll deal with him, too."

She shaped her lips into a scornful smile. "He'd swat you like a fly."

Jennifer had the satisfaction of seeing surprise flit across Frank's face before she jerked her arm from his grasp. When the elevator bell binged, she stepped inside and pressed the button for the tenth floor.

Several people surged around Frank and crowded into the elevator.

Frustration twisted his face into a furious mask. "I'll see you soon, Jen."

CHAPTER FOUR

An hour later, Jennifer returned to the Wilson house. She hadn't seen Banning after all. He was still in court and likely to remain there for a while. The thought crossed her mind that he might be avoiding her, but she pushed it away. He had no reason to do that. If he didn't want to give her information about Stuart, Banning would tell her so.

The butler advanced to meet her as she moved toward the staircase. "There's a lady to see you, Miss Denton. She's in the small parlor."

A tall, dignified figure with graying temples and a precise British accent, Roberts represented Jennifer's idea of the perfect butler. "Thank you. I'll go now."

She walked to the back of the hall and stepped into a lovely room filled with delicate furniture and the scent of roses, which were placed in several vases around the room. A woman wearing a dark coat arose from one of the chairs by the fireplace. She looked to be about thirty and had an attractive face, blonde hair, and bright blue eyes.

"Miss Denton? I'm Louise Caldwell. Mr. Banning intended to come along to introduce me, but he had to be elsewhere."

The woman's voice sounded soft and cultured. Jennifer took an appreciative sniff of the delectable, floral scent wafting her way and then took another. This particular perfume had been a favorite of her former patient's and cost a few hundred dollars an ounce, a bit pricey for a nurse's income.

From an inside pocket of her cape, the woman produced a long white envelope and handed it to Jennifer. "Mr. Banning asked me to tell you that he'd talk to you later."

The letter introduced Louise Caldwell, a nurse of exceptional qualifications and a person to be trusted implicitly. Jennifer noted the squiggly lines below the lawyer's typed name. She had seen his signature on the bottom of the will, but she couldn't identify this writing as being the same.

"Mr. Banning gave me his cell phone number." Louise smiled again. "If you want to check on me."

Jennifer didn't want to disturb the lawyer while he argued a court case. Besides, who could doubt such a friendly face as Louise's or her willingness to wait until her presence could be verified?

Remembering Stuart's warning about strangers, Jennifer said, "I wonder why Mr. Banning didn't tell me about you?"

"It's just like a man." The woman's smile revealed a dimple in her right cheek. "Please call me Louise."

"My name is Jennifer. What can I do for you?"

"Mr. Banning hired me to help you with the child."

"That was thoughtful of him, but Johnny has a full-time nurse."

"The foreign woman?" Louise's smile revealed excellent teeth. "Her visa will soon expire."

Banning hadn't mentioned that. "I didn't know." From the corner of her eye, Jennifer saw the butler enter the room. "Yes, Roberts?"

"There's a . . . *person* to see you, Miss Denton. He is in the front hall."

Whoever the man was, he hadn't made a favorable impression upon Roberts. "Who is he?" she asked.

"He calls himself Julio."

Jennifer turned to offer her excuses to Louise and saw a

peculiar expression flit across the nurse's face. "Is something wrong?" When the woman smiled, Jennifer said, "I'll be right back."

Stepping out into the hall, she looked toward the tall figure standing by the front door and then glanced back into the room.

Louise licked her lips as though she was nervous.

The click of Jennifer's heels sounded unnaturally loud on the tiles as she covered the distance to the door.

Julio had the swarthy skin of someone often exposed to hot sun. Deep lines radiated from his dark eyes, no doubt from squinting against the sun's glare. His accent sounded the same as Maria's. Like Maria, he had gray hair mingled with the black. There the resemblance ended. Maria was small and slight. Julio was as big and tall as Stuart, with wide shoulders that strained the seams of his dark jacket. Hands the size of small hams held a shapeless hat in their clutch.

"I am here to watch over you and the boy."

For such a deep voice, he spoke softly.

"Apparently, this is my day for offers of help."

He nodded. "Maria gets along well with the child."

"I meant a nurse named Louise Caldwell."

Julio stared over her head. "She is here now?"

Why was he so curious? "This way."

Jennifer turned to look over her shoulder and gasped in alarm when Julio drew a revolver from the inside of his jacket. Motioning for her to be quiet, he ran forward soundlessly on tiptoe, and flattened his body against the wall outside the room.

A moment later, he darted inside.

Jennifer waited for a few seconds before running after him.

A cold draft of air swirled around her from the open French doors. Louise Caldwell was nowhere in sight.

Jennifer shivered and hugged her arms around her waist. "She was here a moment ago. Why would she leave?"

Julio closed the doors. "Because the man said my name."

Jennifer watched Julio replace his revolver with an easy motion similar to the one Stuart had used. "Why should your name bother her?"

"The nurse is tall? Blue eyes and light hair?"

She nodded.

"A bad woman, ma'am. The people she works for look for Stuart. He has information they want."

"What information?"

The door behind her opened. She whirled around and saw Roberts wheeling in a serving cart.

"Would you like your coffee now, Miss Denton?"

She hid her trembling hands behind her back. "Yes, Roberts. And bring an extra cup, please."

If he thought it strange for Jennifer to offer her visitor coffee, Roberts didn't let it show on his face. "Very good, ma'am." His gaze shifted to the fireplace. "You need more wood."

"Never mind, Roberts. It's cold in here because Miss Caldwell decided to leave through the patio doors. In her haste, she left them open."

The butler stared at her for a moment. "Very well, ma'am." He left the room.

Jennifer swung around toward Julio. "Nobody leaves the patio doors open on a cold day like this. Roberts must be wondering what's going on." She made a face. "So am I." Hugging her arms around her body, she headed for the fireplace. "If I ask you something, Julio, will you tell me the truth?"

"Who can say what is truth, ma'am?"

That didn't sound encouraging. "I'm not sure what you mean, but I'm not going to ask you to explain. I'd probably feel more inadequate than I do right now." Jennifer paused and then added, "A stranger arrives, pretending to be a nurse, and I fall for it."

Julio said nothing.

"I nearly made a bad mistake. I'll be afraid to accept anyone at face value ever again." Extending her cold hands toward the blaze, Jennifer checked the mirror over the mantle and saw him watching her. "If Stuart should decide to take his son elsewhere, I'd understand."

"Stuart thinks well of you."

Jennifer wasn't sure why those few words pleased her so much. "Oh?"

"It is true."

"What is truth?" she countered.

A ghost of a smile touched Julio's mouth. "Stuart told me a strange word . . . *touché.*"

An answering smile curved her lips. "That sounds like him."

She left the fireplace, sat down, and waved Julio to the chair opposite her. He sat on the edge of the seat and reached out to rub a broad finger over the rich brocade. She marveled that such a rough looking man had an obvious appreciation for the beautiful fabric covering the chair.

A young, uniformed maid with dark hair and eyes and a friendly smile stepped forward, carrying a cloth-covered tray. A discreet clearing of the butler's throat wiped away her smile.

She sat the tray down on the table beside Jennifer and bobbed a quick curtsey. "If there's anything else you need . . ."

When her voice trailed off, Jennifer's gaze followed hers.

The butler's austere features wore a disapproving frown. "I explained to you before, Betty. You will not address Miss Denton unless she first speaks to you and requires an answer."

The girl bent her head. "I'm sorry, sir."

He said, to Jennifer, "She is young, ma'am. Please excuse her familiarity."

Looking at the girl's quivering lips brought back vivid memories for Jennifer. She could almost hear her Aunt Agatha's harsh tones. A child newly orphaned and missing her mother longed for comfort and companionship, but her aunt had none to offer.

Roberts gave the maid a curt gesture to leave.

Jennifer said, "I'd like Betty to remain."

The butler bowed. "As you wish, ma'am." He nodded toward Betty. "You will await Miss Denton's pleasure."

The girl looked ready to burst into tears.

Jennifer smiled at her. "It's nothing dreadful. I wanted to ask if you'd like to work upstairs."

A doubtful frown wrinkled the girl's forehead. "Cleaning, ma'am?"

"Taking care of Johnny's clothes, helping Maria with his food. Helping out in general."

Betty began to giggle. "Oh, thank you, ma'am! I'm always breaking something down here."

The butler's features assumed their bland expression. "You wish her to assume her new duties immediately, Miss Denton?"

"Yes."

He bowed and left the drawing room.

"When you get upstairs, Betty, take the corridor to the left. Johnny's in the nursery, the last room on the right. You'll find an older woman there. Her name is Maria."

Betty flashed a smile and ran out of the room.

Jennifer poured two cups of coffee and held one out to Julio.

His hand swallowed the fragile cup. "You have a weakness, ma'am."

The soft words surprised her. "What?"

"Stuart told me other words. Sucker for sob story."

Warmth crept into her cheeks. "I suppose that's true."

"You hurt when people suffer."

Jennifer shrugged. "I can't deny it."

"That is your weakness."

"I think it's my strength, but I can understand why you disagree. Compared to you, I've led a very sheltered life."

"You are not too old to learn."

The coffee tasted bitter in her mouth. Julio's world, and no doubt Stuart's world, didn't allow for shades of gray. Everything was right or wrong, yes or no. "What would you have me learn, Julio? How to be unyielding and ruthless?"

"Any weakness can give the wrong people a weapon to use against you."

"What do you mean?"

"People can force you to do things you do not want to do."

"I never thought about it. Probably because I never met those wrong people you talk about." She looked toward the patio doors. "Until today."

Julio said nothing.

"I know that Stuart's in trouble. Can you tell me what it's all about?"

The big man made no answer.

"What will happen if Stuart doesn't tell these people what they want to know?"

"They will try to kill him."

Fearful images darted through her thoughts. She finally sat back in her chair and studied Julio's solemn features. "Stuart told me to give you a job, but I don't know what kind of job."

"I am here to protect you, ma'am."

"From what?"

"From whatever threatens you."

The quiet words made her shiver.

"There she is, the grand lady of the manor. Should we bow, do you think?"

Jennifer's steady gaze met Phil's mocking one. "Perhaps," she said, "you'd rather eat your dinner in the kitchen."

"It's intolerable." Amelia looked down her bony nose at Jennifer. "When an upstart can tell us . . ." She gasped when Julio entered the room. "Who's this?"

"Julio is my new employee."

"He looks like a gangster," Amelia said. "He doesn't belong in the drawing room."

"Perhaps not." Phil snickered. "Unless Jen wants the piano moved. He could probably pick it up all by himself." His laughter died out when Julio stepped closer to him.

"You want me to throw this young man in the fire, ma'am?"

Phil's eyes rounded in sudden fear. "Stay away from me."

Jennifer took a look at the big man's impassive features and understood Phil's alarm. "Please go upstairs, Julio."

He gave Phil a long look before he left the room.

"Imagine, hiring that brute to threaten us." Amelia's face pinched into a sneer. "But what can one expect from a common nurse?"

"I'll tell you what you can expect." Jennifer lifted her chin. "Either you apologize to me, or you leave this house tonight."

The older woman gasped. "Of all the nerve."

Harold Wilson stepped into the room. He took a look at his wife's face, twisted with anger, and said, "What's going on?"

"It's her fault." Amelia pointed at Jennifer. "She hired this terrible man. He was going to hurt Philip."

Harold looked toward his son. "What prompted that?"

Phil shrugged. "We just wished Jen a good evening."

"You must have said more than that."

"He just greeted her, Harold," his wife explained, "and Jen turned on him."

"Hello, everyone." Barbara stepped through the doorway and looked from one to the other. "Did I miss something?"

Jennifer eyed the young woman's hot pink silk dress and wondered how she kept from freezing. The strapless front fit low over her breasts. Instead of sleeves, matching feathers stretched across her upper arms. The uneven hem struck her legs about knee level, but long slits at the sides allowed the skirt to gape open to mid-thigh.

Barbara moved to stand near the fireplace. "I'm starving. Isn't dinner ready?"

Harold moved to Jennifer's side. "Allow me to apologize for my family."

"Thank you." Jennifer turned toward Amelia. "But it's your wife who must apologize."

The red in the older woman's face brightened. "Not likely."

"Mrs. Wilson trusted me to protect Johnny's inheritance." Jennifer's gaze touched each of them. "For as long as I'm in this house, I'll do exactly that."

Barbara made a face. "It'll be a long time before that brat upstairs can be called a legitimate heir."

"You'll behave in a respectful manner toward me and Johnny," Jennifer added, "or you'll find somewhere else to live."

"You're a grand lady now, aren't you?"

"We understand." Harold's soft voice overrode Barbara's angry words. "We'll abide by your rules."

His daughter gave an angry gasp. "Speak for yourself."

"I'm speaking for all of us, Barbara."

"Not for me." She took a step closer to Jennifer. "You cheap—"

"Barbara!"

Her gaze jumped to her father.

"While I'm supporting you, you'll do as I say."

Phil laughed. "That's telling her, Dad."

"That goes for both of you," his father added.

"I'll be the model of decorum," Phil stated, "even if it kills me."

"It's your fault," Barbara said to her brother.

He gave a nonchalant shrug. "So shoot me."

"That isn't the worst idea you've had lately."

A discreet cough from the doorway announced the butler's entrance. "Dinner is served, Miss Denton."

"Thank you, Roberts." She turned to face Amelia. "Do you wish to join us?"

The woman's thin, rat-trap of a mouth pressed tightly together.

"Amelia?" her husband prompted.

She took an indignant breath, looked at her husband again, and muttered, "Sorry."

"Thank you." Jennifer glanced at the others. "Shall we go in?"

With an angry sniff, Amelia turned toward her husband. Phil executed an elaborate bow and extended an arm to his sister.

In the dining room, Roberts bowed in Jennifer's direction and pulled out the chair at the head of the table. She heard a startled gasp behind her but didn't look around.

"Right and proper, Jen," Harold commented.

Roberts seated her with as much ceremony as he would have used for royalty. Raising an imperious, white-gloved hand, he gestured for the servers to move forward.

For the next hour, Jennifer picked at the delicious food. It had been a long time since she'd eaten a meal under such uncomfortable circumstances. Previously, Roberts had always looked toward Amelia for a sign to clear the used dishes and serve the next course. Tonight, he ignored her and deferred to Jennifer, and each time the red in the older woman's face darkened.

By the time the maid served dessert, Jennifer wondered if Amelia might be headed for a stroke. The click of her fork on the dish grew louder with each bite she cut from her slice of strawberry torte.

"Was the meal to your satisfaction, Miss Denton?"

Around a bite of the delicious confection, Jennifer murmured, "Excellent, Roberts. Please convey our compliments to the cook."

Harold nodded in agreement. "This cake is superb."

Barbara and Phil said nothing, though they ate their dessert with apparent enjoyment.

"Would you like coffee in the drawing room, Miss Denton?"

Spend another hour with the Wilsons? Not if she could avoid it. "No, thank you, Roberts."

The butler bowed and withdrew, motioning for the two serving girls to go before him.

"I always enjoy a cup of coffee by the fire after dinner." Amelia's mouth twisted until the red of her lipstick almost disappeared. "I suppose I can't do that any more." Giving Jennifer a venomous look, she threw her napkin onto the table and pushed back her chair.

"I'm sure Jen meant no slight toward us," Harold said.

"She meant it," Amelia insisted. "And it's only the first of the indignities we'll have to suffer."

Jennifer swallowed her bite of dessert. The sweet berries and delectable cake no longer had any appeal. Shoving her plate aside, she arose to her feet and headed out of the dining room.

"What's wrong, Jen?"

Jennifer spun around from the counter in the upstairs kitchen and saw Stuart standing in the doorway. "I didn't hear you come in."

"I wouldn't last long if people heard me moving around."

Why did he always make some reference to the cloak and dagger world in which he lived? Perhaps the wounds on his back formed a constant reminder. "I decided to have a cup of coffee before lunch." She made a face. "Without the Wilsons.

Would you like some?"

"Yes, thank you. Can I help?"

She pointed to a top shelf. He retrieved two cups and set them down on the counter beside the simmering pot. Seen from the distance of less than two feet, the scar at his right temple looked deep. It stretched from the corner of his eye into his hair. He could easily have lost an eye.

Jennifer poured their coffee and sat down at the table. When he sat down opposite her, she asked, "Why do you do it, Stuart?"

"Do what?"

"Your job."

"I enjoy it."

"I might believe that, if I hadn't seen your back."

He shrugged. "I wasn't as vigilant as I should have been. It won't happen again."

"If it happened once, it could happen again."

"It won't."

She took a drink of coffee and studied him over the rim of her cup. "If someone asked me about you and I said that I didn't know anything, would they believe me?"

"Why wouldn't they?"

She frowned. "Do you realize how difficult it is to talk to someone who answers every question with another question?"

"Do I do that?"

Her lips quivered.

He smiled in response. "I'll mend my ways."

She stared at him for a moment. "Are you some sort of government agent?"

"Let's just say I do a necessary job."

"And you don't want to involve me in whatever it is."

He made no answer.

"But I am involved, Stuart, simply because I know you."

"I hope not."

"Did you come here just to see Johnny?"

He took a drink of his coffee. "No."

"You're staying until you receive orders of some sort?"

"Smart lady."

"It wasn't hard to figure out."

He frowned. "I hope it's harder for the other side to figure out than it was for you."

"When you ran into that wall, were they after you?"

"Yes."

"They must know Johnny is here. Won't they assume that you're here also?"

"No. They're following a false lead."

"What happens to Johnny after you leave?"

"He'll be safe with you."

"Thank you for that." Jennifer studied the remaining coffee in her cup. "But what if something happens to me?"

"Julio will know what to do."

"You have no idea how much better that makes me feel."

"That had a bitter tinge." Stuart leaned forward. "Is something bothering you, Jen?"

About to deny it, she shrugged. "I ran into someone yesterday."

"Male?"

"Yes." She gave a humorless laugh. "His name is Frank. At one time, I thought I was in love with him."

"But you know better now?"

"Yes." She blew out her breath in a sigh. "He telephoned a while ago. He's on his way out here."

"Do you want me to see him?"

Jennifer didn't have to think about it. "No."

"I could have a talk with him."

"Wouldn't it compromise your position if he finds out you're here?"

"Not necessarily."

That didn't make sense. "What do you mean?"

"I'll tell him a convincing story."

"You'd have to pretend to be my—"

"Right."

She didn't like the sound of that. "What would you say?"

"Whatever it takes to make him believe me."

"You know, Stuart, I'm beginning to wonder how fluent a liar you really are."

"As fluent as I need to be."

She frowned. "That's what I mean."

"I haven't lied to you."

"I believe you. That's how gullible I am."

"No, Jen." He put a warm hand over hers. "That's how trusting you are."

"Same thing."

"Not the same at all. I flatter myself that you don't trust everyone." Stuart finished his coffee and set down his cup. "I'd enjoy getting rid of Romeo."

She gave him a suspicious look. "What does that mean?"

"Bad choice of words. You want Frank out of your life, right?"

"Right."

"And he didn't believe you when you said you were no longer interested in him."

"Right again. He accused me of having another man in my life. I didn't deny it."

"Then he'll expect to see me."

Her lips curved into a smile.

"What's funny, Jen?"

"I said you'd swat him like a fly."

"Then he can't say you didn't warn him."

She still wasn't sure. "What would you do to him?"

"Nothing permanent."

"That doesn't answer my question, Stuart."

"I'll just fix it so he won't bother you again."

"How can you do that?"

Stuart slid the cup across the table and stood up. "Trust me, Jen. Discouraging people is one of my best assets."

She frowned at him. "I don't know."

"I won't put a mark on him." Stuart put a hand over his heart. "I promise."

Chapter Five

Jennifer rinsed the coffee cups and left the kitchen shortly after Stuart. As she turned the corner and headed for the nursery, she saw Frank standing on the landing at the top of the stairs.

He waved. "There you are."

If he had arrived a bit sooner, he might have seen Stuart. She glanced aside at the door to the nursery as she passed by. Stuart used one of the doors leading into the garden to get into and out of the house. He could come into the hallway at any moment.

She stepped up her pace and hurried to meet Frank. "What are you doing on this floor?"

"That butler didn't want to let me in. I told him I was your fiancé. He said you were up here."

"I must have a word with Roberts."

Frank made a face. "He's too snooty for my taste."

Her chin lifted. "He suits me fine."

Jennifer looked past Frank's shoulder to see Barbara tottering toward them on impossibly high heels. She wore a hot pink pantsuit with the top unzipped halfway down.

"Well, now," she said.

The sound of a feminine voice made Frank reach up to straighten his tie before he turned around.

"Hello, Jen." Barbara gave Frank a brilliant smile. "Aren't you going to introduce me to this gorgeous man?"

Jennifer caught the strong odor of alcohol as she waved a

hand between them. "Barbara Wilson . . . Frank Caldwell."

An appreciative smile parted his lips. "I didn't know Jen had such beautiful friends."

Barbara's giggle turned into a hiccup. "That's a lovely compliment, Mr. Caldwell."

"Frank," he corrected.

"Frank." She moved closer to him. "Why haven't I seen you before?"

"Jen and I had a disagreement."

"A quarrel between lovers." Barbara sighed. "How romantic." She lifted a hand to her mouth to cover another hiccup and then reached with the same hand to touch his cheek. "If Jen doesn't make up with you right away, give me a call."

Her sensual whisper brought a dull flush to his cheeks.

Giving him another brilliant smile, she moved toward the stairs.

Frank's gaze followed her entrancing wiggle in the fitted suit. When she started down the stairs, he gave a soft whistle.

"Why don't you follow her," Jennifer suggested, "and get better acquainted?"

"Don't be jealous, darling." He gave her a warm smile. "Every man appreciates a good looking woman."

"I want you to leave."

His features reflected a smug smile. "You're jealous."

"Don't be silly."

"You can't mean that." He reached out to take hold of her shoulders. "One would think you aren't glad to see me."

"One would be right."

"You don't have to worry, darling. I'll be faithful." He jerked her against his chest. "You have my word."

She strained back against his hold. "Let go."

Amusement sparkled in his eyes. "You used to like me to put my arms around you."

She pushed harder against his chest. "I don't like it now."

"I'm here and I'm staying." His eyes narrowed. "Get used to it."

He bent over her.

His lips just grazed her cheek as she twisted away. "Let go!"

"Now, darling." His arms formed a painful vise around her ribs. "Don't be that way."

"Hello, folks."

The sound of Stuart's voice loosened Frank's hold enough for Jennifer to push away.

He stared over her head. "Who are you?"

"More to the point," Stuart replied, "who are *you?*"

Jennifer gave a surprised start when his arm slid around her waist. She saw Frank's gaze drop to her middle and didn't wonder at his interested look. Stuart's fingers rested on her rib cage, just below her breast. The adoring look on his face needed no translation.

"Trouble, darling?" he murmured.

"This is Frank Caldwell. He was just leaving."

Frank looked pointedly at Stuart's arm. "Jen is my fiancée."

"Perhaps Frank and I should have a little talk." Stuart bent and brushed his lips against hers. "Save my place."

Frank shot an accusing glance at Jennifer. "Who is this man?"

Stuart shifted to put her behind him. "Let's go for a walk, Frank."

The blustering look on Frank's face sickened and died when his gaze locked with Stuart's, several inches higher.

Stuart reached back to briefly cup Jennifer's cheek in his hand. "I'll be back soon, sweetheart." Putting a hand on Frank's elbow, Stuart guided him to the stairway.

Jennifer quickly walked to the railing and watched them descend. A smile touched her mouth. She'd bet her meager bank account that Frank wouldn't bother her again.

Stuart swung the front door open. "Outside."

When Frank headed toward his car, parked in the circular drive in front of the house, Stuart slipped an arm through his and steered him away. "You can't leave yet. We haven't had our talk."

"Where are we going?"

"Where we can talk privately. We have to get acquainted. How can we do that if we don't talk?"

"Look, whoever you are—"

"My name's Stuart." He nudged the man toward the trees at the side of the house. "And you're Frank."

"Look, mister—"

"Why so formal? We're on a first name basis."

When they were out of sight of the house windows, Stuart shoved his companion against the trunk of one of the huge oak trees. "I hate long goodbyes, so I'll make this short. Jen belongs to me. She doesn't want anything to do with you."

Frank nervously licked his lips. "I . . ."

"If I hear that you've bothered her, I won't like it."

Stuart reached into a pocket of his jacket and produced a set of metal knuckles. Fitting them onto his left hand, he held them up close to Frank's nose.

"The first time you bother her, I'm going to work on your face." Stuart allowed a moment for that to sink in. "You won't be so pretty when I finish."

Frank's eyes widened at the sight of the polished metal close to his cheek.

Stuart returned the knuckles to his pocket and slipped the revolver out of his shoulder holster. Stepping closer, he pressed the muzzle against Frank's teeth and heard the man's frightened intake of breath. "The second time you bother her, you'll make me angry."

Frank's terrified gaze was riveted to the shiny barrel of the pistol.

Stuart pressed the gun's muzzle a bit harder against Frank's teeth.

"Mmmmph . . ."

"You want to say something, Frank?"

Between frightened gasps, he said, "I won't . . . make . . . you angry."

"I'm delighted to hear you say that, Frank. However, if you consider going to the police or something equally stupid, I have friends who are nastier than I am. They'd pay you a visit. You wouldn't like them as well as you like me. They're not as understanding as I am."

"Uh . . ."

"Yes, Frank? Are you trying to tell me something?"

"I . . . I won't bother her."

Stuart replaced the revolver with a quick flip. "I'm glad we had this talk." He gave the man a smile. "Communication is the doorway to understanding."

Despite the cold wind blowing through the trees, sweat stood in beads on Frank's brow. He managed a sickly smile before he sidled away and headed for a break between the trees. He paused once to look back.

Stuart twisted his features into a scowl.

Frank tripped over his own feet. With a frightened glance over his shoulder, he pushed himself upright and began running.

Stuart leaned against the tree and laughed.

". . . and this last page as well, Jennifer."

She signed where Banning indicated.

"That starts the procedure for your guardianship."

She studied the lawyer's keen eyes staring at her over his half-glasses. "Stuart's alive."

Banning made no comment.

"You knew all the time, didn't you?"

"Yes."

"Why didn't you tell me?" She gestured toward the documents in front of her. "There's no reason to pursue this any farther."

The lawyer's shaggy eyebrows shoved closer together. "There's every reason to pursue it."

"But Stuart's alive," she persisted.

"Not officially. And with that in mind, don't you think it would look a little peculiar if I withdrew this petition?"

She said, "Who would know?" then nodded. "Court records are part of the public domain."

"Right." Banning put the signed papers into a manila folder and carried it to a filing cabinet. "We won't take this action to conclusion, of course. It's enough that you've signed the final papers."

Jennifer said, softly, "Who is Stuart?"

The lawyer secured the bar lock on the safe. "You can trust him completely."

"I know that."

Her emphatic statement drew a sharp glance.

"What I meant to say is that I've watched him with his son. Any man capable of that kind of gentleness and with that much love to give can't be bad."

The lawyer snorted. "I once prosecuted a man accused of killing five people. Even though he confessed in open court, his mother maintained that a man as gentle and full of love as her son couldn't be bad."

"Are you saying Stuart isn't what I think he is?"

"Is anyone who we think they are?"

She frowned. "You're as bad as he is, always answering a question with another question."

"Comparing me favorably with Stuart." Banning chuckled. "I take that as a compliment." He moved back to his desk and sat down. "By the way, he's leaving soon."

"When?"

The lawyer silently stared at her over his glasses.

"I know." Jennifer got up from the chair. "You can't tell me."

His chair creaked as he heaved his bulk up out of the chair. "Be sure to drive carefully."

"I will."

She took the elevator to the lobby and headed for the entrance. From the corner of her eye, she saw movement and looked up to see a woman staring at her. The woman turned away immediately, but Jennifer had a good look at her face.

It was Louise, that phony nurse.

Jennifer went through the revolving doors and out onto the sidewalk. Without even glancing toward her car, she flagged a passing taxi. She got in, gave the driver her address, and turned to look out the back window.

The blonde stood staring at the cab. Two big, tough-looking men joined her. While Jennifer watched, a long, dark car pulled up. The three got into the vehicle and then the car pulled into traffic.

Jennifer dug into her purse, pulled out her cell phone, and dialed Banning's office number. His secretary answered. Banning had left the building for a meeting with a client. The woman offered to take a message. Jennifer thanked her and ended the call.

Stuart might be at the Wilson house.

She punched in the first few numbers and then ended that call as well. Even if Stuart was at the house, she couldn't ask

Roberts to call him to the phone. So far, Stuart had entered and left the house without anyone seeing him. Except for Phil, and the young man hadn't mentioned the incident in her presence.

There was no one she could call for help. She'd have to deal with this by herself. Exactly how she was going to do that, Jennifer didn't know. The three in the car behind her were obviously following her and hoping to find Stuart. She couldn't lead them to him.

But where could she go?

She scanned both sides of the street but saw no likely place. When the driver stopped at another light, she saw a sign advertising a large mall in northern Virginia. Leaning forward, she said, "I've changed my mind." She almost lifted an arm to point to the sign, but decided it wouldn't be smart to give anyone an idea of where she was going.

"I want to go to that mall." She nodded her head toward the right. "The one advertised over there."

"Yes, ma'am."

Jennifer settled back on the seat and whispered, "I won't let you down, Stuart."

"You talking to me, ma'am?"

"No," she told the driver. "Just talking to myself."

He grinned into the rear view mirror. "We all do it."

She took another look out the back window and frowned.

The black car was gaining on the taxi.

Stuart dropped the curtain over the window. "Jen should be back by now, Julio."

"You want me to find her?"

"I'll go." Stuart checked his revolver. "Stay with Johnny."

"Be careful, my friend."

"I'm always careful." Stuart hunched his shoulders against

the itch of healing skin. "Almost always."

"Jennifer is a smart lady."

"Yes, but I suspect she has very little experience with the seamier side of life."

"You will protect her, Stuart."

"That takes a load off my mind." His friend's soft laugh prompted an answering chuckle. "Stay in the nursery, Julio. If I need you, I'll send someone to stay with Johnny."

A few minutes later, while stopped at a light, Stuart pulled the soft wool cap lower over his ears. He shivered, rubbed his gloved hands over his arms, and stretched out a hand to shove the heater control to a higher level. It took longer now for him to adjust to cold temperatures.

Too many years spent in tropical climates.

It didn't matter whether or not he adjusted to the icy December winds. In a few days he'd be where it was a lot warmer. He sighed and settled back in the seat. In the past he'd looked forward to getting back on known ground. Now he admitted that returning to South America didn't have the appeal it once had. He didn't have to think too long to figure out the reason.

His attraction to Jennifer was growing stronger every day. It could only lead in one direction. If he were smart, he'd leave before it was too late.

Jennifer continued to occupy his thoughts while Stuart drove the beat-up replacement truck to the Falls Church, Virginia, building where Banning had his office. Jennifer's car sat half a block away. It had a ticket on the windshield, so she hadn't fed the meter for a while.

According to Banning, she'd left his office over an hour ago. Something had happened to make her avoid using her car. Stuart didn't see a bus stop anywhere nearby. She wouldn't expect to get any distance walking, nor would she cross the street for a taxi going in the opposite direction. So she must have flagged one on her side of the street, heading in the direction Stuart was driving.

A strolling policeman stopped and looked Stuart's way. The cop was obviously curious about a truck stopped in the middle of a block and the driver's apparent interest in a parked car. Stuart pulled away and saw another uniformed officer patrolling the other side of the street. In the distance, a black and white official vehicle turned onto the street.

Someone might have forced Jen into a car, but an action like that attracted attention, the one thing a smart agent avoided. The courthouse was close by and the city jail was on the corner. Professionals wouldn't try to grab her with so much visible law enforcement.

A more likely explanation was that Jen thought someone might be following her. She wouldn't come directly home and place him in danger of being discovered. So she had left her car and taken a cab.

But where did she go?

His gaze flicked from one side of the street to the other. He saw a number of small businesses, but didn't think it likely she would stop at any of them. She'd go someplace where she could merge into a large crowd. Then, at the appropriate time, she'd try to slip away and get home.

His roving glance noted a sign advertising a huge mall in northern Virginia. He nodded. What better place to join a crowd than in a mall? He didn't waste time wondering how he'd find her among thousands of people. Taking the route he assumed the cab had taken, he finally turned onto the mall grounds. Directly ahead, he saw an entrance and a car backing out of a parking place. Stuart darted into the spot.

A loud honk, followed by a yell of annoyance greeted him when he slid off the truck seat. He looked in the direction of the other driver, and the man hastily rolled up his window and drove away.

Stuart grunted and rubbed his bearded chin. He must look seedier than he thought.

Shivering in the icy breeze, he replaced the sunglasses with a pair of horn-rims. The lenses looked like corrective ones, but their only function was to change his eye color to a faded, blue-green. The cap covered all of his hair.

The mall entrance stood a short distance away. He entered and moved to the center. Checking the length of the mall in both directions, he headed for a nearby snack stand and bought a large pretzel topped with mustard. Nothing looked more normal than eating. The size of the pretzel and the covering napkin shielded the bottom part of his face whenever he took a bite.

Stuart nipped off a large chunk. He enjoyed the tang of the mustard on his tongue while his gaze swept the nearby stores. If his hunch was right, Jen would dart into a store and stay there until she thought the coast was clear.

He'd bet the rest of his pretzel she would say those words when he found her.

An elegant department store stood across from the mall entrance, but it was too obvious a choice. Judging by her clothes, Jen was a conservative dresser. If she wanted to disappear, she wouldn't go into a store that sold the kind of clothes she normally wore.

Looking to his right, Stuart spotted a likely choice. The window sported a collection of trendy, brightly colored clothes. He detoured into a boutique showing a curly black wig in the window. Scooping the wig off the model's head, he headed for the counter with the cash register.

The saleswoman eyed the pretzel with some alarm.

Stuart ignored her frown and slapped the hair down on the

counter. "I'm in a hurry." The sizeable tip he gave her resulted in an abrupt change of attitude.

"We have some real bargains on coats and sweaters, sir." She pointed a finger. "The best selection is on that rack, against the wall."

Stuart strode over and selected a dark coat. Adding it to the bag containing the wig, he put more bills into the woman's outstretched hand.

She gave him a smile. "Come in again, sir."

He nodded and left, still munching on the pretzel.

"Ma'am?"

Jennifer made a face at the changing-room mirror. The orange and purple jumpsuit looked hideous. "Yes?"

"Your fiancé is here."

Fear jumped through her. When she had carried in a double armload of outfits, she'd meant to spend a lot of time trying on the garish clothes until she could figure a way to sneak past Louise and her friends. But if they sent in the message by the sales clerk, they wouldn't use a weak excuse like a waiting fiancé. They'd send Louise in to check the try-on cubes.

Or would they? Maybe they were standing outside, waiting for her.

"Ma'am?" the salesgirl called.

"Hmmn?"

"What shall I tell the gentleman?"

Jennifer turned toward the face peering around the curtain. "Tell him I'll be right out."

The salesgirl gave her a strange look before she dropped the curtain back into place.

Jennifer didn't blame her. No doubt, the girl wondered why her customer wasn't anxious to see her fiancé.

Curiosity prodded Jennifer to sweep aside the curtain and

move the short distance to the entrance of the dressing area. She peeped out and saw a tall, familiar figure standing just outside the doorway.

Stuart spotted her and held out the bag. "I got the coat and wig, just like you wanted."

The sound of his voice pushed her forward. She rushed toward him and threw her arms around his neck.

His arms lifted to surround her. "You pick strange times to get amorous, Phyllis."

Shock held her still while he reached up and took her arms from around his neck. He pointedly checked his watch. "Can you get a move on?" His voice held more of an edge than before. "My boss is expecting me back."

Behind the thick lenses, one of his eyelids slowly closed and slowly opened again.

Jennifer doubled her hands into fists and propped them on her hips. "You mean that secretary *Gloria* is expecting you back."

The lenses didn't hide the flash of surprise in his eyes. A moment later, he said, "You aren't going to start that stuff about me and Gloria again."

"Do you think I don't know what's going on?" Jennifer grabbed the bag out of his hand. "You don't fool me, either of you."

From the corners of her eyes, she saw the two salesgirls edging closer.

"Will you try on the wig and the coat? See if they fit?" Stuart checked his watch again. "I have to get back."

She jutted her chin at him. "All I asked of you was to help me with my costume for the party, and you don't want to."

"I'm helping, I'm helping. Now go try these on."

Giving him an exasperated look, she walked back to her cube.

She dumped the coat and the wig out of the bag. Tearing off the horrid jumpsuit, she got into her sweater and slacks and put on the wig. The short black curls looked strange, but they certainly changed her appearance. Slipping on the black coat, she buttoned it and studied her image. The wig and the shapeless coat made her look like a different person. Hurriedly stuffing her other coat into the bag, she walked out into the store.

"I'll just wear them," she told Stuart.

"Whatever."

His attitude was clearly that of a man who'd had enough of a woman's foolishness. He turned away. "Let's go. I don't want to lose my job."

Jennifer stuck out her tongue at his broad back. She heard the two salesgirls giggling as she stalked after him.

Once outside, he took hold of her elbow and steered her into the doorway of the next shop. He stood in front of her, blocking the view of anyone passing by. "Put these on."

She took a pair of heavy-rimmed glasses from his hand and slipped them on. Peeping around his broad shoulder, she whispered, "Is the coast clear?" and frowned at his rumble of laughter. "I could have been killed and you're laughing." She looked around his other shoulder. "They might be out there right now."

"Put this scarf over the wig."

He handed her a nondescript piece of dark blue material.

"But, Stuart—"

"Don't argue, Jen."

"My name is Phyllis. Remember?"

He shrugged. "Whatever."

Jennifer tied the scarf over the wig. She caught a glimpse of herself in the glass and then took a longer look. "Hey . . . I look like someone else, not me."

"That's the idea."

He took her arm and pulled her out into the concourse.

"But you don't know what happened. I can't just walk

outside. Some people are following me."

He nudged her toward the entrance. "They're following Jennifer Denton."

"Do I look different enough to fool them?"

"Let's hope so."

"You don't exactly fill me with confidence, Stuart."

"Think about it. They aren't looking for a dark-haired woman with glasses."

She darted a glance behind her.

"Turn around," he murmured. "The surest way to attract attention is to start looking at everyone."

A blast of cold air from the open door made her duck her head against flying sleet. "Great. Now it's snowing."

"It *is* great," Stuart replied. "It cuts visibility. Keep your head down. We aren't far from the truck."

He pulled her close against his side. She didn't protest, assuming he was trying to protect her against the gusting wind. A short time later, he opened the passenger door and helped her onto the seat.

She waited until he dropped behind the wheel before she said, "Don't you want to know what happened?"

"I assume you spotted someone following you."

"Not just someone. That blonde nurse."

Stuart started the truck. "Was she alone?"

"No. There were two men with her. Do you know her?"

"Let's just say our paths have crossed."

"She said her name was Louise Campbell."

"It isn't. Her name is Gladys Brown. She was born and raised on a farm in Kansas." He gave Jennifer a smile. "That bit about the secretary wasn't bad. Showed quick thinking."

"You mean I might have a future as a government agent?"

"I wouldn't go that far." He backed out of the parking place. "Now tell me what happened and don't leave out anything."

CHAPTER SIX

Stuart dropped her half a block from her parked car. She understood that he didn't want to come any closer to her vehicle, but it felt like the longest distance she'd ever walked. Opening the door, she slid onto the seat.

He had promised to follow her. Though she glanced often in the rear and side view mirrors on her way home, she didn't see Stuart's truck. That didn't prove anything, of course. If he said he'd watch out for her, he would. A thoughtful smile tilted her lips. Yesterday she wasn't sure she could trust him at all, but today she felt safe just knowing he was nearby.

Of course he wouldn't be around for much longer. After listening to her story and asking a couple of pertinent questions, he'd told her that he'd be leaving soon. She wasn't at all sure how she felt about that.

If Louise and those two thugs had followed her to try to find Stuart, they obviously knew he was alive and in the United States. According to Julio, they wanted Stuart enough to go to whatever trouble might be necessary to secure his capture.

Goosebumps traveled up her arms when Jennifer remembered the terrible injuries to his back. He had assured her that there was no danger, that he would be safely out of the country very soon, but she didn't believe it. To stay alive as a government agent, a man would have to be resourceful. Stuart certainly was that, but he was also human.

Julio believed caring about someone gave your enemies a

weapon to use against you. If that was true, Stuart had a built-in weapon in the presence of his son. Yet he couldn't leave the boy in South America.

Jennifer wrestled the problem back and forth but came to no satisfactory conclusions. Leaving the car on the circular driveway outside the house, she told Roberts to hold lunch for half an hour and walked upstairs. Stuart might not be there yet, but she'd wait for him. She had to know what to do if trouble arose while he was away.

Shoving the unsettling thought away, she opened the door and entered the nursery. Stuart sat on the sofa against the far wall and read to his son. He looked up and waved her forward. "Come and join us, Jen."

"Wouldn't you rather be alone?"

"No, of course not."

Glancing toward Johnny, she said, "I'm sure you don't have as much time to spend with your son as you'd like."

"A pretty lady is never an interruption." Stuart looked down at his son. "Right, Johnny?"

The boy's small face puckered into a frown. "In-ter-rup?"

Stuart chuckled. "I guess that is a big word."

"What does it mean, Daddy?"

"Something that stops you from doing what you want to do. Understand?"

Johnny's gaze returned to Jennifer.

The message in his eyes needed no translation. She murmured, "I'll see you later," and backed out of the doorway.

Stuart put down the book. "Why did you do that, Johnny?"

His son's face radiated innocence. "Do what, Daddy?"

"Don't play dumb." Stuart studied the small upturned face until Johnny's gaze slid away from his. "You were rude to Jen. If I didn't know better, I'd think no one taught you any manners."

Johnny twisted off his father's lap. "I don't like her. I want her to leave."

"She's a very nice lady and she's been good to you."

"But she isn't a nice lady, Daddy. She's looking for a husband. She'll trap you."

Stuart's glance swept toward the two women seated against the wall. Betty's mouth opened in surprise, before she turned to look at the woman sitting beside her.

Maria's gaze evaded Stuart's.

"Who told you that, Johnny?" he asked

The little boy darted a glance toward Maria. He looked back at his father but said nothing.

When Maria arose from her chair, Stuart said, "Stay here." He opened the inner door, beckoned to Julio to come out, and turned back to face her. "I'm going to ask you once, and I want the truth. Did you make those remarks to Johnny?"

She said nothing.

Any other woman of his acquaintance would get angry and try to bluff her way out of the situation. Failing that, she'd probably burst into tears. Maria wouldn't do either of those things.

"Well?" he prompted.

"Yes. I tell him."

"You want to tell me why?"

"The woman is not right for you."

"That isn't your decision."

Her head lifted. "I take care of your son since he is born. I promise his mother to take care of him always."

"That also isn't your decision."

"You must pick a wife who loves your son."

Now he understood. "I hired Sasha in Panama to take care of Johnny because she's your niece. I never had a personal interest in her."

85

"She is young enough to give you sons."

"And I'm old enough to be her father. Don't mention her again, Maria."

She flinched. "I do what I think is right. Do not be angry."

"It's too late for that."

"You will send me away?"

"No!" Johnny cried.

The glow of satisfaction in the woman's dark eyes whetted Stuart's anger. "I trusted you, but you brought trouble into this house."

Bowing her head, she whispered, "Do not send me away."

"Julio will arrange for you to leave tomorrow. In the meantime, you'll sleep in another room. Betty will take care of Johnny."

Maria's gaze held his. "You always trust me before. It is that woman's fault."

Julio muttered something to her that made Maria cringe and move toward the door. He followed her outside.

Johnny ran after them, but Stuart caught his son at the door and swept him up into his arms. He nodded to Betty. She stepped out into the hall and closed the door behind her.

"You and I have to talk, son."

The boy twisted in his hold. "You sent Maria away!"

"She told you bad things about Jen, things that aren't true."

"I don't want Maria to go."

"She's a baby nurse, Johnny. Are you a baby?"

The little boy frowned, clearly trying to decide whether he wanted Maria enough to admit to being a baby.

"You must learn not to believe everything people tell you." Stuart gathered him closer in his arms. "Are you still a baby, son?"

"No."

"It takes a man to admit he's made a mistake. You must

apologize to Jen."

The small boy shifted to look up at his father's face. "Maria said I need Sasha to take care of me." Johnny's bottom lip began to tremble. "She said I was too much trouble for you, Daddy."

Stuart bent and kissed his son's cheek. "We're a family, you and I. You could never be too much trouble for me."

"Daddy . . ."

"Yes?"

"Are you sure you don't love Sasha?"

"She's making a new life for herself. Maybe she'll get married."

Johnny stared up at him. "Are you going to make a new life too, Daddy?"

"What do you mean?"

"Are you going to get married?"

Stuart studied his son's earnest expression. "If I do, she'll be someone whom I love very much and someone whom you can love."

Johnny's frown told Stuart that the boy wanted to say something else but wasn't sure if he should.

"What is it, son?"

"Do you love Jennifer?"

He considered the boy's question. "I haven't known her for very long."

"Does it take a long time to love someone, Daddy?"

"Not always," Stuart murmured.

"But sometimes?" the little boy persisted.

Stuart smoothed Johnny's hair back from his forehead. "What's bothering you?"

Johnny's gaze slid away from his. "Sasha would come here to us, if she knew we wanted her."

"She's an eighteen-year-old girl, Johnny. When I marry again, it'll be someone nearer my own age." The unhappiness on his son's face urged Stuart to pull the boy closer and give him a hug. "You and I are a family, Johnny. We don't need anyone else."

"But families need a mommy." Johnny's gaze searched his father's face. "Don't they, Daddy?"

Stuart said, softly, "Yes, I suppose they do."

A few hours later, Jennifer sat in one of the large wing chairs by the drawing room fireplace and studied the leaping flames. The ugly moment in the nursery this afternoon still bothered her. She couldn't expect Johnny to care for her, not this early in their relationship, but she didn't expect hostility.

She thought about the cold resentment in the little boy's eyes. Did she say or do something to upset him? She sighed and stretched out a hand to the warmth of the fire. He just didn't like her. She might as well accept it.

"Jen?"

She jumped, looked around, and saw Harold Wilson standing a few feet away.

"I hope I'm not intruding."

"Of course not." She waved a hand toward the companion chair.

"I hope you're going to join us for dinner." He dropped into the chair opposite her. "We haven't seen much of you."

Harold retained most of his youthful good looks and appeared well-groomed as always. He gave the impression of good health and vitality and had the trim body of a man half his age.

"We've missed you, Jen."

"I've been busy."

His eyes met hers briefly and then skidded away, only to return a moment later as though he was hesitant to maintain eye contact with her. "You've had a lot thrust upon you in a very short time, my dear." He smiled again. "I'd be glad to offer my services."

"I can handle the responsibility."

He lifted his hands in a gesture of apology. "I meant no insult." His hands clenched and unclenched before he reached up to adjust his tie. "I'm sure you'll do a beautiful job."

Why was he so antsy? "Is something wrong, Harold?"

"Of course not." He gave a soft laugh. "There doesn't have to be something wrong before we can have a little chat, does there, Jen?" He cleared his throat and shifted on the chair. "Fortunately, you're sensible as well as sympathetic."

Intuition told her that he was trying to appeal more to her sympathy than her sensibility.

"From the moment you entered this house, Jen, I knew you were a very special person."

Jennifer took another sniff of the pleasant citrus aroma of his after shaving lotion. Stuart was the only man of her acquaintance who didn't wear any. The reason wasn't hard to figure out. He didn't want to attract attention.

"You look lovely this evening, Jen."

Curiosity arched her eyebrows. "You've never given me so many compliments before."

"A fault which shall be remedied immediately."

Again, his gaze shifted away from hers. She said, "Do you want to talk to me about something, Harold?"

A relieved look flitted across his features. "I should have realized that you'd make it easy for me."

"Make what easy?"

He chuckled. "I feel reluctant to bring up such an indelicate subject as money."

She frowned. "Money?"

"My family is very upset about the terms of the will."

Jennifer shrugged. "There's nothing I can do about that."

He smiled at her again. "Of course you can."

"I'm not the heir."

"You could influence the distribution of monthly income."

"Mr. Banning is the executor."

The fingers of Harold's right hand tightened around the end of the chair's arm, drawing her attention to the gold ring on his little finger. The sizeable red stone glowed in the firelight. She wasn't an expert, but it looked like a genuine ruby. The fire added a rich glow to the gold watch at his wrist.

The Wilsons weren't destitute, no matter how much they pretended to be dependent upon their late aunt's charity.

"Phil's in trouble, Jen."

"What kind of trouble?"

"He owes a large gambling debt to a rather nasty person who insists upon having his money paid back." Harold laughed, but his eyes narrowed, as though he was gauging her reaction. "It wasn't Phil's fault. People enticed him into the game and then cheated him."

"That's too bad."

Harold gave her another smile. "You have a kind heart."

"I heard you talking to Phil about running up gambling debts once before."

A frown wrinkled Harold's forehead. "We must make allowances for a boy's high spirits."

"Phil is twenty-six."

Uncertainty flitted across Harold's face.

"He had a new car for his last birthday," Jennifer added.

"I like to give my children nice things."

She looked pointedly at his jacket. "Unless I'm mistaken, that's cashmere."

"You surely don't begrudge an old man's attempt to keep up appearances."

"You look very healthy to me."

"Healthy." His blustering attitude dissolved like chimney smoke in a strong wind. "That's no more than I deserve, I suppose."

She frowned. "I beg your pardon?"

"It isn't your fault, my dear. I hoped to charm you, and you think I look healthy."

Jennifer watched the firelight playing upon his face. He reminded her of a deflated balloon, flat and featureless. "Why should you want to charm me, Harold?"

"I'm quite fond of you, Jen." His gaze didn't quite meet hers. "But no man likes to admit that he's made mistakes."

He put a hand to his face, but she saw the glint of his eyes from between his fingers. He obviously wanted to see her reaction.

"We all make mistakes, Harold."

The hand dropped from his eyes. "I'm glad you can understand a father's concern for his son."

"Of course." She interpreted the flicker in his eyes as renewed hope. "I'm sure you'll find a way to deal with Phil's problem."

The corners of Harold's mouth tightened. "You won't allow me to keep my dignity, will you?"

"Is it dignified to brag about indulging your children?"

From the darkening red in Harold's cheeks, her remark had struck a nerve. "I didn't expect that from you, Jen."

He fished in his jacket pocket and brought out a silver cigarette case. Raising his eyebrows in her direction, he silently asked permission to smoke.

She nodded.

He selected a cigarette, retrieved a gold lighter from his pocket, and flipped it open. "We all have . . . uh, quirks we wouldn't want aired in public."

She didn't like the smile tilting one corner of his mouth.

"Barbara told me about your friend Frank. Phil told me about

91

the bearded man who visits you at night, not to mention Julio." Harold's smile turned sly. "Talk about still waters running deep."

"What are you trying to say?"

"I'm merely pointing out that families occasionally have to circle the wagons and protect each other."

"Banning thinks I should toss you all out of the house."

Harold's pale eyes narrowed. "Harsh words, Jen."

"What do you expect when you threaten me?"

"Who's threatening you? All I'm doing is asking you to help me protect my son. In return, I'll keep quiet about your male friends."

"Are you insinuating—"

"There's no reason to get angry." Harold stood up and tossed his cigarette into the fireplace. "We're in a position to do each other a favor."

"There's nothing I can do about the will."

"You help me, Jen, and I'll help you. If you refuse, I'll be forced to take steps to protect the Wilson heir."

"What do you mean?"

"I'd be remiss in my duties if I didn't ensure that little John's guardian is morally sound." He paused for effect. "I'll sue for custody of the boy. It should be easy once I cite your . . . adventures with unknown and questionable men."

"There haven't been any adventures, Harold."

"The Federal Bureau of Investigation may not agree with you."

"What?"

He smiled. "You had two male visitors yesterday while you were out."

Did those men with Louise actually come to the house? "Roberts didn't mention it."

"I told him I'd take care of it."

She didn't like the sound of that. "Take care of what, Harold?"

"I'm sorry, my dear. I didn't mean to usurp your authority. I thought I'd do you a favor."

"Who were these men?"

"I told you. They were FBI agents."

"How do you know?"

"They showed me their identification."

"That can be forged," she pointed out.

"They had badges with pictures." Harold dragged a finger down his cheek. "One of them had a long scar."

"What did they want?"

"Someone reported seeing a mysterious stranger in the vicinity of the house. These men came to check the story, since the report could mean that we have prowlers on the estate. They asked me if I knew anything about it or had seen anyone. I told them that the only stranger I knew anything about was the bearded man whom Phil saw with you." Harold paused to smile slyly. "They thanked me for the information and left."

Jennifer arose from her chair. She had to talk to Stuart.

Harold stepped forward. "I'd advise you to reconsider my request, Jen. Once these facts about your strange friend are aired in court, it won't take long for a judge to declare you unfit to have the charge of any child."

She drew in a breath, preparing to tell Harold exactly what she thought of him. The smirk on the man's thin lips said he expected her to revert to type and yell at him.

It occurred to her that Stuart wouldn't allow Harold to bother him. With that in mind, she held the older man's gaze while she shaped her lips into a smile. Surprise flashed across his features. She had the satisfaction of seeing him give his lips a nervous lick before she walked across the room and stepped out into the hall.

★ ★ ★ ★ ★

"Daddy?"

"Yes, son?"

"Can I eat in here?"

"If you wish." Stuart finished buttoning Johnny's pajama top and helped him to put on his robe. "Betty can fix you a bottle."

Johnny made a face. "I'm too big for that."

"Are you big enough to apologize to Jen?"

"I'm still a little boy."

"I suppose you are." Stuart headed for the door.

Johnny ran after him. "I want to go with you, Daddy."

Stuart frowned and turned around. "Little boys belong in the nursery."

His son's eyes looked wise beyond their years. "Can I go with you if I tell Jen that I'm sorry?"

Stuart bent and swept his son up into his arms. "I don't think we need baby bottles any more."

Jennifer's satisfied smile dwindled and died as she climbed the stairs. Pausing by the door to the nursery, she gazed back down the hallway toward the stairs. Harold meant what he said. Standing her ground in this house was one thing. Facing him in a courtroom was another. He would portray her as unsavory. Judges wouldn't tolerate illicit behavior on the part of juvenile guardians and rightly so. Unfortunately, there was very little she could say in her own behalf without involving Stuart. And she couldn't do that.

She sighed and whispered, "I have to talk to you, Stuart."

"Always a pleasure."

Spinning around, she saw him and Johnny standing in the open doorway. The boy looked up at his father and then back to Jennifer. "I'm sorry I was rude."

Stuart must have urged him to say those words. Jennifer

wished that it had been his son's idea. "Thank you."

Johnny frowned. "You're glad I was rude?"

"I'm glad you apologized."

She saw no friendliness in the boy's eyes and wished that Stuart hadn't insisted upon his son's gesture. "I made vegetable soup yesterday. Come and have some with me."

"Sounds great," Stuart commented. "I have to make a call, Johnny. You go along with Jen. I'll be there in a few minutes."

After his father walked away, Johnny stood looking up at her. The scowl on his small face didn't bode well for their time together.

Jennifer smiled and held out her hand. He looked at it as though it might bite. Sidling around her, he moved several steps away and stayed at that distance while he followed her to the small kitchen.

She waved him to a seat and yanked the refrigerator door open. The air flowing around her didn't feel much colder than the room behind her. If music had charms to soothe the savage beast, perhaps food could do the same for a hostile child.

She set the soup on the counter and then walked back to the refrigerator for a package of cheese. She placed it on a saucer and put it on the table.

"Have some, Johnny."

"I don't like it."

"Okay." She broke off a bite, put it into her mouth, and nodded her appreciation of the nutty taste. "The less you eat, the more there'll be for me."

She opened the lower cabinet doors to get a pot and pretended not to notice Johnny reaching out to the cheese. He nipped off a chunk. His small nostrils flared as he sniffed it. He sent another guarded look in her direction and put the lump into his mouth.

A minor victory, but she savored it.

Stuart appeared and set the table while Johnny helped by carrying forks and spoons.

"I suppose you've eaten some strange things, Stuart."

"I've eaten things you wouldn't want to step on."

The idea made her shiver. "We won't pursue that any farther."

"It's just as well," he agreed. "I wouldn't want to spoil your appetite."

"Thank you."

After their meal, Jennifer went with them to the nursery. Johnny was nearly asleep on his feet.

Stuart took off his son's robe and tucked the little boy into bed. "They're totally dependent upon us, aren't they?"

What had prompted that remark?

"I never knew my parents, Jen."

The simple words made her long to comfort him. Uncertainty about his reaction kept her silent.

"I wasn't quite two years old when my mother left me at an orphanage."

"Oh, Stuart," she whispered, "how awful for you."

"It might have been, but a wonderful lady adopted me. She had kids of her own who accepted me as their younger brother. When her husband died, she worked two jobs to support all of us." A muscle worked in his jaw. "She died last year. I couldn't have loved her more if she was my birth mother."

His voice sounded flat and unemotional, but Jennifer sensed a high level of pain behind his words.

He turned to look at her. "You have her gentleness and sweetness. Knowing you is like having a part of her back. I'll always be grateful to you for that."

There was that word again. She'd never been on the receiving end of a man's gratitude before. She wasn't at all sure how she felt about it.

"Is something wrong, Jen?"

Glad for a diversion, she nodded. "I was in the drawing room a while ago and Harold strolled in and joined me." She paused. "He asked for money. Phil's in trouble with someone to whom he owes a large gambling debt. The man threatened him, unless Phil pays what he owes."

"It could be true," Stuart conceded, "but Harold is one of the most accomplished liars I've ever met." He studied her surprised features. "I know because I'm also an accomplished liar."

"You admit it?" She stared back at him. "How do I know if you ever tell the truth?"

"So far, I haven't found it necessary to lie to you."

Would he find it easy to do? "You'd really do that?"

"Only if I had to."

"To protect me?" When he nodded, she said, "You may get your chance. Harold thinks you and Julio have compromised my good name."

"He said that to you?"

"In exchange for money, he offered his support should anyone claim that I'm not morally fit to care for the Wilson heir."

"Look who's talking about morals."

Stuart's green eyes appeared as cold as a mountain lake in winter. He made her uneasy. "Harold seemed desperate," she said.

"Because it suited his purpose, Jen. Don't let him fool you. Harold and his family moved in this house to exert influence on Mrs. Wilson."

She couldn't deny that. "He threatened to take me to court. If that happens, the only defense I have is to reveal your identity as Johnny's father. And I can't do that without jeopardizing you and your mission, whatever that is."

Stuart made no comment.

"There's more. Two men came to the house yesterday while I

was out. Harold talked to them. He said they had badges identifying them as FBI agents."

"Go on."

"Apparently, someone reported seeing a mysterious stranger lurking in the neighborhood. These FBI men meant to talk to every household in the area to see if anyone had any suspicions of a prowler around their property. They came to this house and asked Harold if he'd seen anyone . . ." Jennifer paused. "Harold said the only mysterious stranger he knew about was the man whom his son saw visiting me late one night."

"Did Harold give you a description of these men?"

"One of them had a scar on his face." She put a finger under her eye and pulled it down to the corner of her mouth. "Like that."

Softly, Stuart said, "They weren't FBI agents."

Jennifer nodded. "I suspected that."

"They were two of Garizon's men. They came here hoping to get information about me." He paused. "And Johnny. If they had him, they'd soon have me."

There was only one way to interpret that. "Surely they wouldn't harm a child."

His features looked bleak. "Ruthless people employ ruthless means."

Fear formed a knot in her stomach. "You're scaring me."

"Good. That means you'll be careful."

CHAPTER SEVEN

The following morning, Jennifer had finished breakfast and was halfway up the stairs when Roberts spoke to her from the downstairs lobby.

"There's a telephone call for you, Miss Denton, from a Mr. Banning. Would you care to take it in the morning room?"

She retraced her steps and turned toward the back of the house. A small room stood opposite the library. She walked inside, moved to a table near the fireplace, and picked up the receiver. "Hello."

"Good morning, Jennifer."

Banning's voice sounded different from the one she remembered. Nevertheless, she said, "Good morning, Mr. Banning. How nice to hear from you."

A muffled sneeze greeted her. "And it's nice to hear your voice, Jennifer. Unfortunately, as you can hear, I have a cold."

His voice sounded muffled as though he might have a handkerchief pressed to his nose. "I'm sorry you're ill."

"So am I, my dear. I need to see you. Can you come to my office right away?"

Jennifer frowned. "I didn't tell you. Someone followed me when I left your office yesterday."

"You obviously eluded them."

Them? She had said some*one.* How did he know there was more than one person involved? Before she could ask, he said,

"I need to talk with you, Jennifer. I promise not to get too close to you."

"Couldn't you come out here?"

He sneezed again. "I'm due in court within an hour. I'll be there for the rest of the day."

"Can't you tell me over the phone?"

"You never know who might be listening on an extension."

She couldn't deny that possibility, but going to his office had little appeal. "I don't know," she began.

"You'll be perfectly safe. I'll send a car for you. He'll also take you back home."

"How will I know he's from you?"

"Good point. How about if he says something we agree upon?"

"Like what?"

"How about the name Stuart? What better choice could there be?"

"I'm not sure—"

"I don't like to insist, Jennifer, but there are new papers you have to sign." She heard another sneeze. Then he cleared his throat and said, "I know, I know. I'll be right there."

Jennifer felt uneasy about his request. "I'd better check with Stuart."

"You'll meet him here."

She blinked in surprise. "Stuart's going to be there?"

"Yes, but it wouldn't be smart for the two of you to travel together."

Why was Stuart going to the lawyer's office? Maybe it had something to do with Harold's threat. Yes, that made sense. Stuart would want to protect his son from Harold's greed and Amelia's neglect. Of course! *That's* why there'd be "new papers to sign."

"I'll send the car immediately," Banning continued. "The driver will open the back door for you and say just one word, 'Stuart.'"

"This sounds like something out of a bad movie."

"You wound me, Jennifer. I think it's one of my best ideas." Banning coughed again. "The man will be there within twenty minutes."

Hurrying downstairs a short time later, Jennifer spotted the butler supervising one of the young maids arranging flowers in a tall vase. "I'm going to Mr. Banning's office, Roberts, but I'll be back for lunch."

"Would you like your van brought around?"

"He's sending a car for me."

"Very good, ma'am."

Jennifer paused by the hall mirror to give her upswept hair a final pat. The eyes looking back at her held a gleam of excitement. Tucking a stray curl under her soft wool hat, she winked at her image and hurried to the front door.

A dark car headed up the driveway. The driver swept to a stop, presenting the side of the vehicle to her. She didn't see any identifying markings.

He stepped out and moved around the hood of the car. "Miss Denton?"

He was medium-sized, with dark hair and eyes, and wore a dark jacket and slacks but no hat. Banning said the driver would say only Stuart's name, but she could understand that he wanted her to identify herself. A house this large might have several other occupants.

"I'm Jennifer Denton," she replied. Her gaze swept the length of the car's body. "This isn't what I expected."

His gaze followed the direction of hers. "Did you think the car would be a regular taxi?"

"Yes."

"Taxi drivers keep a record of all their fares."

Now she understood. "Mr. Banning doesn't want the wrong people to know about this meeting."

"That's right." The man moved to open the back door. He smiled and murmured, "Stuart."

Jennifer returned his smile.

Stuart walked slowly along the front of a gaily decorated department store window before he sauntered toward a pay telephone at the next corner. He ducked his head against a blast of cold air and took the opportunity to check the sidewalk in both directions.

People carrying colorfully wrapped boxes moved purposefully past him in both directions. Shifting his two packages to his left arm, he moved out to join the crowd.

He looked both ways before he stepped inside the booth, deposited money, and dialed a number. When a man answered, Stuart said, "I sing tenor."

The man on the other end said, "You used to sing bass."

"Anything to tell me?" Stuart asked.

"Mama left the house."

Mama was the code word for Jennifer.

"When?"

"A short time ago," the voice continued. "She left in a large, unmarked car."

"Is someone following her?"

"They were, but they got caught behind an accident."

Stuart wrenched the booth's door open and headed for his truck.

Jennifer opened her purse and took out a thick envelope. Banning would probably want to talk to her about this wad of documents. She found pages relating to her guardianship of Johnny and read through them, curious to see how Banning had set it up.

There followed a long discourse regarding the boy's eventual inheritance. Jennifer gave a soft whistle at the property and amounts of money mentioned on those close-typed pages.

She didn't see the name of Banning's law firm anywhere. Apparently, this was information for her alone. Folding the papers again, she stuffed them back into the envelope and put it in her purse.

Snow swirled outside the car windows, but the roomy interior pampered her with comfort and warmth. She slid her palm across the upholstery. The fabric felt surprising soft, yet the seat fit her back exactly right for maximum comfort. She couldn't remember ever riding in a car as comfortable as this one.

Looking toward the front seat, she started to comment on her comfort, but changed her mind when the driver's gaze met hers in the rear view mirror. He didn't look so friendly now. Perhaps he felt tired or hungry.

Her insides rumbled. She felt hungry, too. Glancing out the window, Jennifer frowned and bent closer to the glass. Nothing looked familiar. She leaned forward and said, "Which way are you going?"

"You won't be late for your appointment," the driver answered.

When the car stopped at a light, she glanced up at the street sign and saw the letters "SE," denoting the southeast area of the city. Why was he driving through this part of Washington? He was supposed to take her to Falls Church, Virginia, to Banning's office.

The driver's abrupt turn to the right would have tossed her onto the floor if she hadn't fastened her seat belt. This time when she looked outside the window, she saw derelict and boarded-up buildings lining both sides of the street.

"Where are you going, driver?"

A thick panel of glass lifted out of the top of the front seat, closing her off from the driver.

She unfastened her seat belt and hunched forward to rap on the glass. "Where are you taking me?"

He lifted a telephone to his ear and didn't reply.

Jennifer couldn't hear what he was saying. She slid back onto the seat and grabbed for the door handle. Her searching fingers felt nothing but smooth upholstery. She couldn't open the door from the inside. Why would Banning send this kind of car for her?

He wouldn't. Whoever had called earlier wasn't Banning!

How could she have been so stupid? At the time Banning's request had sounded logical, but she should have followed her gut-instinct. She should have insisted that Banning come to the house.

She dug her cell phone out of her purse and began punching in the numbers for Banning's office. The driver watched her through the rear view mirror but made no move to stop her from calling for help. It wasn't difficult to figure out the reason. He wanted her to call. Anyone could retrieve the last numbers dialed from a cell phone.

She broke the connection and put the phone back into her purse. Fear stabbed through her as the driver turned into another street and then slowed almost to a stop as he aimed the nose of the car into an alley.

Jennifer sent a desperate look out the window for anybody to whom she might signal to indicate she needed help. She saw no one on the street.

Her darting gaze spotted a bulging garbage can. A child's stuffed bear stuck out from under the lid. The toy animal, made of some vivid purple fake fur, had one ear hanging by a few threads. It turned and twisted in the frequent gusts of wind.

The car moved down the alley. She saw the back of a large truck with its ramp down. The driver slowed but didn't stop. She yelled to him, but he didn't turn around.

Jennifer cringed at the impact that must surely happen. She saw a woman and two men standing by the truck. The blonde nurse, Louise, smiled at her, just before the car drove up the ramp and into the back of the truck.

Stuart pounded his fist on the steering wheel of the truck. "After Jen's bad experience, I thought she'd be more careful and stay close to the house."

"It is the way of a woman, my friend."

Stuart frowned. "I'm in no mood for philosophy."

"A woman's nature is to be curious, especially about things she should avoid."

"Someday you'll tell me how you learned all these facts about women."

Julio's craggy features didn't change. "I have had three wives."

"I guess that qualifies you as an expert," Stuart conceded, "but it doesn't solve our immediate problem. Wherever Jen is right now, she's in danger, and that danger gets worse as the minutes tick by."

"Do not blame yourself."

"I don't even know where to start looking for her." Stuart's bleak gaze studied the snow pelting the truck windows. "Talk about a needle in a haystack."

Julio said, softly, "Can this be *Sombra?* The shadow?"

"I don't feel much like a shadow today." Stuart pointed a finger. "And these buildings aren't the jungle."

"It is a kind of jungle, Stuart."

"One made of cement. Man is the predator here, Julio."

"We will hear something about Jennifer soon."

"It had better be soon." Stuart frowned. "When you kidnap somebody, it's important to disorient them as soon as possible. That means taking them somewhere unfamiliar."

"Where would such a place be for Jennifer?"

Stuart didn't have to think about it. "The seamier part of town. I doubt she's ever been there. Even if she has, she wouldn't know it very well. Also, and more important, she wouldn't feel safe moving around on her own. Taking her to that part of town lessens the possibility that she'll try to get away." He said after a moment, "Any company indoors is better than anyone she'd meet outside on her own."

"So what do you want to do?" Julio asked.

"They won't take her to an area with stores. They wouldn't want to deal with crowds of Christmas shoppers." Stuart's mouth hardened. "That narrows the field to only a few square miles."

"Men are watching Garizon and his companions. We will soon have word."

"You said that an hour ago, Julio."

"You are impatient, my friend."

Stuart drew in a long breath and tried to dredge up the reserved detachment that served him so well. Unfortunately, he no longer felt reserved or detached where Jen was concerned.

Julio said, softly, "They will not harm her. She is not the one they want."

Stuart turned to meet the dark, intense gaze of his friend. "I should have warned her."

"Jennifer is a smart lady," Julio commented. "She will not do anything foolish."

"You mean anything *else* foolish. She has no experience with this sort of thing." Stuart scanned the street again. "Wherever she is, she's scared."

"We are all scared."

Surprise pulled Stuart's head around. "Not you, Julio. For as long as I've known you, I've never seen you scared."

"Like all men, there are things I fear."

"No one would ever know it."

Julio shrugged his massive shoulders. "The trick, as you say, is not to mind the fear." He added, after a moment, "Have we not always done our job?"

Stuart nodded.

"We will find her."

He looked into Julio's eyes and nodded again.

Jennifer twisted around and watched the back of the truck close. The sharp clang of metal against metal shut out the last of the daylight. A moment later, she felt a jerk.

The truck started moving.

Her heart began to pound. She sent a frantic gaze around the dark interior of the car and then sat back on the seat and tried to relax. She had to be able to function, if and when she got a chance to run away. She had to hold together until Stuart found her.

On the heels of that thought came a sobering one. Her kidnappers weren't amateurs. They knew how to deal with any attempted escape from their custody.

Jennifer noted the flare of a cigarette lighter in the front seat. The intermittent glow, as the driver took drags on his cigarette, gave her something ordinary to concentrate upon. She kept her eyes focused upon the small red spot as it lifted and then dropped, again and again. Finally, she didn't see it any longer. He must have put out the stub.

How long did it take to smoke a cigarette?

She searched her memory for someone she knew who smoked. Yes, that circulatory specialist, back when she was a student nurse. What was his name? Stephen. Yes, Stephen

Walker. She used to see him in the hospital cafeteria. He sat at a long table, with several other doctors.

They usually had about ten minutes left of their lunchtime when he fished a pack out of his pocket and passed cigarettes around. She always thought it strange that doctors would smoke but tell their patients the habit was bad for them. Within the next seven or eight minutes, Dr. Walker would take his last drag and crush the cigarette in an ashtray. It might not be an average time for everyone, but it gave her some sort of a gauge.

She judged no more than a couple of minutes had passed before the driver's lighter flared again. As before, she watched his movements until the red glow disappeared. Using her estimate of time, and counting the first cigarette he'd smoked, about twenty minutes had passed since he had driven into the back of the truck.

She clenched her hands until the nails bit into her palms. That was long enough to get far away from the city.

Where was the driver headed? Someplace in Maryland, perhaps? What did it matter? She was getting farther away from Stuart every minute.

The sensation of movement stopped. Jennifer tightened her clasp on her purse. If she got the chance, she had to try to run. With luck, maybe she could maneuver past them. She considered that for a moment and then gave a soft laugh. Who was she kidding? Louise and those men wouldn't let her escape.

A sudden clang jerked Jennifer's head around. Rising to her knees, she watched the back of the truck open. Two men walked forward. Ducking their heads against flying snow, they moved a ramp into position and jumped aside.

She twisted around when she heard the driver's door open. Moments later, he reached in to help her out. He kept hold of her elbow while they descended the slippery ramp.

Louise held a black length of material in her hands. "Hello

again, Miss Denton."

In the last few seconds before the woman tied the scarf over Jennifer's eyes, she looked around, trying to spot something recognizable. She almost laughed with delight when she saw the garbage can.

There couldn't be *two* toy animals that color in a trash can near a curb.

They hadn't gone anywhere. The truck had driven around for a while and then wound up back where it started. Relief welled up inside her, but she quickly averted her gaze as the blonde settled the blindfold over her eyes.

Someone took Jennifer's purse off her shoulder. She felt a strand of narrow rope looped around her wrists. Responding to a tug on the line, she began walking.

"Negative, *Sombra*. Negative."

"Understood."

Stuart clicked off the short-term phone. His narrowed gaze searched the street in both directions, but he saw no familiar head of red hair. Not that he expected to, of course. A woman who looked like Jen couldn't walk on these streets alone for very long before she acquired the kind of company she didn't want.

He stood in front of a derelict schoolhouse, one of the known haunts of Garizon, his old enemy. The building wasn't the only place in the area the man used, nor was it the most recent, but Stuart walked inside and checked it. From the accumulated dirt and trash, he judged that no one had been there for a long time.

Another dead end.

He frowned at the choice of words but didn't dwell upon it. The last thing Garizon wanted was to kill Jennifer. She would be far more valuable as a bargaining tool.

Stuart shifted his shoulders against the itch on his back. Garizon had almost made a bad mistake that last time Stuart was his unwilling guest. A bit more of the drug, and Garizon would have killed the one man he wanted to keep alive.

The man wouldn't make any stupid mistakes with Jen.

Stuart shrugged off his thoughts and checked the phone. The time was about gone. A block farther down the street, he saw a garbage truck making rounds and walked that way.

The two workmen became chatty when Stuart grinned at them, made the customary remark about the chill in the air, and then stripped the paper bag off the half-empty bottle he carried. The men moved forward. Stuart held out the liquor and told them to keep it to ward off the cold. When they headed toward a nearby alley to sample their prize, he tossed the cell phone into the back of the truck and moved away.

He stepped into the doorway of a closed-out dress shop and took a fully-charged phone from another pocket. After punching in the numbers, he waited until a familiar voice said, "I am here."

"See anything?"

"No. I see nothing," Julio answered.

"Meet me at the truck. We'll shift to another area."

"I will be there."

Stuart clicked off and pocketed the phone. He gritted his teeth against the bite of the wind.

"Where are you, Jen?" he murmured.

"Step up."

Obedient to the heavily accented command, Jennifer lifted her booted foot but still stumbled over a raised hump in the floor and fell to her knees. Pain shot down both arms when her escorts jerked her back up onto her feet.

She couldn't see who supported her on the right side, but the flowery scent drifting past her nostrils identified that person as

Louise. The woman gave a soft laugh and tightened her hold. Jennifer bit her lips against the pain as a string of foreign words flowed around her.

Louise answered the man with a curt phrase but released her hold on Jennifer's arm.

Their words had a strange echo, as though they were in a large, empty room. A strange scraping noise drew Jennifer's attention. She knew that sound but couldn't place it until it stopped with a thud that vibrated through the soles of her boots.

Of course. A garage door closing. From the clang, it had to be a heavy, metal door. Maybe they were in a public parking garage. That would explain the chill in the air and the echoes.

Someone urged her forward. Placing her feet carefully in front of her, Jennifer walked in the direction indicated until her escorts halted.

"Welcome."

A soft, male voice spoke near her left ear. She jumped and looked around but saw nothing through the blindfold. "Who's speaking? Where am I?"

"Who I am does not matter, Miss Denton."

He had a slight accent.

"Please bring a chair for the young lady."

She heard the scrape of chair legs behind her. A heavy hand on her shoulder guided her backward onto a hard seat.

"I regret I cannot make you more comfortable."

Jennifer lifted her hands to the material covering her eyes. "Taking this off would do for a start."

"Please do not remove the blindfold."

The words contained no particular stress, but Jennifer obediently dropped her hands back into her lap.

"I see you are going to be a cooperative guest."

Counting Louise and her two companions, there were now at least three people watching her. With her hands tied in front of her and the blindfold in place, she had no chance of surprising them.

"Someone took my purse."

"It is here." A moment later, the man said, "Write down these numbers, Paco."

So, he had checked her cell phone.

She heard the rustle of papers. He must be looking at the information in the envelope that Banning had supplied. Jennifer tried to recall what else she had in her purse, besides the papers and her cell phone. What did it matter anyway? She couldn't stop him from examining the contents of her bag.

"I see that the child in your care inherits a considerable fortune, Miss Denton."

This wasn't the time for small talk. "Who are you?"

"It will be better if you do not ask."

His soft laugh sent a shiver down her back. If she knew the answer to her question, she wouldn't leave here alive.

"Let us not speak of unpleasant things," the man continued. "We mean you no harm."

"I find that difficult to believe."

"I need your help."

She held up her bound wrists. "You have a strange way of asking for it."

"I hope to convince you, Miss Denton, to assist us."

"In what?"

"I depend upon you to achieve what my men have not been able to accomplish. The capture of *Sombra.*"

"*Sombra?*"

"You know him as Stuart Kendall."

CHAPTER EIGHT

Shock held her motionless. For the first time, Jennifer welcomed the blindfold covering the upper part of her face. Did this man know Stuart was alive, or was he just probing for information and hoping she'd get careless?

Striving for a casual, conversational tone, she said, "I understand Mr. Kendall is missing and presumed dead."

"Ah, yes, the accident." After a pause, the man said, "Mr. Kendall's body was not found."

"Wasn't he swept away in the river?"

She sensed surprise at her question. Perhaps the facts surrounding Stuart's disappearance weren't common knowledge. If so, she'd made a mistake and provided information to this man when she should have kept silent.

"Who told you about the accident, Miss Denton?"

That was simple enough to answer. "I heard about it at the reading of Mrs. Wilson's will."

"Ah, yes." The papers rustled again. "Mr. Foster."

"Banning," she corrected and heard a satisfied sigh.

Another mistake. The lawyer's name wasn't on any of those papers in her purse. Of course, this man might just be testing her to see if she would lie to him or tell him the truth.

On the heels of that thought came another, more disturbing one. These people knew far more than she would ever know about the reaction of people under stress. They'd see the crimped edges of her mouth and know she was upset. They might even ask her more questions, hoping for more information. If that's what they wanted, she had to deny it to them.

She leaned back against the chair and tried to relax.

"The man Banning is of little importance."

Maybe her mistake didn't matter. Or maybe this man meant to trap her again.

"You perhaps wonder about my interest in Mr. Kendall?"

Not wishing to appear too eager, she shrugged. "If you want to tell me."

"We have a contact in the American Embassy in Panama. He has worked for us for many years. Some might call him a spy." The man chuckled. "I prefer to think of him as a patriot. He observed Mr. Kendall's activities over several months and reported them to us."

"What does that have to do with me?"

"A woman who gets straight to the point." The man laughed again. "How refreshing."

"You haven't answered my question."

"I saw Stuart Kendall two days ago. He wore a beard and thick glasses, but the man was Kendall."

Worry tightened into a knot in Jennifer's stomach. They knew Stuart's disguise consisted in part of a beard and glasses. Or did they? Did they really see him, or were they hoping she'd make another slip?

"One of my men also observed Kendall near the Wilson estate. Did he perhaps call you on the telephone and request to see you, Miss Denton?"

She could answer that question honestly without involving Stuart. "I've never had a call from Mr. Kendall."

Seconds passed before the man said, "I believe you."

"I still don't see—"

"Why do you play games with her?"

Louise's voice came from behind Jennifer's chair.

"I can make her tell you what you want to know."

A sharp pain knifed through Jennifer's shoulder. She tried to shift away, but someone pulled her roughly back against the chair.

"Do not touch Miss Denton again."

An angry, "Hmmph!" said that Louise resented the command.

"I did not hear you agree," the man prompted.

"I will do nothing," Louise answered.

Jennifer shivered. She couldn't see the man's face, but the cold tones of his voice were enough to make her uneasy. She wouldn't want to be the target of his anger. Apparently, neither did Louise.

"You must be trustworthy, Miss Denton, or you would not have been named as the child's guardian. It is logical that Kendall will wish you to continue in that capacity. Therefore he will try to find you. When he does, we will be waiting for him."

She heard faint, punching sounds. Then he spoke again.

"Miss Denton asked me to tell you that she is unsure when she will return."

The sounds she heard must have been the man dialing the telephone number of the Wilson house. He must be talking to Roberts.

Jennifer tensed her muscles, ready to jump up, run forward, and yell. A punishing grip on her shoulder kept her in the chair.

"Miss Denton is not at home, sir. A gentleman called to say she is unavoidably detained."

Stuart closed his cell phone with a snap. "The butler says some man called to say Jen wouldn't be home any time soon." He turned to look at his companion. "They have her, Julio."

"Garizon will not hurt her."

"We can't be sure of that."

"Why would he do it?" Julio asked. "She has no information he can use."

"That's true," Stuart said, conceding the logic of Julio's statement.

"Our men are watching Garizon's headquarters."

"He might not take her to the warehouse."

"It is possible," Julio said, "but not likely. He is a man of old habits."

"And it would appeal to his ego to use a place he knows *we* know about." Stuart put the truck in motion. "I'll need you to provide a diversion."

"One of my many talents."

Stuart glanced around when he heard Julio's soft laugh. "You're getting more Americanized every day."

Jennifer shifted on the hard seat. The back of the chair consisted of three round pieces of wood that provided little support for her shoulders and none for the lower part of her spine.

Worse than that, the room grew colder as the time passed. Her muscles felt stiff and tight from the surrounding chill and from lack of movement. She had to get up soon and move around, or she wouldn't be ready when her chance came.

If it ever did.

The people guarding her weren't fools. She couldn't expect them to make any stupid mistakes.

"How much longer will you wait?" Louise spoke somewhere off to Jennifer's left side. "Kendall is not coming."

"He will be here."

"You stay too long, Fernando. We should—"

"Silence!"

The single word bit the woman's sentence off as cleanly as an axe chops wood. Jennifer held her breath. She hadn't thought so much anger could be contained in one word.

Louise stammered, "I . . . I am sorry."

Her quickened breathing sounded unnaturally loud. Though she couldn't see the man Louise had called Fernando, Jennifer leaned forward, waiting for his reaction. The darkness before her eyes made the waiting worse.

"As a measure of my trust in you, Miss Denton, I tell you my name. I am Garizon."

"Should I have heard of you?"

"No. I am not famous. Nor am I a diplomat. I merely carry out the orders of my superiors." He paused and then said, "I apologize for your discomfort. However, I very much doubt you would have agreed to meet with me had I given you the choice. I want you to understand that *Sombra* is a dangerous man."

She shifted her sore shoulder. "And you aren't?"

"In my experience, Americans respond to only two things."

Unable to contain her curiosity, she asked, "Which are?"

"One is a show of force."

"And the other?"

"A loved one in danger."

Both were heavy arguments, but maybe she could shift his emphasis a bit. "There's one more. We also respond to a fellow American in trouble."

Seconds passed before the man said, "Are you loyal to your country, Miss Denton?"

"Of course."

"I hope you are telling me the truth."

"Why would I lie to you?"

"An interesting question." He said, in a very different voice, "Keep back."

Jennifer gasped in sudden alarm and twisted around.

"Do not fear, Miss Denton. No one will harm you."

She said, "I hope you're telling *me* the truth."

"I brought you here to ask for your help."

She held up her bound hands. "Keeping me prisoner is a poor way of asking for my assistance."

"I cannot release you until I am sure of you."

What was that supposed to mean?

"Your own government admits that Stuart Kendall is guilty of criminal activities in my country."

The knot in her stomach twisted again. "What sort of criminal activities?"

"You would find the discussion extremely distasteful. Any decent woman would. Please believe me, Miss Denton. You do not want to know."

Stuart had said those same words.

"I must, of course, explain some of Kendall's activities if I expect you to help me capture him." Garizon sighed. "I apologize in advance, for I must upset you."

She didn't want to hear anything he had to say. "I'd much rather leave now."

"I am sure you would, but that is not possible. I told you that Kendall is guilty of crimes in my country."

She nodded. "Yes, but what crimes?"

"All sorts, I'm afraid."

"Tell me," she persisted.

"To give Kendall his due, I believe he did not want to get involved in these activities. It was his wife's unfortunate problem that triggered his decision."

Jennifer knew from the bits Stuart told her about his wife that Martha had emotional problems. There must be something else, something he hadn't mentioned.

"I regret to say that Mrs. Kendall was an addict."

Given Martha's problems, that could be true. Patients taking narcotics often became dependent upon them.

"Supplying her habit proved difficult on Kendall's salary. He was forced to . . . ah, supplement his income to procure the drugs she needed."

Jennifer didn't want to hear any more. "The woman is dead. What purpose does it serve to tell me these things?"

"Because he needed money, Kendall found places to use his peculiar talents, and people who would pay any price for his services. He committed murder for money."

She remembered Stuart's gentleness toward his son and said, softly, "I don't want to hear any more."

"It was my own brother whom Kendall murdered." Garizon paused. "I could tell you other acts that he committed, gruesome and horrible things, some of them involving innocent women." When Jennifer's hands knotted into fists, he said, "Please forgive me. I said you would find these facts shocking. Now you understand, at least in part, why we mean to capture Stuart Kendall and return him to our country to stand trial for his crimes."

Stuart had been kind to her. She didn't want it on her conscience that she'd provided the means of his capture. "If he's alive, Mr. Kendall would be much more likely to file a missing persons report with the police than to personally look for me."

"I know him. He will try to rescue you."

Jennifer stiffened. "You didn't bring me here to seek my help. You intend to use me for bait."

"That is a crude way of expressing the facts, but you are correct. Kendall knows about this place, so we made sure that some of his friends saw the truck and got a good look at the driver. That is why he drove you around for some time. *Sombra* will soon step into our trap."

"You said that word before. What does it mean?"

"It is a name associated with terror and murder. In some parts of the world, Stuart Kendall is known as *Sombra*, the shadow. He is an evil shadow who brings death and destruction wherever he goes."

Lies. All lies. She silently repeated the words.

"Yet he always finds someone to assist him, either by charm or by threats. He usually chooses an attractive woman, a woman like you, Miss Denton."

The faint queasiness in Jennifer's stomach rushed upward to become a bitter taste in her mouth.

"I regret involving you." The man's voice held pity. "But time is short. I mean to take Kendall back with me. This time I will not fail."

The words had a cold and cruel sound, even more so when she remembered the injuries to Stuart's back. Were these the people who hurt him before? "You intend to take him back to your country to face trial?"

Some man muttered a long string of words Jennifer couldn't understand. Another man answered him. She had no idea what they said, but she detected a note of excitement in both voices and thought she knew why. Stuart must be close by.

"Excuse me, young man."

Stuart swung around. A beckoning hand summoned him to the open back door of a dark, well-polished limousine. The lady inside smiled at him. "I need your help."

Stuart noted the gray-streaked, dark hair peeping from under her fur hat and her delicate skin that would look young when she was ninety. A subtle, tantalizing perfume drifted toward him when he bent and leaned closer to the open door. "What can I do for you, ma'am?"

Her pleasant features crinkled at the corners of her eyes. "I brought Christmas gifts to the orphanage." She waved a hand bedecked with glittering diamonds toward a large stone building, standing back from the street. "I have a lot of packages." She gave Stuart a smile as sweet as her soft voice. "Would you assist my chauffeur in carrying them inside?"

Stuart smiled back at her. "My pleasure." He had to stay in the area of the warehouse until Julio arrived. What could be better than this?

"I'll gladly pay you for your time," she offered.

"No pay is necessary, ma'am."

He walked to the open trunk and accepted several brightly wrapped packages from a young man in a uniform and matching hat. Stuart positioned one of boxes to block part of his face and moved out at the chauffeur's side.

Once inside the building, Stuart watched as a tall, older man with a sour expression on his thin face moved forward. He directed them toward a room at the far end of the central hall.

Stuart's nostrils wrinkled at the strong odor of some industrial strength cleaner. His frowning gaze noted the brown walls and serviceable floor. The powers that be obviously didn't think it necessary to waste money decorating this hall.

Maybe all orphanages were the same, cold and forbidding and filled with children who wished for someone to rescue them from their misery. Not every child would be as fortunate as he had been.

He thought about the first time Stella folded him into her arms and told him that she wanted to be his mother. He could still remember the delightful scent of roses on her person. No one in his acquaintance ever wore perfume. It was the first time he'd smelled the delicate aroma. From that time on, he associated roses with the wonderful lady who'd changed his life.

Pausing by a pair of glass-topped doors leading into a playroom, Stuart put a hand to the crack between the doors. The air moving through the space felt chilly. Management apparently didn't waste money on heating bills, either. He noted two dozen or so small children smearing finger paints, tearing pages out of magazines, and running here and there.

A young woman moved among them. Mousy brown hair had come loose from the twisted bun on top of her head. The gray, high-necked dress hung loosely on her tall, slender frame. It was probably some sort of uniform, bought more for practicality than appearance. The wrinkled skirt had colorful stains and what looked like the remains of a crushed banana.

Judging by her resigned expression, she'd had a trying day.

He felt a strong surge of pity for her before he turned away from the doors and hurried in the chauffeur's wake.

They deposited their packages on the floor around a Christmas tree placed in one corner of a large room. The tree looked tall enough but the back had almost no branches. Someone had turned that side toward the corner. The decorations consisted of hand-strung popcorn on a long string, wrapped around the branches.

Stuart's mouth twisted with anger on behalf of the children who would do their best to be merry without much assistance. He headed back down the hall. The chauffeur followed and stood to one side while Stuart walked up to the man who had told them where to take the children's presents.

"That's not much of a Christmas tree."

The man's face adopted a pious look. "We do the best we can, sir, with the funds which are available."

Stuart looked pointedly at the man's well-pressed suit and silk tie. "I'm from the Bureau."

Doubt wrinkled the man's forehead.

"You're due for an inspection. I hope you're ready."

"Well . . . I've only been here for two months."

Judging by the man's frown and his frantic gaze darting here and there, he had no idea what bureau Stuart represented.

"They won't be happy at headquarters when I tell them about that tree."

The man licked his thin lips. "I see your problem, sir. You

thought we'd finished decorating the lunch room, but we haven't. There will be more added to the decorations."

"What's your name?"

He licked his lips again. "Adam Shockley."

"Don't add anything else to that scrawny tree. Get another one, Shockley, and decorate it properly."

"But, sir—"

"Someone will come back to check on it, but don't expect to see him wearing an expensive suit."

"You mean he'll be in some sort of disguise?"

"He might be your Santa Claus."

The man looked blank.

Stuart allowed his eyebrows to drift slowly upward. "You *will* have a Santa?"

"Oh . . . oh, yes, of course."

"I'm going to give them your name, Shockley. They'll hold you responsible."

The man's face paled with anxiety. "I'll take care of it right away, sir."

"See that you do." Aware of the chauffeur listening with interest to his remarks, Stuart added, "We also expect the children to have a proper Christmas dinner."

From the stunned look on Shockley's face, a good meal hadn't been part of the plans, either. He managed a smile. "Oh, they'll have a good meal, sir."

"See to it, Shockley. Whoever inspects you will sample the food to make sure it's good and nutritious."

"There won't be any problems, sir."

"I may be the one who comes back to check on you."

"What is your name?"

"We never give our names."

"Yes, sir. The children will have a Christmas to remember."

Outside on the sidewalk, the chauffeur said, "Exactly what

bureau is that?"

Stuart shrugged. "It worked, didn't it?"

The man chuckled. "Good for you, sir."

On the third and last trip back to the limousine, Stuart spotted a short, chunky man standing by a car parked thirty feet or so from the limousine. The skin on Stuart's neck began to tingle. A doctor had told him once that it was physically impossible for someone's neck to tingle as a sign of danger.

Stuart knew better.

He accompanied the chauffeur to the front doors of the orphanage. Once inside, Stuart moved to a side window and inched his face around the sill. The stocky man stood facing the front door.

The chauffeur peered over his shoulder. "Friend of yours?"

"Not so you'd notice."

"Use the back door. Directly across from the parking lot, you'll see an alley leading to the next street over."

Stuart extended a hand. "Thanks."

"You did these kids a favor." The man grinned. "It's only right that I do one for you."

Rough fingers shoved the strap of Jennifer's purse into her hands. She heard another spate of foreign words. Callused fingers fumbled with the rope around her wrists and finally whipped it away.

What was going on? Had the man changed his mind and decided to let her go? She began to rub her hands. "What's happening?"

"Your cooperation may not be needed after all, Miss Denton. We are moving you to a place of safety."

"What's going on?"

"We expect Mr. Kendall to arrive at any moment. Once we have him in custody, you will be permitted to leave."

She hadn't expected that. "You'll let me go?"

"Of course. I told you earlier that I meant you no harm."

"And Mr. Kendall?"

"He will not be harmed, unless he refuses to surrender to our custody."

Someone jerked her to her feet. "Come on, sweetie."

Louise again.

Jennifer heard what sounded like people shoving heavy objects around the floor. Maybe they were building barricades to protect themselves against something. Or someone. It must be true. They expected Stuart. They meant to capture him. It was all her fault, and she couldn't do anything to warn him.

The hold on her arm tightened, urging her to move faster. Something rolled under her foot. Jennifer stumbled, lost her balance, and fell, banging her head on the cement floor. The dull ache in the back of her head grew worse when someone grabbed her by the hair and tried to pull her up.

She wanted to comply, to ease the intense pain in her scalp, but her legs didn't seem to work. The pain grew more acute when Louise gave her a painful slap on her left cheek and another on her right.

"There's no one around to protect you now." She grabbed a handful of Jennifer's hair and jerked. "Get up!"

A man said something.

Louise yelled back at him and hit Jennifer in the face two more times. The salty taste of blood ran across her tongue before she fell.

Strong arms scooped her up. Each of the man's steps sent a jarring pain through her head. She clenched her fists and tried to stay alert, but sounds began to merge together.

Someone pulled at the straps of her handbag.

Jennifer tightened her grip. Her head rocked with the force of another blow before darkness closed around her.

CHAPTER NINE

Stuart cracked open the back door of the orphanage and looked out. The air sweeping around his head didn't feel much colder than the bleak hall behind him. He didn't see any movement. The space behind the building contained a small parking lot and a trash collection area with overflowing garbage cans and a couple of dumpsters.

A late model car backed out of a space close to the door. Adam Shockley didn't look toward the building. He was in too much of a hurry. Stuart grinned. The kids would have a nice Christmas this year, with a good meal and the gifts the lady had provided.

He looked over his shoulder and whispered, "Thanks, mom."

Pulling the cap lower over his eyes, he stepped outside and closed the door after him. He checked both sides of the building but saw no one. That proved nothing. His imagination could be working overtime, but he didn't think so. He frowned and lifted a hand to massage the back of his neck.

A narrow driveway ran along behind the orphanage with another alley intersecting it almost directly across from where he stood. It would take only a few steps and he'd be out of sight from the sides of the building.

"Keep very still, Mr. Kendall."

From the corner of his eye, Stuart saw a stocky figure advancing toward him. So the man hadn't disappeared after all. Shrugging his shoulders deeper into his jacket, Stuart moved down the steps and away from the building.

"Mr. Kendall. You will stop, please."

He kept walking.

The man ran forward. "Stop."

Stuart stopped walking and turned around. Speaking with a nasal twang, he said, "You talkin' to me?" His gaze shifted to the large bore pistol, equipped with a silencer. "What's with the funny lookin' gun, mister?"

"Very good, Mr. Kendall. Very good, indeed."

"You aimin' to rob me?"

The man laughed. "The contents of your pockets hold no allure for me."

Stuart adopted a puzzled expression. "Huh?"

"Come now, Mr. Kendall. I have no time for this."

"I don't much like someone pointin' a gun at me." Stuart dropped his brows into a frown. "In fact, I don't like it at all."

The man motioned for him to move back. "Put your hands on the top of your head, Mr. Kendall, and move back against the wall. My partners will be here shortly."

Stuart didn't like the sound of that. "If this ain't the limit!" He jerked a thumb to indicate the direction behind him. "This mornin', a long-haired kid with a knife took my watch and a ring a girl gave me. Now you and your friends are goin' to take my money."

For the first time, doubt flitted across the man's pudgy face.

Not giving him time to think about it, Stuart rammed a hand into his pants pocket and brought out a couple of crumpled bills. "You can have one of these tens, if you let me keep the other one." He moved forward while he spoke, holding out the money. "I don't want any trouble, mister."

When the man's attention shifted to the money, Stuart jumped the last couple of feet. His left hand grabbed the extended right wrist and twisted. At the same time, he aimed a karate chop at the side of the man's neck.

Stuart draped the unconscious form across his shoulder. Shooting a glance at the sides of the building, he trotted toward the garbage area, heaved the man into the top of one of the dumpsters, and tossed the gun in after him. He took another look around and then turned away.

It took less than ten seconds to sprint through the narrow alley to the next street. Slowing to a rapid walk, Stuart started down the sidewalk, but couldn't prevent the rapidly appearing steam near his mouth. If the man's partners showed up now, it wouldn't be good for the home team.

A red painted door up ahead advertised the Good Times Bar. Stuart trotted to the door, pulled it open and stepped inside.

"You lonesome, honey?"

The husky voice in the vicinity of his right shoulder turned him around. The woman formed a vaguely lighter shape against the gloom behind her.

"How about buying me a drink, honey?"

"Sure." Stuart lifted a hand toward the bartender. "Beer for me. Give the lady whatever she wants."

"Hey, I like that. You've got manners." She moved to the bar. "You're also cute."

Country-western music blared from the far end of the room. Stuart frowned at the assault on his eardrums.

"Turn it down, Charlie!" the woman yelled.

The bartender waved a hand toward the back of the room and yelled, "Tell him, Mike."

The noise level dropped, but Stuart's ears still rang.

"Charlie lost his hearing aid," the woman explained.

Stuart followed her to the bar and leaned an arm on the counter. He regretted the gesture a moment later when she moved closer. The potent scent of her perfume filled his nostrils, making him stretch his neck to get a breath of fresh air.

"Stick around, honey. I like you."

He gave her a smile and shifted a few inches away. "I like you too, but I'm busy right now."

"Doing what?"

"I'm looking for someone."

She leaned close again and murmured, "Won't I do?"

"I'm looking for a redhead and a tall, thin guy. Have you seen anyone like that?"

"What do you want with them?"

"The redhead is my wife."

The woman let out a cackle of laughter. "You don't know when you're well off." She cocked a well-padded hip onto one of the worn, leather stools. "You know what I like, Bill."

The florescent lights in the bar area cast a harsh beam on her pale hair, heavy makeup, and the strings of cheap beads hung around her neck. Stuart also noticed her trembling hands.

The bartender brought a beer and a smaller glass full of what looked to Stuart like whiskey. The woman upended the glass and drank it down. She crooked a finger to the bartender who brought her a second drink which disappeared as quickly as the first one.

"You're better off without a wife like that, honey." She nodded toward the hovering bartender. "I'll have another one."

This drink lasted no longer than the first two. She gave Stuart a smile. "You should find yourself another woman."

Her words sounded slurred. When she lifted the empty glass and smiled at him, he pushed his beer toward her. "You're probably right, but I'm going to keep looking until I find her."

The blonde's hand wrapped around the glass. "Some guys never learn." Taking the beer with her, she slid off the stool and wove an unsteady path toward the back of the room.

When the bartender turned away, Stuart shifted back into a shadowy corner. He shucked out of his dark jacket, turned it wrong side out, and put it back on, purple side out. Taking a dark wig out of a pocket, he pulled it over his hair. Next came the glasses.

Stuart reversed the cap to a pale blue and adjusted it over the wig. When he felt satisfied that everything looked right, he moved to the door and stepped outside.

He heard voices in the direction of the alley and something metal rolling around. A man began cursing but stopped immediately when someone said something to him in a clipped, angry tone. Then two men ran out onto the sidewalk. They looked in both directions and then turned toward Stuart again.

He brushed past them, deliberately banging the shoulder of one of the men. When he said something, Stuart gave him an angry look. He made a few pointed remarks about blocking the sidewalk and continued on down the street.

Jennifer woke up with a dull pain in the back of her head and a sharper one in her right hip. It hurt her shoulders to lift her arms, but she managed it. Sliding her fingers under the hair on the back of her neck, she touched a wet, sticky place. Was she bleeding?

"Where am I?" she asked.

Nobody answered.

She pulled the blindfold away from her eyes, blinked to focus her eyes, and looked around. She lay in a small room with a high ceiling. Her cot sat against the wall. Nearby stood a metal chair. She didn't see any other furniture.

They'd brought her here because Garizon expected Stuart to arrive at any moment, and they couldn't watch her while they waited to trap him. Could it all be over? Or were they still waiting for Stuart?

She strained to listen but heard no sound. Twisting her head carefully, she turned toward the door. It looked like some sort of heavy metal. They could be shooting off fireworks outside and she wouldn't hear them.

Or even worse, they might be shooting off guns.

Stuart could be in one of these small rooms. Garizon had said he planned to take Stuart back to his country to stand trial. Stuart could be close to her and she wouldn't know it. He might even be in the next room and she couldn't help him.

Of course, Stuart might think she'd done enough. In her own defense, the man on the phone did sound a lot like Banning. After all, a person with a heavy cold sounded different. She had no reason to think it could be someone else, except for that one remark about her getting away from *them*.

Banning had no way of knowing that more than one person had tried to kidnap her. She should have questioned him, but she hadn't. That had been her first mistake. She should have followed her first inclination and talked to Stuart about going to the lawyer's office, but she hadn't, and that was her second mistake.

She heaved a tired sigh. This had not been one of her better days.

Stuart wouldn't thank her for putting herself into jeopardy and thereby forcing him to come looking for her. She should have been in the house, taking care of his son.

The sobering thought occurred to her that he had far greater troubles. Garizon meant to see Stuart dead, in part to avenge his brother, but she suspected some other motive as well. Garizon could be the one who had tortured Stuart. If so, how had Stuart gotten away?

His wounds weren't yet healed. They couldn't be much older than a week to ten days, which meant that Stuart had been a prisoner somewhere while the Panamanian authorities looked for his drowned body.

A person in trouble in a foreign country, perhaps in danger

of his life, would seek help from the American Embassy. Stuart may have tried and found them helpless to intervene in the legal affairs of another nation. So he'd slipped out of the country and returned to the United States.

Jennifer gave a tired groan. His locale didn't matter. He had problems here, too. Maybe she couldn't help him, but she could at least try. The first order of business was to get out of this room.

She lifted her left arm to check her watch, but couldn't focus on the dial. She turned to look over her right shoulder. Light came from a window high up on the wall behind her. From the dimness in the room, she judged that the time must be late afternoon. She carefully pushed upright and swung her legs over the side of the cot. The room made lazy circles. This was no good at all. How could she try to escape if she couldn't even stand up?

She squeezed her eyes shut for a few seconds and then opened them again. The circles moved slower this time. She rested her head back against the wall and fingered her sore jaw. She probably had bruises and looked terrible.

She sighed at the mess of hair hanging in red disarray over her left shoulder. Hopefully, she had some hairpins left in the matted strands. Shaping the ball of hair proved difficult. Her shoulders hurt. Movement aggravated the ache in her head, but she finally managed it and turned back to study the door.

She had to know what had happened to Stuart. Those men had been excited about something just before they'd brought her to this room. Could it be Stuart? As if in answer to her question, she heard a key turn in the lock.

The door opened and Louise stepped inside. She wore a form-fitting, red wool dress that made the most of her trim figure. "I decided to drop in and see how you're doing, Jennifer."

Maybe it would be smart to pretend to be worse than she was. "If I look as bad as I feel, I may never buy another mirror."

Her voice sounded strange. Of course. Her lips were swollen. One more debt she owed to the blonde.

Louise sat down on the metal chair and crossed her shapely legs. "I thought we'd have a chat."

"Why?" Jennifer shot back, forgetting her resolve to be meek.

"We have something in common." The woman's red lips parted in a sly smile. "Or perhaps I should say someone."

"I don't think that you and I have anything in common."

"Oh, but we do. And my name is Louise."

"Don't you mean . . ." Jennifer bit off her sentence just before she revealed the name Stuart had mentioned. "Never mind. I'm dizzy. I'm not thinking too clearly."

Her answer seemed to please Louise. "You shouldn't have argued with me."

Jennifer didn't remember arguing with the woman, but it wouldn't do her any good to say so.

"I'm looking forward to seeing Stuart again." The smile on Louise's face could have only one meaning. "I haven't seen him for several months."

"You know him?"

The words were out before Jennifer could stop them.

"Very well, indeed." Louise leaned forward, in the manner of someone sharing a confidence. "Part of Stuart's job was to entertain visitors to the American Embassy. His wife never attended the parties, so he always asked me to be his partner."

From what she knew about Martha, Jennifer could believe that Stuart's wife had trouble associating with other people. But that didn't mean he had turned to Louise for comfort.

"Stuart and I were very close," the woman murmured.

Jennifer took a sniff of the woman's perfume and silently conceded that it would take a dedicated and loyal husband to resist Louise's charms.

"I was the nurse at the American Embassy." Louise gave a soft laugh. "That made it handy."

"What about his wife?"

Louise looked at her as though she'd said something incredibly ignorant. "Wives are always the last to know." She laughed. "Stuart didn't love her, anyway."

The door opened, and a man came into the room. Jennifer estimated his age at about thirty. He stood tall, had handsome features, black curly hair, and a thin mustache.

His dark eyes looked from her to Louise and then back at Jennifer again. Stepping close, he bent down and gently fingered her cheek and her swollen lips. "You don't look well, Miss Denton. Did you have an accident?"

It was the voice of the man who had spoken to her when she'd worn the blindfold.

"She fell," Louise explained, looking around his shoulder.

Jennifer interpreted the woman's stare as a warning to keep quiet.

"You must be very clumsy, Miss Denton," the man commented. "You apparently fell down several times. And each time, you hit the same side of your face." He straightened and turned around to stare at Louise.

She nervously licked her lips. "Miss Denton stepped on something that rolled under her foot."

"More than once?"

Louise slid off the chair. "She fought with me and tried to get away. I had to stop her."

"How could she fight with her hands tied?"

"They weren't tied. I took the rope off."

"I told you to leave the rope on her wrists until Miss Denton arrived in this room."

He took a couple of steps closer to Louise.

She gave him a smile. "I didn't hurt her, Fernando." She gasped as soon as the word left her mouth.

"You are careless, Louise. That is the second time you have said my name. Once more will be one too many."

His soft words hung in the air of the room.

She straightened and jutted her chin at him. "I don't see what difference it makes if she knows your name, now that she's seen your face."

"I allow Miss Denton to see my face because I hope to convince her to help us."

"Why do you need my help? I thought you expected Mr. Kendall at any moment."

Jennifer regretted the words as soon as they were out of her mouth. If Stuart's capture hadn't happened as Garizon had planned, he wouldn't be in the best of moods.

She tried again. "I mean I heard all the movement around me, like you were fixing barricades or something, and you told me that he would be here soon."

"He is not here yet, but if all goes well, my men should bring him here within the hour."

Louise moved closer. "Don't trust her."

Garizon's hand snaked out and hit her on the mouth.

Jennifer gasped in shock and revulsion when Louise fell against the wall. She moaned and reached up to massage the side of her face. When she pushed upright, a thin trickle of blood ran from the corner of her mouth.

Garizon turned and gave Jennifer a charming smile. "If you want to know why Louise hurt you, Miss Denton, it is because she is jealous of you."

The blonde made a strangled sound, which he ignored.

"Her job was to investigate Mr. Kendall, to find out all that she could about him." Garizon smiled again. " 'Get next to him' is how I believe you Americans say it. Unfortunately, she forgot her duty and became involved with Kendall."

The bitter taste of bile shot up into Jennifer's throat. Could it be true? Had Stuart indulged in an affair with Louise?

"I have distressed you again. I regret that very much." The man's look held pity. "But I must distress you even more. I must tell you facts about Stuart Kendall, things you will not want to hear, but I want you to see that he is dangerous and must be stopped."

"It's nothing to me. I'm not involved with him."

"I am sure you are not. Cheap affairs would have no appeal for a lady like you." He jerked a thumb at Louise. "You are smarter than that one. She made the mistake of falling in love with Kendall."

Jennifer twisted away from him and then winced when the hammer started up again in the back of her head.

"Louise believes you are Kendall's woman."

"I'm nobody's woman."

"Of course not." The man nodded. "He would not choose a female like you."

No matter how she turned that statement, she couldn't make it sound complimentary. Did Garizon mean she wasn't the type to attract a man like Stuart? And what did it matter, anyway? She didn't want to be a member of his harem. Nor did she want a temporary place in his life.

She wanted much more.

Jennifer took a deep breath and allowed it to ooze out between her lips in a long sigh. She couldn't pinpoint the moment or the hour when her feelings toward him had begun to change. He'd given her no encouragement. She had no reason to believe he ever would. She only knew that his survival grew increasingly more important to her.

"Do you love your country, Miss Denton?"

Jennifer felt cold and tired to the bone. She needed rest and quiet. She needed time to think. Why didn't he leave her alone? "Yes. I love my country, but I won't help you. I've heard and read about the way some smaller countries treat their people. They do even worse things to Americans. For all I know, Stuart Kendall may have only done his duty. You may be pursuing him for reasons of your own."

"As intelligent as you are pretty," Garizon said. "I would think less of you if you did not question my motives."

"Then you understand why I won't help you."

He pulled the chair closer and sat down. "I will make a bargain with you."

His bland expression told her nothing. "What kind of a bargain?"

"Once we have had our talk, I do not think you will wish to protect Stuart Kendall." He stared at her for a few seconds. "However, if you still feel loyal to him, I will release you."

"You'll let me go?"

"After you hear what I have to tell you, if you can truly say that Kendall is worth your loyalty, then you will be free to leave." Garizon leaned closer. "May I tell you about him?"

Jennifer shifted under his steady scrutiny. "I'll listen."

Stuart entered a department store on the corner. He paused to look out the window but didn't see the two men from the alley. Reaching up to massage the back of his neck, his hand froze when something hard pressed into the middle of his back.

"Put your hands in your jacket pockets, Mr. Kendall."

From the corner of his eye, Stuart saw two men edging around to cover him on his left side. They stood far enough away to be out of reach, should he decide to lunge in their direction.

"Do not do anything foolish. My instructions are to take you alive, but I will kill you if you do not obey my orders."

Stuart didn't doubt him. The object pressing into his back felt like the bore of a gun. He grunted when the pressure shifted to one of his sore places.

"Very slowly now, Mr. Kendall. Put your hands into your pockets."

Stuart obeyed.

"There's a car outside with two men standing by the back door. Move toward it."

Three men inside and two outside. He didn't like the odds.

The man prodded him again. "We are going outside now. Move."

Stuart walked forward, opened the door, and stepped outside. A gust of wind blew drifting snow into his eyes, but he had a good view of the men moving forward to escort him to the car. They all looked big and tough.

"Get in."

Stuart bent and slid onto the back seat. The door slammed shut behind him. A thick sheet of glass separated the front of the car from the back. He didn't have to touch the smooth surface to realize that the divider had to be bullet proof.

The two men got into the front seat. One of them put a telephone to his ear.

Stuart checked the seat. No belts or buckles. Nothing he could use for a weapon. His sweeping glance checked the inside of both doors. No handles.

It was as neat a job of corralling as he'd ever seen.

CHAPTER TEN

Jennifer hugged her arms around her waist and gritted her teeth against the cold. Logic told her that Garizon would say whatever he needed to say to win her over and influence her opinion of Stuart.

The man would exaggerate or even lie to further his cause.

She knew all that, yet she wanted to stop her ears to close off his soft voice. As she listened to his intricate tale of brutality and death at the hands of the man he called *Sombra,* she admitted to having doubts about Stuart's complete innocence.

Garizon spoke of the murder of his younger brother in a voice that shook with anger and grief. She couldn't doubt his sincerity or his pain. His dark eyes held a haunted look that made it difficult for her not to offer him sympathy. If all of this was an act solely for her benefit and he felt nothing of the emotion he conveyed to her, the stage had missed a truly great performer.

What he said could be truth or lies. She had no prior basis on which to judge his sincerity. Sometimes patients faked pain to get a nurse's attention. Lying in a hospital bed could be a lonely pastime, if you never received visitors. That type of assessment proved a lot easier for her than trying to decide if Garizon was an honorable man. She suspected his face showed exactly what he wanted it to show.

His accusations depicted a man without conscience and common decency, a man who recognized no boundaries for his behavior. Jennifer couldn't accept that. Stuart *did* possess those qualities. He had cared enough about what was fair and right to have his son apologize for hurting her feelings. That wasn't the act of a sadistic murderer.

She had read about atrocities happening in faraway places, but they'd never seemed real to her before. In the hospital, she had treated victims of accidents with horrible injuries, but she'd never before seen a victim of torture, until she'd seen the wounds on Stuart's back.

Like so many other people, she took for granted all of the advantages and the privileges that living in the United States provided. Baring unusual circumstances, she would never be the victim of violence or lose the right to worship in the church of her choice. She would never lose her right to work at her chosen profession and advance as far as her abilities and ambition would take her.

How could she fully appreciate the lack of freedom and the suffering going on in other countries?

When she'd asked Stuart why he wanted to do the particular job he chose for a career, he had said he enjoyed it. Perhaps he had become a government agent because he saw evil in the world and wanted to do something about it.

"I regret you had to hear such things, Miss Denton." Garizon's eyes held compassion. "I am sorry to bring unhappiness into your young life."

A steady, dull ache throbbed behind her eyes. "I know about unhappiness."

"You have not known cruelty, I suspect."

Jennifer opened her eyes and murmured, "I've also known cruelty." She paused, remembering the years spent in her aunt's bleak, brownstone mansion. "Emotional, not physical."

"Believe me, Miss Denton, physical cruelty is worse."

"I'm sure it is." She thought about the sore places on Stuart's back. "It must take a special kind of person to willfully inflict punishment upon another."

"No, it only takes a person with a good enough reason."

She couldn't accept that. "People aren't all like that."

"Not the people you know, perhaps, but there are many in my acquaintance with the aptitude for that job."

His matter-of-fact tone made her shiver. "You speak of torture as though it's a line of work."

"For many men, it is exactly that."

Did Garizon know this subject so well because he had once tortured Stuart?

"I apologize again, Miss Denton. You are upset."

"Yes, I am. There isn't any logical reason for one person to cause another person physical pain."

"You have a soft heart."

Was it so simple for others to dissect her character? "People tell me that's a weakness."

"Only to a madman."

Regardless of the answer, she had to know Garizon's intentions toward Stuart. "Do you mean to kill Mr. Kendall?"

"I am not his executioner. I am merely the means of extraditing him to my country to stand trial."

She licked her lips. "That's just a formality, isn't it?"

He nodded in agreement. "It will be a very short trial. Then the firing squad."

Jennifer pictured Stuart's tall frame backed against a cement wall with bullets tearing into his flesh. Misery tightened her throat. Because of her, Stuart might lose his life.

She heard the sound of running footsteps. A dark-skinned young man ran through the open doorway. She couldn't understand what he said, but his rapid speech and excited arm movements told their own story.

When he left the room, Louise followed him.

Garizon's handsome features wore a satisfied smile. "My men captured Kendall."

Jennifer felt queasy. Stuart wouldn't give up willingly. Garizon's men must have used force.

"You do not look pleased at the prospect of seeing Kendall again." Garizon nodded approval. "I quite understand."

He left the room and closed the door behind him.

She didn't hear the lock turn. He hadn't worried about her trying to get out of the room.

Jennifer glanced up at the small window and saw daylight rapidly fading away. Just like her hopes. She felt as weary as if she'd done hard, physical labor.

She couldn't bear to think of what Garizon would do to Stuart. The man had said he wanted to take Stuart back to his country to stand trial, but that didn't mean he couldn't indulge his hatred first.

Her gaze moved across the ceiling, and she sat up straighter. Fluorescent lights. Why hadn't she noticed them before? Pushing up off the cot, Jennifer took a couple of steps toward the door. The dizziness wasn't so bad now, but she took her time and placed one foot carefully in front of the other until she reached the door.

Sweeping her palm over the area of the wall near the door, she found the switch and flipped it to ON. The sudden intensity of light made her blink and grope her way back to the cot.

The door swung open. She spun around and saw Stuart standing in the doorway. Something flashed in the depths of his eyes. Concern? Worry?

Two men stepped forward, a younger man and one much older with sparse, gray hair. The younger one raised his arm. She had a glimpse of something that glittered in the light before he made a swipe at the back of Stuart's head.

Stuart fell like a downed tree.

The young man laughed and said something Jennifer didn't understand, but she didn't have to speak the language to understand the smirk on his face. She caught the name Rico, referring to the gray-haired man. Rico's reply identified the younger man as Pedro.

Murmuring something to his companion, Pedro thrust the pistol into his jacket pocket and moved inside the room.

Jennifer pressed against the wall, more fearful now than she'd been at any other time. Any woman could understand his intentions from the leer on his face.

Pedro said something else to his companion and then stepped deliberately on the middle of Stuart's back before he moved forward to stand in front of Jennifer. His dark eyes dropped to the vicinity of her breasts. He gave a soft laugh. Reaching over, he began to unbutton her coat.

Rico called to him, said Garizon's name, and pointed down the hallway.

Giving her face a final pat, Pedro turned away. He stepped onto Stuart's back again and took the time to grind his heel into the area over Stuart's kidneys, before he laughed and walked to the doorway. He gave her another smile and then stepped away and closed the door behind him.

Jennifer winced at the thought of Stuart's sore ribs hitting the cement floor. The man's hard shoes must have caused even more damage to Stuart's back.

She looked at him, lying almost at her feet, and thought about the terrible things Garizon had told her. According to him, Stuart had committed unspeakable cruelties against those weaker than himself. Staring down at him, she couldn't reconcile the horrible picture of a mad killer with the Stuart she knew.

Stretched out at her feet, he looked vulnerable. She felt a stab of guilt. He wouldn't be lying there unconscious if it weren't for her. He had gotten caught trying to rescue her. And no matter what he was or what he might have done, he had always treated her like a lady.

Jennifer got up off the cot. Slipping to her knees, she reached out a hand and pushed back the collar of his jacket. A curly, black wig covered the back of his head and his neck. Fearing what she might find, she pulled off his wooly cap and pushed the wig off his head.

Lack of visible blood, while a good sign, didn't mean there was no injury. As gently as she could, she fingered the back of his head. Her probing touch felt a slight swelling.

She frowned when he didn't move. An unconscious person often reacted to a touch on a painful area. She pressed her fingers against his throat and felt the beat of a strong pulse. The next moment, she yelped in alarm as an iron hand gripped her wrist and pulled her to the floor.

She fell hard onto her right hip and yelled at the sudden increase in pain. Then she was on her back and staring up into Stuart's narrowed gaze. His eyes held no recognition in their depths. They had the same dazed look she'd seen once before.

Fear climbed into her throat and squeezed. "Stuart . . . it's Jennifer."

He released her arm and grabbed a handful of her hair.

She groaned at the pain in the back of her head. "You're hurting me."

His fingers tightened in the knot of her hair.

"Let me go. Please."

She sucked in a breath to make one last attempt to reach him, to beg him to let her go. Before she could say the words, his eyes lost their focus. He slumped down across her.

Reaching out a tentative hand, she touched his face. He didn't move. Could he be dead? She shifted her hand, and his warm breath feathered across her palm.

She took a shaky breath. Under normal conditions, Stuart

would never hurt her, but the green eyes that had looked down at her a moment ago had glittered with anger and determination. In that moment, he had looked capable of anything.

She maneuvered her hands along his arms but couldn't lift his upper body. She began pushing against his shoulder and easing her body out from under his. She finally pushed free. Crawling on hands and knees, she headed for the cot. She paused to gather strength in her trembling arms and legs and then levered her weight up onto the thin mattress and sat down.

Accompanied by two husky young men, Garizon stepped into the room.

The two men flipped Stuart onto his back. They picked him up, one of them holding his shoulders and the other carrying his legs. Garizon, with a bow toward Jennifer, followed them outside.

Stuart awoke to throbbing pain. He rarely had headaches, but this one was a beauty. He lay immobile, afraid the back of his head might fall off if he moved. Faint sounds teased his hearing. Thinking made his head hurt worse, but he gritted his teeth and tried to concentrate on his surroundings. At last he separated the soft murmurs into two male voices.

He opened his eyes just enough to see two men standing near a door with their backs to him. Stuart widened the crack between his eyelids enough to take a quick look around. He saw a room with gray cement walls. If there was any furniture, it had to be behind him and out of his range of sight.

The men turned to look at him, but he didn't make the mistake of closing his eyes. People often slept with their lids partially open. He concentrated upon making his breathing slow and regular until the men turned away again.

They spoke a language Stuart knew well. Attuned now to

their soft speech, he had no trouble following their conversation.

"I do not like it, Paulo. We stay too long."

The other man nodded. "You are right, my friend. We have Kendall. I say kill him and leave this place."

"That will not satisfy Garizon," the first man put in. "He blames Kendall for his brother's death."

"But Kendall was not there."

"Quiet." The other man grabbed his arm. "Do not speak those words again. It is better for all of us if he believes Kendall killed Juan."

So these two knew who had murdered Garizon's brother. Stuart stored the information away for future use.

"What about the red-haired woman?"

"Perhaps we will take her with us."

They began to chuckle but stopped when the door opened to admit Garizon. He moved toward the cot.

Stuart recognized his old enemy and rolled his eyes far back in their sockets. He didn't try to focus when the man bent over him.

Garizon pushed one of Stuart's eyelids up and then muttered an oath and straightened. "Pedro hit him too hard."

"What does it matter? You wanted him dead."

"Garcia will be here within forty-eight hours for the meeting with our local distributor. Garcia expects me to give him the names of the Panamanian traitors." Garizon cursed again. "Kendall has that information, but because of Pedro's stupidity, Kendall may never wake up."

"Let us go to the airplane," the man suggested.

Stuart tensed. There were a limited number of places around the D. C. area where a large plane could land. And Garizon rarely traveled in a small plane.

"Without food or water or medical attention, Kendall will

soon die," the man added.

Garizon nodded agreement. "The woman will go with us."

They left the room and closed the door.

Stuart took in a long breath, pushed himself upright, and swung his feet out onto the floor. His head not only hurt but felt too heavy for his neck. Were those the symptoms of a concussion? Whether they were or not, he had to get up.

He clenched his hands into fists and stood up. His head didn't fall off, but pain radiated from the back of his neck to a point over his eyes. He waited a moment to see if anything else unusual might happen. Then he slowly lifted his chin until he could look around the room.

Other than his cot, the only piece of furniture was a battered desk standing against the back wall. He tilted his head back to look up. The pain felt worse, but he took the time to study a small window up near the roof. If he stood on the desk and stretched on tiptoe, he could pull himself up to the window ledge.

Then what? His mouth curled into a cynical smile. He'd have a job climbing onto the desk. No use thinking about the window. It would have to be the old-fashioned way, through the door.

He had a fuzzy memory of seeing Jen in a room like this one. He remembered the surprised look on her face when she saw him but nothing else. That must have been when someone hit him from behind.

Stuart took a stiff-legged step toward the door and grunted with pain. He took another and then another. If this was the best he could do, Garizon and his men didn't have much to fear. They had left him alone because they thought he was unconscious and likely to remain that way, but Garizon could decide to come back and use his gun. Leaving his enemy alive wouldn't sit well with the man.

Stuart dipped a hand into the hidden pocket inside his jacket and pulled out his pistol. The men who had found him in the store hadn't wanted to get close enough to look for weapons before they put him into the car. And, apparently, no one had searched him after the hit on his head.

Garizon could be leaving for the airport at any time. Stuart shoved the sight of Jen's pale face to the back of his mind. He'd learned long ago not to waste time worrying about what he couldn't control.

His first priority was to get out of this room.

Jennifer paced back and forth. Stuart had another injury now, possibly a fatal one. Surely Garizon wouldn't torture an unconscious man.

Her vivid imagination conjured up a vision of Stuart suffering from multiple injuries. He might be dead by now. She pictured him lying on a cold cement floor like this one, his bright green eyes dull and unseeing.

And it was all her fault.

The door opened without warning. She swung around, hoping to see Stuart walking toward her. When she saw Garizon, Jennifer lifted her chin. "It's almost dark outside. How much longer are you going to keep me here?"

"My men spotted friends of Kendall a short distance away."

"You said he had no friends."

Garizon shrugged. "He has colleagues as evil and as desperate to survive as he is. You may be the means of securing our escape, Miss Denton."

She thought she understood. "You're going to hold me for ransom?"

He smiled. "I doubt that Mr. Kendall's friends would pay money for you, but they may not wish to see you harmed."

"You said you'd release me."

"I also said you could be my means of capturing Stuart Kendall."

Something didn't track. "But your men brought him here. You have him in custody."

"I intended to take him back for trial."

Ice water slid down her back. "Intended?"

Garizon stared at her for a moment. "He has not regained consciousness."

At least Stuart still lived. She let out her held breath in a sigh. "Does he need medical attention?"

"Not for much longer."

Now she understood. He must be in critical condition. "You're just going to let him die?"

"I am kinder to him than he was to my brother, Miss Denton."

Garizon called to someone out in the hallway. The older man, Rico, peered in. Jennifer couldn't understand what Garizon said to him, but Rico nodded and moved inside the room. Garizon turned to her again. "We are leaving before Kendall's friends arrive. You understand, of course, that I will not take him with me." Garizon lifted his hands in a gesture to say there was no other way. "An unconscious man would be a liability."

Her lips felt stiff and cold. "You're just going to leave him like that?"

"Rico will bring you to the airplane, Miss Denton."

"What airplane?"

"We return home tonight. You will go with us."

Stuart twisted the knob. It turned easily. Garizon didn't usually make foolish mistakes. Stuart meant to take advantage of this one.

He opened the door far enough to look outside and saw the opposite wall. He listened for a few seconds but heard no sounds of movement or of voices. They had Jennifer in a room of a similar size to this one. It would be too much to hope for that he would find her in this same corridor, but he had to find her soon.

He inched his face out into the gap between the door and the jamb. Looking to his left, he saw a cement wall. He checked the other direction and saw a long, empty hallway with closed doors on both sides. He stepped outside and began walking. His thick-soled shoes made no sound on the cement floor.

Stopping at the first door, he reached out and turned the knob. He squared around, braced for whatever he might find, and swung the door open. The room contained nothing, except for some broken crates and empty beer bottles.

He checked each of the rooms in the hallway and found all of them empty. He walked the few feet to the end of the hallway and stopped just before the intersection with another, wider hall.

He bent, got onto both knees and slowly stretched out on his stomach. The imaginary hammer started working on his head again. He waited a few seconds and then inched forward until he could lay his cheek on the floor and look out.

To the right, he saw another wall. He slowly turned his head to look to his left. The main room of the warehouse stood about thirty feet away. He lay for several seconds, watching and listening for any signs of activity but heard none.

He walked down the hallway, stepped out into the big room, and slid into the shadows by the open door. Crouching low, he walked on tiptoes to the shelter of a large crate. He waited a few seconds and then stood up.

Garizon had left the warehouse.

Stuart retrieved his cellular phone from his left boot. He punched in some numbers. After the first ring, a voice spoke into his ear in heavily accented English. "You call wrong number."

"The number is one," Stuart replied.

"We had a problem." The voice no longer had an accent. "Things went bad."

"They got worse." Stuart winced against the pounding in the back of his head. "The bird is heading for the nest."

"Then we'll chop down the tree."

"Not just yet. Mama went along for the ride."

"By the way," the voice said, "I found your Christmas present. It's smaller than you thought."

Stuart's grip tightened on the phone. They knew the location of Garizon's plane, and it wasn't a large jet. "Where did you find it?"

"On your other list. It was the *second* place I looked."

For identification purposes, the agency divided the airfields in the Washington metropolitan area into two lists, the first for large or major airfields and the second for smaller fields.

"We'll send you some wings. Pickup at Lot 2. Ten minutes."

A helicopter in the parking lot, two blocks away. "I understand," Stuart replied.

Jennifer sat alone in the back of the limousine. Up ahead, she could see the taillights of the dark van holding Louise, Garizon, and his men. The driver kept the glass raised between him and Jennifer. Not that she had any desire to talk to him. Or to anyone. Her thoughts were back in the warehouse.

She had to believe Garizon when he said he didn't expect Stuart to live. Pain knifed through her. Whatever else happened, she had to get out of this. If she couldn't help Stuart, she could at least fulfill her obligation to protect his son from the Wilsons.

But she had to do something soon, or she'd be an extra passenger on that airplane. She had to get away from these people, but her chances weren't good while she sat in the back of this car.

Stuart depended on you.

She pushed the tormenting words away. This wasn't the time for soul searching. She had to think clearly. Garizon didn't want the burden of Stuart because he was unconscious. What if she pretended to be sick? They might not want to drag a sick person along with them.

It wouldn't be easy, but it was worth a try. The most foolproof way was to stumble when the driver pulled her out of the car. If she did it right, she could fake hitting her back on the way down.

The car took a tight, right turn. She saw a few lights in the distance, but this couldn't be a major airport.

The car slowed. Off to the right, Jennifer saw the dim outline of a large building. Less than a minute later, the car stopped. The driver left the headlights on when he opened the door and stepped outside.

When the door beside her opened, Jennifer made exaggerated, slow movements as she twisted around on the seat. The driver reached in to grab hold of her arm. She stepped out and teetered on one foot. She gasped with apparent alarm at the icy sleet driving into her face and fell away from him. She managed to thump the side of the car with her fist on the way down.

He bent over to help her up, but she groaned and let her body go limp. With both hands in her armpits, he lifted her up and then suddenly dropped her. Unprepared for his action, she fell backward into a deep snowdrift. He ran around the car and disappeared from her sight.

She pushed up out of the drift and searched the darkness for some clue as to what had happened. Voices broke the stillness. She saw lights in the distance, heard a scream and a terse order to stand still.

Louise passed her in a dead run and disappeared into the darkness.

What was going on? Jennifer pushed to her knees and then used the car to pull herself upright. She heard yelling and saw the vague figures of people rushing around.

"Don't move!"

Gasping in surprise, she spun around. English. They spoke English.

She took a couple of steps and ran into a tree. But trees didn't have arms. She looked up and saw a familiar pair of green eyes staring at her.

Shifting her gaze, she looked at the barrel of the pistol pointed at her face.

CHAPTER ELEVEN

Jennifer heard loud shouts and occasional shots, but they didn't unsettle her as much as Stuart's solemn gaze. She remembered the sight of his eyes staring down at her, his hand tightening cruelly in her hair. Icy particles punished her face, but she ignored their bite and squinted into the driving snow.

Was this Stuart . . . or *Sombra?*

Her held breath gushed out in a sigh of relief when she looked into his eyes. They weren't blank and staring. They held worry and concern.

Something whispered past her cheek and tore through her hair. The next moment, she heard a ping and blinked when snow from the hood of the car kicked up into her face.

Stuart yelled, "Get down!" and pushed her behind him. His right hand lifted. A moment later, she heard a sharp report. Someone yelled as though in pain. She held up a hand to protect her eyes from the driving ice particles and stretched around him to find the source of the sound.

A man stumbled into the circle of light at the hangar entrance. He tottered for a moment and then fell face forward into the snow.

"That was one of Garizon's men," Stuart explained. "He didn't miss you by much."

She reached up shaking fingers to the side of her head. "You mean . . . that was a bullet that went through my hair?"

"Yes."

The trembling spread from her fingers, down the length of her body, and on to her legs. "Shouldn't you check on that man?"

"It isn't necessary."

She said, through stiff lips, "You must be an expert marksman."

"We're in the open. We have to get away from this car." He reached out an arm and pulled her against his side. "We'll run for the unlighted side of the hangar. Keep low, Jen."

She couldn't match the length of his steps, but his arm swept her along until he was almost carrying her across the sparkling snow. When they slid to a stop in the shadows, he put her against the wall and took up a position to one side.

The noises sounded farther away now. She listened for a few seconds but heard no more shots. She peeped around the corner of the building. Through the swirling snow, she saw Garizon's van several yards away. A mid-sized airplane stood parked on the apron in front of the hangar. A helicopter stood nearby. Its rotors still turned, as though the occupants had jumped out in too much of a hurry to turn off the engine.

"Is that how you got here?" she asked.

"Yes. A guy picked me up about twenty minutes after Garizon left the warehouse." He pointed a finger. "The others came in those two vans."

"For a man who wasn't supposed to wake up again, you did very well."

Stuart drew in a long breath and blew it out before he said, "I'm sorry about all this, Jen."

She sensed he was watching her and waiting to see how she would respond to her fright. A humorless laugh trembled on her lips. How could she tell him how she felt, when she wasn't sure herself?

Back in the warehouse, she had seen the man come up behind

Stuart and hit him on the back of the head. Garizon had told her later that he didn't expect Stuart to wake up and he didn't want the burden of an unconscious man. So he intended to leave Stuart to die of natural causes.

Yet here he stood, looking no worse for his experience.

How could that be? Was this whole thing an elaborate hoax, put together to stop her from asking any more questions? Maybe Garizon himself was a government agent. And that woman Louise as well. But if that were true, why would Louise attack her?

Perhaps Garizon had told the truth when he said that Louise was in love with Stuart. If the woman knew he'd transferred his affections to someone else, she may have acted out of jealousy.

The person who knew all the answers stood in front of her. All Jennifer had to do was ask him about Louise. She opened her mouth to say the words but said instead, "How did you know where to look for me?"

"Just be glad I did know."

The answer was too sure, too quick. Something didn't fit. "How did you know where to find Garizon's plane?"

"I didn't know. One of our operatives told me."

"How did he know?"

"Does it matter?"

"I think it matters a lot." She paused and then said, "You woke up briefly after that man hit you on the head. Do you remember?"

"No."

"You apparently thought I was the one who hit you. You grabbed my hair in your fist and twisted it. I spoke to you and told you who I was, but you didn't respond."

"I regret that."

She said, quietly, "A year ago, the police brought a young man, accompanied by a guard, to the hospital. He seemed like a pleasant, gentle person, until the day he grabbed a student nurse and tried to strangle her. The guard stopped him. I was in the room at the time. The patient's eyes looked wild, like those of a trapped animal."

"I assume that you're telling me this for a reason."

The lack of emotion in Stuart's voice chilled her. "Your eyes looked that way today." She took in a breath. "I thought you were going to kill me."

"I could never hurt you, Jen."

"I'd like to believe that." She studied his face, but the dimness hid his expression. "What's it all about, Stuart?"

"There's nothing for you to worry about."

"I worry about *you*."

Well, there it was. She'd finally said it. He probably didn't want to hear it, and she certainly didn't want to say it, but now he knew. Let him make of it whatever he wanted.

His mouth opened as though he was going to say something. She tensed and leaned forward.

He said, "Did Garizon hurt you?"

She slumped back against the hangar wall. Those weren't the words she wanted to hear. "No. He treated me very well."

"How did you get the bruises on your face?"

"From Louise."

Stuart leaned closer. "She did a good job."

"Maybe one day I can return the favor."

He studied her for a moment. "That doesn't sound like you."

"I'm cold, tired and hungry. I've been tied up, slapped around, scared half out of wits, and shot at. You might say I've had a bad day."

"I can't picture you getting violent with anyone."

In the darkness, she saw the gleam of his teeth. "How about if I start with you?"

"Stuart!" someone called

"Here," he answered and lifted an arm.

Jennifer saw a spectral figure near the line of trees.

"We need you. They split up," a man called. "I'll send Mitch back to stay with Miss Denton."

"Right."

A moment later, the man faded back into the darkness.

"Who are you, Stuart?"

"What do you mean?"

"Garizon kidnapped me because he wanted to use me as bait to lure you into a trap."

"It worked."

"But why did it work? Why does he want you so badly?"

"Didn't he tell you?"

She gave a short laugh. "You're still answering a question with another question."

He made no comment.

"Garizon believes you killed his brother."

"I didn't."

"How can you be so sure?" The words were out before she could prevent them. A moment later, she added, "How many men have you killed?"

He made no answer.

"How many, Stuart?" she pressed.

When he still didn't answer, she said, softly, "He wanted my cooperation, so he told me a lot of things about you."

"What do you mean?"

Tired and shivering with cold, she reached up to swipe snow off her face and eyelashes. She felt her spurt of anger draining away, like a balloon losing its air. "You got into trouble because of me. I regret that. If you leave now, you can get away before they find you. I won't say anything." She blew out her breath in a long sigh. "I owe you that much."

His hand shot out and grabbed her arm in a painful vise. "What are you talking about?"

She cringed away from him. "Please don't hurt me."

He flinched as though she'd slapped him. Even in the driving snow, she could see that his face had lost its color. If she had wanted to hurt him, she'd done a good job.

But she didn't want to hurt him. She wanted to hear him say he'd never killed anyone out of vengeance or malice but only in self-defense.

He let her go with a suddenness that made her fall back against the hangar. His head lifted. The green eyes glittered like frozen emeralds. The weak moment, if she could call it that, had passed.

He flipped the revolver back into his jacket holster and took hold of her wrists. When she gasped with alarm, his mouth twisted into a caricature of a smile before he untied the rope and threw it away. "Relax, Jen. I've never killed anyone with a rope."

She wanted to tell him that she was sorry, but the hard line of his jaw kept her silent. He'd never spoken to her in that cold tone before. She wanted to say something to restore their easy relationship, but too much had happened.

Why couldn't he explain? Why couldn't he trust her enough to tell her what she wanted to know?

He reached out a hand to the back of her head. "I saw you fall and hit your head. I just want to be sure you're not bleeding."

"I faked that one, but I did fall in the warehouse."

Gentle fingers probed her skull and paused when she grunted in pain. Reaching into a pocket of his jacket, Stuart produced a small, pencil-sized flashlight. He withdrew his hand from her hair and directed the narrow beam of light onto his fingers.

Jennifer stretched up to see for herself. A thick, dark substance covered the ends of Stuart's fingers. It didn't look like blood.

"Oil," Stuart said. "That warehouse is also a garage."

She felt ashamed that she hadn't remembered his head injury until now. "How does your head feel?"

"It's still attached to my neck, I know that."

"Is the pain severe?" The thin line of his lips and the slightly flared nostrils indicated temper held in check, but she had to know. "Are you sure you're okay?"

"All I know is that I have a headache that must have been meant for a large elephant."

Her training overcame her embarrassment. "You could have a concussion." When he didn't respond, she said, "Tell me."

"Tell you what?"

Why was he playing word games with her? "You must know the things Garizon told me about you. Are they true?"

"I don't know what he told you, Jen. So how can I answer your question?"

She said, past trembling lips, "Don't do this, Stuart."

"Do what?"

"Are you denying everything?"

"Would you believe me, if I did?"

"You said you were an accomplished liar."

"That's true." His shoulders lifted into a shrug. "It's a handy skill."

How could he treat the events of today so lightly? "You came close to being killed."

"Close only counts in horseshoes."

Jennifer gripped her hands tightly together. "You told me that you weren't running from the law and you weren't a wanted criminal."

A cynical smile lifted the corners of his lips. "What else would you expect from an accomplished liar?"

Her hand whipped upward, but he easily deflected her palm before it touched his face. She blinked in amazement at the speed of his movement. He didn't have to think about it. His instincts were honed to such razor sharpness that he reacted automatically.

The angry narrowing of his eyes made her stumble backward. His hands lifted. For a moment, she thought he meant to grab her shoulders and shake her. Then, with a disgusted grunt, he thrust his hands into the pockets of his jacket.

She'd hurt him again. The bleak expression in his eyes tore at her heart. No matter what he'd done before today, he'd searched and found her, and now she repaid his generosity and caring with accusations.

There might be reasons for what he'd done, reasons she could understand, even condone. She wanted to believe he'd looked for her because he cared for her, that her survival was important to him. In reality, he'd probably tried to save her because he felt responsible for her.

Jennifer searched his face and eyes for any sign of tenderness. What she saw left her cold and trembling. She closed her eyes for a moment. The dreadful words were too fresh, too new. How could she say them? When she looked up, he was watching her face.

"Have you killed, Stuart?"

"My job usually involves people you wouldn't invite to your home."

The silence between them lengthened. Part of her wanted to let it go at that and not press him for answers he obviously didn't wish to give, but she couldn't drop it. Everyone she'd cared about had eventually deceived her. She had to know the truth. "Garizon said you killed several people."

"What people?"

Had there been so many he couldn't remember their names?

"What's the matter, Jen? Afraid of hurting my feelings?"

"He called you *Sombra*."

Above the gusting wind, she thought she heard Stuart sigh.

"In some places I'm known by that name." He stared down at her for several seconds and then said, "Ah . . . you've read my character and I've fallen short of your ideals."

"If Garizon lied, you tell me the truth."

"I think you've had enough truth for one day."

His quiet words held censure, but she was past caring about his opinion of her. Misery fueled her anger, and she lifted her head. "I was easy to fool, wasn't I?"

"What do you mean?"

"You told me a bunch of stories about you and your wife. You smiled at me and let me hang around while you read to your son." Anger quickened her breath. "Were you taking pity on the lonely nurse? Giving her a little excitement in her dull life?"

"You can't believe that." Stuart stepped forward and grasped her shoulders. "Why would you want to?"

"Is it true?"

"You're not making sense. Are you afraid?"

"Yes, I'm afraid."

He said, quietly, "Of me?"

When she didn't deny it, his fingers tightened into a cruel grip before he let her go and stepped back. The sudden sound of voices swung him away from her. He lifted the gun in his hand.

"What are you doing, Stuart?"

"Believe it or not, there are people out there who are even worse than I am."

The unaccustomed edge in his voice sent warmth into her cheeks. "I shouldn't have said those things." When he didn't answer, she said, "I know you meant to help me."

His gaze swept the distant ring of trees. "Mitch should be here by now. Something must have gone wrong. Stay here till I come back."

A moment later, he stepped away.

Jennifer's gaze followed him through the swirling snow until he disappeared into the trees. Stuart had a right to be angry with her. Why had she said all those things to him? Why hadn't she given him the benefit of the doubt?

Garizon could have made up all of those incidents he related to her. Well, not all of them. Stuart admitted to the "Sombra" name, but that didn't prove anything.

She should have given him a chance to explain.

A sudden blast of frigid air whipped loose strands of hair into her eyes. Jennifer pulled a soft hat out of her pocket. The darkness concealed its bright blue color. She wore it solely because Stuart had twice remarked that she looked good in blue.

What did it matter now? After the way she had treated him, she'd be lucky if he ever spoke to her again.

As the minutes passed, she grew uneasy. Why didn't Stuart or Mitch return to stay with her? Stuart considered it his duty to see her safely home. He wouldn't leave her alone, if he could get back to her.

Something must have happened to him. She stared into the driving snow, but all she got for her effort were eyes streaming tears from the bitter wind. She wasn't doing any good standing here, shivering and shaking.

She crouched as low as she could and peeped around the corner of the building. Her gaze searched the area in front of the hangar and beyond to the limit of the circle of light, but she saw no sign of Stuart. With Garizon and his men still around, she didn't like the idea of stepping out into the open. It would be better to angle into the trees and then circle back toward the road.

She'd seen the lights of several houses from the limousine windows as they drove toward the airport. She'd stop at one of them, ask to use the phone, and call the local police for help. She could hide until they arrived.

She started walking. When she had covered what she estimated to be half a mile, she stopped within the fringe of trees for a breather. She shivered and stomped her feet. The air felt colder, but the blowing snow didn't look as dense as before.

Somewhere behind her, men called to each other. They could be the government agents, or they could be Garizon and his men. She had to stay out of sight until she found out.

In case it might be Garizon, she darted a look around for anything large enough to use for a weapon. When she whirled to look behind her, her purse thumped against her side. She whipped the bag off her shoulder and stepped into the stand of trees. The purse wasn't large enough to do any damage, but she might be able to surprise anyone who followed her into the trees. With luck, she could knock him down and slip away.

Stepping behind a large tree, she shifted her grip on the purse, drew it back, and held it ready.

Stuart parted his lids. Something cold and slushy ran into his eyes. He blinked several times to clear the icy liquid away. More white flakes fell onto his face. Why was he lying on his back? He saw the night sky through a snow-covered lattice. Blinking against falling snow, he reached up to touch the lattice. At least, he tried to reach up. Something was wrong with his arms. He couldn't move them.

Stuart moved first one leg and then the other. They were okay. Why couldn't he move his arms? Then he saw a weird shape stretched across his upper body with strange looking parts sticking out at different angles. Stuart twisted his neck to get a better look, and pain exploded in his head.

He eased his head back down and gritted his teeth until the worst of the spasm passed. What type of pain did you get with a concussion? Wasn't it localized? This pain centered on the left side, in the area of his temple. Why did his head hurt there? The man in the warehouse had hit him on the right side.

From the corners of his eyes, Stuart looked to the left and to the right. The snow bank extended several feet up on either side of where he lay. He must be in a ditch.

He looked again at the weird thing lying on top of him and blew out his breath in relief. It was a tree branch. His relief didn't last long. The branch looked almost as big around as his body. He couldn't lift it, even without the thick crust of snow and ice adding to its weight.

Being careful not to move his head, he tried to wiggle an arm free. Nothing happened. He rested a few seconds and then tried again with the same result. If he couldn't lift his arms, maybe he could push with his legs. His booted heels slipped and slid on the snow. That wasn't going to work.

Lifting his right leg as high as possible, he brought it down, digging his heel into the snow. His temple pounded again. He waited for a few seconds and then dug his left heel into the snow. He pushed, but one of his feet slipped. He lifted his leg again and brought his foot down hard. Ignoring the pounding in his head, he pushed as hard as he could.

This time, his body moved a few inches.

He pushed again and moved a bit more. His grin died as quickly as it came. His knees were now too close to the branch to get any leverage. He worked his right arm again and finally jerked it free.

Stuart lay and puffed for a while until his breathing returned to something near normal. It took longer to free his left arm, but he managed it. Pushing against the branch with both hands, he began wriggling and twisting his body. He continued to push with his arms and twist his body without much success.

He had to lie still for a time and get his wind back. Putting his hands on the limb, he took a deep breath and shoved with all his strength while he continued to wriggle and push with his feet. Sucking in another breath, he twisted to the side and yanked until his boots were free.

Exhausted, he fell back. The only sound he heard was the rasping of his breathing. When his pulse and heartbeat were no more than that of a man with a moderately high fever, he rolled over and pushed to his knees.

The world tilted. Strange lights danced before his eyes. He reached up and felt the crusty edges of a wound. Lowering his head, he waited until the lights were no more than worrisome fireflies before opening his eyes and pushing to his feet. His head was above the level of the ditch. The heavy snow reduced visibility to a few yards, but he saw trees and bushes on both sides.

The next moment, a man called out and another man answered. They weren't speaking English.

Stuart ducked down below the top of the ditch. He had lost sight of his companions a long time ago. They wouldn't spend time looking for him, not with Garizon and his cronies on the loose.

Using the tree to help, he clawed his way out of the ditch and crouched down. His head pounded worse than ever. He remembered walking several paces beyond a large tree, where there was a narrow, partly frozen creek. He had waded into the middle of the sluggish water and then backed up and placed his feet in the same prints. Then he had climbed the tree.

Yes, that was it. A branch had broken off, carrying him down into the ditch. He had scraped his head on a sharp spike of wood before hitting the ground.

Garizon and his men must have bypassed the tree, but they were still looking for him. This was no place to be when they returned.

Stuart shoved a hand into the special jacket pocket under his arm, but the pistol wasn't there. He must have dropped it when he fell. He had a smaller caliber one in his right boot, but this wasn't the time to stop and dig it out.

He circled back toward the hangar. Each step made his head pound, but he had to get back there before Garizon decided to return and look for Jennifer. Breaking out of the trees, he ran toward the building and slipped and slid into the darkness where he'd left Jen. He called, softly, "Jen . . . it's Stuart."

She didn't answer.

He checked Garizon's cars and both of the government vehicles and found them all empty. Using the pencil flash, he saw footprints heading away from the hangar. He upped his speed to a trot. A short time later, he found the place where she'd swerved into the trees.

Stuart cursed softly. Surely she had more sense than to get lost in the woods. He nodded in satisfaction when her boot prints headed back toward the road.

"Good girl," he murmured.

He started out again and then paused and looked back at the footprints behind him. Anyone who wanted to find the two of them had a double trail to follow, but he didn't have time for evasion. He had to find Jennifer before Garizon and his friends found her. And him.

A few minutes later, Stuart came to a stop. Jen's footprints looked farther apart, like she might be trotting. Maybe she had seen or heard something that scared her.

He followed Jennifer's tracks to the place where they disappeared among the trees. Ducking to avoid a large branch, he sucked in a breath to call out to her.

Something hit him in the chest. The sudden pain in his sore ribs made him suck in a breath. Before he could get his balance on the slippery snow, he fell backward. He missed the tree, but

167

pain surged through the right side of his head when he hit the ground.

The surrounding trees began a slow spin. Then everything went dark.

CHAPTER TWELVE

Jennifer's swinging purse hit the man in the chest. She heard his surprised grunt a moment before he fell. If there was any justice at all, this was the man who had stepped on Stuart's back. If this was the same creep, at least she'd paid back a little of what he deserved.

Pulling the purse straps back onto her shoulder, she took a few running steps and then paused to look back. He wasn't moving. The fall had probably knocked the breath out of him. Her purse couldn't hurt him. If he was momentarily stunned, she had time to find a place to hide in the surrounding trees.

She moved sideways and craned her neck to look around the tree. She could see most of his body. He wore jeans and a jacket. The light was dim, but his jacket looked just like the one that Stuart had on.

Ripping off her gloves, Jennifer ran forward and dropped to her knees. She felt for a pulse in the side of his neck and then sighed with relief at the firm throb beneath her fingers. She moved her hands over his face and head looking for any other injury. Her searching fingers paused when she felt the rough edges of a wound over his left ear. The area wasn't bleeding, but the crusty area around it proved that it had bled profusely.

Her imagination conjured up vivid images of how he might have gotten this new wound, but she pushed them away. What did it matter how it had happened? He was hurt and needed her help. She couldn't panic now.

His pulse felt strong and steady, and his breathing appeared to be regular, but she wanted to check the back of his head. She dug in her purse and found the small flashlight she carried and rarely used. She clicked the switch on and off a few times and then threw it back in her purse. It served her right for never checking the batteries.

Then she remembered that Stuart kept a pencil flash in a pocket of his jacket. Stretching across his chest, she thrust a hand into the left pocket. Nothing there. She searched the right pocket, found it empty, and groaned in frustration.

"Think, Jennifer," she whispered.

Maybe he'd had the flash in his hand when he fell. She beat the snow on the right side of his body but found nothing. Dodging the icy particles blowing up into her face, she crawled on hands and knees and searched the area beyond his feet. Then, moving up on the other side, she raked her hands through the snow and gave a heartfelt "Yes!" when she found the light.

She had a few seconds of worry before she figured out how to turn it on. Shielding the narrow beam of light with her hand, she turned it on his face. A bloody groove made a new part in his hair on the left side of his head, just above the temple. She shifted around in the snow, eased his cap off, and lifted his head onto her lap. With injuries on two areas of his skull, any doctor would admit Stuart to a hospital for observation. All she could do was to stay with him and hope he woke up soon. She couldn't move him and she couldn't leave him here alone.

Head injuries could produce abnormal reactions. Would he know her when he woke up? Or would he look at her with no recognition in his eyes? Stuart had endured atrocities at the hands of his captors. Remembering his reaction when she produced the hypodermic and the vial of numbing agent, she knew they'd also given him drugs. She could only imagine what Martha had endured. How painful it must have been for her each time he left her, not knowing when or if he would return, or what condition he might be in when he did come back.

Cradling his head closer, Jennifer gently brushed snow off his face. Uneasiness made her drop a hand to his shoulder. She gave him a gentle shake. He didn't respond. He looked vulnerable lying so still in her arms. Her fingers curved into a caress against the hard line of his jaw.

"Stuart . . . wake up. Can you hear me?"

Jennifer looked over her shoulder and saw two sets of headlights shining through the breaks between the trees. At this distance, she couldn't see the vehicles. Stuart had said that the government agents traveled in two vans. Maybe they were looking for him. But wouldn't they send men through the grove of trees? They wouldn't just stay on the road and hope that Stuart would see their headlights.

If these vehicles were Garizon's car and van, he and his friends would be too glad to escape to bother looking for her. Or would they? The man blamed Stuart for his brother's death and wouldn't leave without making an attempt to either capture Stuart or kill him.

Twisting her head to one side, she had a clear view of the lead car, a long black limousine. If they stopped to investigate this stand of trees, she'd move out where they could see her. After all the trouble she'd caused Stuart today, it was the least she owed him.

Why were they moving so slowly? She squinted into the wind and saw a light held at the side of the car and aimed down at the road. Garizon must be following a trail.

Footprints. She and Stuart had walked on the road.

Jennifer pulled on her gloves and bent over him again. She shook his shoulder. "We're in trouble. You have to wake up."

He didn't respond.

She leaned down and touched her lips to his. The cold of

melting snow on his flesh gave way to warmth as her lips lingered upon his. Lifting her head, she murmured, "Stuart . . . wake up. We have to get out of here."

He gave a soft moan. "Jen?"

She hugged his head close to her chest. "Yes, it's Jen. We have to get away fast. We have to run."

One of his eyes opened and stared up at her. "Run? I'll be lucky, if I can sit up." The other eye opened. "I had the strangest dream."

Warmth rushed over her face. Fortunately, it was too dark under the trees to him to notice her heightened color. "I'm glad you're awake, Stuart."

"That makes one of us." He groaned again. "I didn't know my head could hurt in so many places."

"I'll give you some aspirin." She darted a look toward the approaching headlights and then wriggled away from him to grab her purse. "We have to get out of here."

Using his elbows, Stuart levered himself to a sitting position. "Okay . . . if you think you can carry me."

"That isn't funny." Jennifer found the bottle of aspirins and opened it. "Take two of these."

" 'And call me in the morning.' "

"Hush," she warned.

She bit down on a finger of her glove and pulled it off. With the glove dangling from her mouth, she moved forward and lifted one of the tablets to his lips. "Take this."

"Oh, nurse . . . I'm worse."

Jennifer spit out the glove and put an aspirin in his mouth. "Swallow." When he did, she held up another pill. "Now this one."

"Yes, ma'am."

She tossed the bottle back into her purse and pulled on her gloves. "Can you get up?"

"If you're asking if my legs will work, yes."

"What do you mean?"

"I believe you call it vertigo."

"You're dizzy?"

"I didn't think you'd stoop to talking like a layman."

She shot another look over her shoulder and leaned forward. "You have to get up."

Obediently, he got his legs under him, pushed upright, and leaned against the tree. "Are you going to heave me over your shoulder?"

"Don't joke, Stuart."

"I'm not joking. Have you ever tried to walk when you're dizzy?"

She hadn't, but she wasn't going to tell him so. "You'd be surprised what you can do when you have to. Garizon and his men are following our footprints. They'll be here shortly. We have to get out of here and find someplace to hide." Jennifer lifted one of his arms, slid under it, and wrapped her arm around his waist. "Lean on me."

He stared down at her. "I asked you before if you thought you could carry me."

"I'm a nurse. I've handled patients who weigh a lot more than you do." She shifted a bit to her left. "How far is it to the main road?"

"Too far. We'll go back to the government van."

"We can't. Garizon's car is on the road between us and the hangar."

"We'll go through the trees."

"But they don't go all the way down to the hangar. There's a cleared place. We can't cross it without them seeing us."

"There's a dry creek bed not far from here. It goes up behind the hangar."

She opened her mouth to ask how he knew about the creek

bed and heard him chuckle. "What's funny, Stuart?"

He bent and gave her a quick kiss. "You are."

His warm breath feathering across her face made it difficult to concentrate. Giving him a smile, she turned into the wind and started walking.

The snow lay deep under the trees. Stuart kept moving, but he had trouble with his balance. He slipped once, and she took his full weight across her shoulders until he stood up.

"Sorry," he murmured.

Jennifer didn't waste breath answering. She was out of shape for wading through knee-deep snow with a very large man leaning on her shoulders. When she glanced back toward the road, she saw three figures standing in the glare of the headlights and looking at the stand of trees.

"It's no good, Stuart. They'll follow our tracks and catch up with us. We can't move fast enough."

"They won't come into the trees."

"They'll have to, if they want to find us."

"Garizon and his men followed me into a stand of trees once before."

"What happened?"

"I survived, but several of them didn't." As if he felt her involuntary shiver, Stuart added, "Garizon's men fear the night when *Sombra* is around."

With a few words, he reactivated her dread and insecurity. A moment later, he stumbled again and almost went down. "Sorry." He raised a hand to his eyes. "The dizziness isn't getting any better."

"It's because you're moving around." Ahead of them, she saw the end of the trees. "Where's that creek you mentioned?"

Stuart carefully moved his head to the right. "Over there. The bank is high enough to provide cover."

Slipping and sliding and more winded than she cared to

admit, Jennifer swung around and headed in the direction he indicated. "We'll make it," she encouraged. "Just keep walking."

"I'm not about to sit down."

A moment later, she said, "There it is."

Getting down into the creek bed proved easy enough. They slipped and slid to the bottom. She looked at the four-foot high, snowy banks lining the creek on both sides and didn't feel encouraged any longer.

"How are we going to get back up there?"

"I can boost you up."

She had a mental image of the part of her anatomy where he'd have to push and shove. "No thanks."

His sudden laugh told her that he knew what she was thinking. "You're priceless, Jen."

She took his arm over her shoulder again, bent lower than before, and started walking. "You might be able to push me up over the top, but I could never pull you up after me."

He stopped moving and abruptly pulled her down with him. She saw why. The sides of the bank weren't so high now. Up ahead, they were even lower. She pointed toward the lighted area in front of the hangar. "We can't . . . just stroll across . . . in full view . . . of everyone."

It took a few breaths to get it all out. When she looked aside at Stuart, he frowned at her.

"Gripe, gripe, gripe. Can't take you anywhere."

"Very funny," she shot back.

"No problem, Jen."

"How do we do it?"

"With skill and cunning."

"Uh-huh."

After they'd rounded a sharp bend, Stuart stopped and knelt down. Afraid something else might have happened, Jennifer dropped down beside him. "What's wrong?"

"Other than the pain in my head, the dizziness and possible frostbite, I'm fine." He moved around to shield her as best as he could from the driving wind. "We need a rest."

His breathing looked faster than normal. She sat down and gulped in breaths of cold air. When he curled an arm around her shoulders and pulled her close against his side, she didn't protest.

Finally, he pointed over her shoulder. "You'll have to check out the government van."

She stared at him. "How do you know it's still there? Wouldn't Garizon take both of them?"

"No."

She didn't understand. "Why would he leave a vehicle for you to use? You might come after him."

"Trust me, Jen. He won't try to start my van."

"How do you know that?"

"He tried once before and lost a few men when the car exploded."

"You put a bomb in it?"

"Yes."

Stuart pulled a small, rectangular box from his pocket. One end held two tiny lights, one red and the other green. "At this moment, the mechanism is set on safety."

Jennifer leaned closer and noted the softly glowing green light. "How do you activate it?"

"By pressing the red light."

That didn't look safe. "But you've been carrying this case in your pocket. You could have pressed that switch by accident."

He turned the box over and pointed out a depression in the case. "First you have to move this small lever. That takes a definite click. You can't move it by brushing against it."

"No wonder you said that I had no aptitude for this kind of work."

"It isn't a question of aptitude at this point." He shrugged as though the reason were obvious. "From here on, we have to crawl. Once we get there, you have to run from the corner of the hangar to the vehicle. As you can see, I'm having trouble just standing up."

"We'll both go," she suggested.

"You can't crawl forward and hold me up at the same time. I'll follow you, at my own speed, but you have to do the rest by yourself."

Jennifer searched for a hole in his logic but couldn't find one. "Okay, I'll do it, but I don't know which one of us is dizzier."

"I do," he stated. "That's why you have to check out the van."

She following his line of reasoning and nodded. "That's because Garizon thinks I'm with you back there in those trees."

"Give the lady a gold star."

"So he won't have his attention on the government car and shouldn't be looking in this direction."

"Good deduction. I'm impressed."

She frowned in his direction. "Could you please be serious? There could be angry people with guns in that hangar."

"What did you just tell me?" he prompted.

"I said they wouldn't be looking in this direction. If that's true, I'll be safe." When he opened his mouth to make a comment, she snapped, "And don't say anything about a stupid gold star."

"Touchy," he murmured.

She couldn't shake the feeling that he used this light-hearted banter to make her feel at ease with what he wanted her to do and also to cover up the truth about how he felt. "I don't like leaving you."

"Don't worry about me, mama."

"You could have a concussion."

"I have a nurse with me." He grinned. "What more could I want?"

She pushed to her knees. "Here goes."

He caught hold of her arm. "Keep low. Circle around and approach the van with the wind behind you."

"Why?"

"Looking into the wind makes a person's eyes water. If there's someone there, he'll be looking in the other direction."

"Why didn't I think of that?"

His fingers tightened. "I'll follow you, but I can't move as fast as you. Don't try to be a heroine. If you see someone, run back to me." Stuart probed into his right boot and drew out a nasty looking, snub-nosed revolver. "I'll deal with him."

She had a better idea. "Let me have the gun."

"No way."

"But you're too dizzy to shoot accurately."

"Do you trust me, Jen?"

She didn't have to think about the answer. "Yes."

His white teeth flashed in a smile. "You wouldn't have said that an hour ago."

She couldn't deny it. "A lot has happened since then."

He gave her a swift, hard kiss. "Be careful."

More out of breath than before, she dropped her purse at his feet and began crawling.

Within a few yards, Jennifer dropped to her hands and knees and then to her belly. She wriggled forward with her head turned to her left but saw no one. When she neared the area of the hangar, she stopped to allow her breathing to slow to something approaching normal. The snow-encrusted vehicle standing nearby looked empty. But, obedient to Stuart's instructions, she crawled forward and kept watching for any sign of movement.

A few feet farther on, the sides of the bank rose high enough to allow her to get up and jog, bent far forward to avoid being seen. She didn't feel as frightened as she thought she would. Undoubtedly, Stuart's presence gave her courage. He depended upon her. Except for the confines of her job, she couldn't remember any other time when someone had depended upon her. She couldn't let him down.

When Jennifer reached the place where the creek bed curved off to the right, she crawled out onto the bank and lay still, alert for any sign of movement.

In the distance, she saw the car's headlights. Garizon and his men hadn't yet worked up the nerve to go into the trees after Stuart. Their presence worried her, but she could keep the van between her and the car. As Stuart said, they had to look into the wind to see her and they wouldn't because they thought she was still in the grove of trees.

She glanced around again. One side of the terminal lay in darkness. A dozen people might be hiding there and she wouldn't be able to see them. She didn't see anyone around the van, either, but that didn't prove there was no one inside. To be sure, she had to open the door. And to do that, she had to move out where Garizon and the others could see her.

Looking back toward the creek bed, she saw what looked like the white blur of Stuart's face peeping over the bank. Knowing that he was so close jump-started her courage. She ran to the van, slid the door back, and looked inside.

A surprised gasp came a moment before someone jumped up off the seat. "Well, well . . . look who's here." Louise stepped down. "Hello, Jennifer. I'm glad to see you." The woman's red lips parted in a smile of relish. "This time, Garizon isn't around to spoil my fun."

Jennifer backed a few steps.

Louise followed her, squinting against the driving wind. "Too bad about Stuart. Garizon will kill him this time."

"You think so?"

"Of course." Louise sighed. "Too bad. I always fancied Stuart." She smiled again. "He also fancied me. Did you know that, Jennifer?"

"I don't believe you."

"Why would I lie to you?" The blonde woman shrugged. "I didn't intend for anyone to find out about us, but Garizon has spies everywhere."

Jennifer shifted a bit more to her right. "Stuart wouldn't touch a woman like you."

Louise's throaty laughter floated around them. "You think not? Ah, but you're still young enough to believe what you want to believe."

"You passed that age a long time ago."

A tightening of the woman's mouth told Jennifer that her barb had hit where it mattered most.

Louise smiled. "Stuart likes to amuse himself with young ones like you, but he always comes back to me."

"Any port in a storm."

Surprise flashed across the blonde's face. "So the little dove has a few claws." She laughed. "That doesn't matter. You aren't woman enough for a man like Stuart."

Jennifer smiled. "He doesn't complain."

"Now who's lying?"

She easily dodged the woman's rush. Putting out a foot, Jennifer tripped her and had the pleasure of seeing Louise fall face first into a snow bank.

Remembering Stuart's advice, Jennifer shifted until her back was to the wind. Louise erupted from the snow and ran toward her. Timing her move to the woman's forward movement, Jennifer grabbed Louise's arm and neatly flipped her onto her back.

The blonde rolled over and pushed up. Thrusting a hand into her coat pocket, she brought out a slim, flat tube. With a sharp click, she opened the switchblade knife and advanced toward Jennifer again. "I'm going to cut you, sweetie. When I'm finished, your face won't be so pretty any more." She charged forward.

Jennifer grabbed the woman's right arm with her left hand while her flattened right hand struck Louise solidly at the base of her throat. She dropped like a rock. Standing over her, panting from her exertions, Jennifer heard movement behind her. She whirled around to see Stuart weaving toward her.

"I thought you might need help." He moved to her side and handed over her purse. "Obviously, I was wrong."

Her gaze followed his. "I once took a self-defense course."

"Remind me never to argue with you." He grasped her arm and turned her around. "It's time to go."

She pointed over her shoulder at the prostrate figure. "What about her?"

"Never stay around to admire your handiwork." Stuart started toward the van. "Agent's manual, page twelve."

She returned his smile and waited while he retrieved the small case from his pocket and turned it off.

"You have to drive, Jen."

She helped him onto the passenger seat and then moved around and sat down behind the wheel. Nodding with satisfaction, she said, "It's like my van."

He pointed ahead. "Swing by the plane."

What was going on? "Don't tell me you want to fly out of here."

"No. I want to make sure no one else does."

Jen stared at the distant car. "Won't they see us?"

"Yes."

She turned to look at him. "And that doesn't bother you?"

"They'll have a job if they try to turn their car around. The plowed space is down the middle of the road."

She drew up beside the plane. "That's a Lear jet, isn't it?"

"Yes. How did you know?"

"The husband of a friend of mine has a private plane that looks a lot like this one. It seats six people. They took me up in it once."

Stuart slid the door open on his side and stepped outside. Jennifer winced at the arctic air swirling inside the cab. She said, "I'll keep the engine running," and heard him laugh.

"You do that, Jen."

He pulled the revolver from his shoulder holster and shot a few rounds at the windows.

So far as she could tell, with the ice crusting on the plane's glass portholes, the bullets had no effect. She leaned over and called, "Better do it again. The glass didn't break."

"It doesn't have to. The shots will weaken and crack it enough to prevent pressurization of the cabin."

She should have known better. He always had a good reason for what he did.

Jennifer saw movement around Garizon's car. One of the men standing in the light of the headlights lifted an arm and pointed back toward the hangar. "Hurry, Stuart. They've seen us."

He put a few shots into both engines and then moved back to stand by the door. He took two tries before he stepped up and dropped onto the seat.

She looked down the road again. "They might decide to back up all the way to the hangar."

"They couldn't make any speed that way. We'll be gone long before they can get here."

"But what if—"

"There's a back way out of here. Garizon can't follow us."

"What's to stop him?"

"His car doesn't have the right kind of tires."

Jennifer smiled. "Is there anything you don't know?"

"What you eat for breakfast."

The tingling in the pit of her stomach radiated outward until goose bumps slid down her arms. There was nothing different about the tone of his voice, but the look in his eyes made her shiver. She whispered, "Toast and cold cereal." Her gaze locked with his. "What about you?"

Excitement lurched inside her as his eyes narrowed and darkened. "Pancakes, strawberries and champagne." His smile wrapped around her like a warm blanket. "I saw it in a movie once and always wanted to try it."

His eyes held a glow that made her pulse pound harder, but there was also tenderness.

"Has anyone ever told you, Jen, that your face gives away your thoughts?"

His hand lifted to the back of her head. She made no attempt to move away. His kiss was passionate and thorough. He finally lifted his head and ran a gentle finger across her cheek. "You're going to have bruises."

A delighted shiver ran over her. Before she could speak, he began telling her how to operate the van. Her warm feeling oozed away as he pointed out various dials and switches. One moment, he had kissed her. The next, he talked to her as though he had no interest in her at all.

"Don't touch any of these switches," he continued.

They were alone. He must know that she wanted him to kiss her again. And he wanted the same thing. She couldn't be wrong about that. Or could she? The familiar feeling of insecurity surfaced despite her efforts to keep it at bay. Did he kiss her to insure that she'd do what he told her?

"Did you hear me, Jen?"

"Not all of it."

He stared at her for a moment before he pointed out the

special switches and gauges again. When he'd finished, she
turned the van around and aimed it away from the hangar.

CHAPTER THIRTEEN

"Follow the creek bed." Stuart pointed ahead. "I'll show you where the road turns off into the trees."

If there was a road, it must be buried under several inches of snow, Jennifer thought. She steered farther to the right but couldn't see much through the swirling snow.

"Careful," he cautioned. "Don't get too close to the edge. If you slide down there, we're in trouble."

He had a point. The bank along the creek stood nearly four feet above the bottom in places. If she skidded down there, they wouldn't get out again.

She jerked the wheel to the left and found it surprisingly easy to turn. She turned too far, corrected too much to the right, and fought her natural impulse to overcorrect again. Her hands began to cramp, but she didn't dare relax her grip. The steering wheel had too much play in it. When she tried to slow their forward progress, the brakes grabbed, pitching them sharply forward.

"The wheel and the brakes are probably more responsive than you're used to."

"Yes, they are," she agreed.

He lifted a hand and made a lazy gesture toward her left. At least, that's how it looked to her.

She squeezed forward over the wheel. Peering through the snow, she saw a gap between the trees and steered toward it. The wheels spun in the loose snow but finally dug in, propelling them forward.

The steering wheel and the brakes weren't the only sensitive equipment on this vehicle. The lightest touch of her foot on the accelerator had an immediate effect. This felt like learning to drive all over again. Giving her head a shake and mumbling to herself, she steered for the middle of the narrow clearing that Stuart called a road.

"Relax, Jen. Nothing to get excited about."

The mist of their breath fogged up the windshield so badly she had difficulty seeing the way ahead. She reached down to turn on the defroster, but his hand whipped out and grabbed hers in an iron grip.

"Don't move that knob." He pulled her fingers away from the dashboard. "It isn't the defroster."

"It is on my van."

His gaze bored into hers. "As I told you before, there are controls in here which you must not touch. That," he pointed to the knob her fingers had momentarily rested upon, "is one of them."

"What's it for?"

"Just drive." He put his head back against the headrest. "And be careful."

"That's right. Don't tell me."

"I don't intend to."

She swallowed her anger. "I've had quite a day, Stuart. I've been kidnapped, tied up, slapped around by that blonde witch, and almost abducted to a foreign country."

"What's your point?"

Jennifer swung the wheel in time to prevent sideswiping a large tree. "Now I'm driving the getaway car," she said with a laugh.

Stuart groaned.

"And don't say that isn't what you call it."

He sat with his eyes half closed, watching ahead.

"Has any woman ever told you that you have a couple of exasperating habits?"

"Only a couple?"

Her lips twitched. "A typical, male response."

"I am a typical male."

She looked at him and said, "I can think of many adjectives to describe you, Stuart, but that isn't one of them."

He gave her a smile and said, "I'll take the easy way out and assume you mean that as a compliment."

The van gave a bone-jarring jolt.

"I think you just hit something."

Jennifer faced front just in time to avoid a huge tree stump. The van slid to the right. Tightening her grip on the wheel, she carefully steered back to the left and blew out her breath in relief.

"I presume we're heading for a road, Stuart."

"It's about five miles from here."

"Is there a sign?"

"An arrow."

She fought another slide and got straightened out only to slip the other way. "On top of everything else, I'm driving along a trail a deer wouldn't use, and I'm supposed to find my way back home."

The tires slid again.

"If you wrap us around one of these trees, you won't have to worry about the way home."

Jennifer took the hint and kept her eyes on the road. She could see the cloud of her breath in the air. Reaching out to move the heater bar to a higher level, she hesitated with her gloved finger almost on the small lever.

Was this one of the things Stuart said not to touch? She decided to err on the side of caution and withdrew her hand. As the minutes passed, her hands began to ache from her white-knuckled grip on the wheel. She risked a glance at Stuart. His head lay back against the neck rest. His eyes were closed.

"Stuart?"

He didn't answer.

She leaned over and shook his shoulder.

He didn't wake up.

Jennifer alternated looks ahead with observing him. So far as she could tell, his breathing seemed regular and his color looked good.

A loud scrape across the top of the van sent a stab of fear through her. Licking her lips, she stretched out to swipe the mist away from the windshield. Low-hanging branches, heavy with snow, appeared in the glow of the headlights.

Didn't the road look narrower?

Desperate, panic-driven thoughts whirled through her head. What if something happened to the van? With Stuart unconscious, how would she find that arrow he mentioned?

She took a couple of slow breaths. Wallowing in a pool of emotion might satisfy her feelings, but it wouldn't get her home. Checking the mileage, she judged she'd traveled about three miles. Another two miles until she would see the sign.

But on which side of the road would it be?

Her eyes strained to see through the snow hitting the windshield. She gasped in alarm when twin gleams at the side of the road turned into the eyes of a large deer. The animal seemed confused by the headlights. In desperation, Jennifer hit the horn. The frightened beast jumped across the road in front of her. She twisted the wheel and just missed his rump before he disappeared into the trees.

Despite the chill in the van, she felt perspiration beading her forehead. Maybe the van's radiator would survive an impact with a full-grown deer, but she didn't want to find out.

She ran the window down a bit. Icy bits stung her cheeks, but she held her face up to the opening and took a couple of breaths. The wind felt colder. Did that mean another snowstorm coming their way? That was all they needed. Frowning at the thought, she closed the window.

The turning, twisting stretch of untouched snow didn't resemble any kind of a road. Had Stuart made a mistake? She dismissed the thought immediately. The Stuarts of this world didn't make mistakes.

The mileage gauge showed the passage of another mile. One more to go, according to her original estimate.

Another bump made Jennifer gaze in amazement at the tree scraping along the right side of the van. She spun the wheel, plunging them to the other side. The left front of the van hit another tree and came to an abrupt stop.

She took a moment to breathe deeply before she opened the door and slithered off the seat. Her foot skidded on the step and pitched her out into a deep drift. She sat up, spitting snow out of her mouth. Shivering from a cold trickle on her neck, she dug inside her collar and removed a fist-full of slush.

The air definitely felt colder. She shifted around to protect the left side of her face and wondered if the bruising made her skin feel stiff as well as cold. Her teeth chattered as she pushed upright and waded knee-deep snow to look at the front of the van.

The bumper lay against the stump of a young tree. The upper part of the trunk leaned drunkenly backward, exposing a long gash of wood.

"Congratulations, Jennifer," she whispered. "You killed a tree."

She climbed back up into the van, closed the door, and shifted into reverse. Carefully lowering her foot over the gas pedal, she pushed down. The engine revolutions increased, but nothing happened. She applied pressure to the pedal again and heard the wheels spinning.

Was the front end stuck on something?

Deciding it would take a harder pressure, she jabbed the accelerator. The van slid backward, despite her efforts to stop it. She twisted the wheel, but the back end slued to the right. Changing gears, she tried to halt the backward slide and made some headway before the right, back tire slid into what must be a sizeable hole. The van came to a halt with the headlights pointing up above ground level.

She pounded her fist on the steering wheel. Of all the stupid things to do! She reached over to shake Stuart's arm, but he didn't move.

The light was too dim to see if his face had a flush of fever. She didn't want to touch him with her wet gloves, so she got out of the seat and bent over to place her lips against his forehead. His skin felt cold. He needed food and warmth, and he needed them now.

Shoving upright, she moved back through the van. A shovel lay in a horizontal rack along one of the walls. Jennifer glanced at it and then passed by and opened the rear door.

A gust of wind tore the door out of her hand. The next moment, a whirlwind of cold air and snow whipped around her. She glanced over her shoulder and wished she had some kind of a cover to put over Stuart. The best thing she could do for him was to get him out of here.

With a hand lifted to shield her eyes, she put a foot down outside and sank up to her knee in snow. After several tries at closing the door against the downhill angle of the van, she gave it up.

She waded around to the right side of the van and bent to look at the snow-covered back wheel. It could be okay, but she had to get rid of some of the snow before she could tell how much of a problem she had.

An eerie prickling ran down the back of her neck and spread into both arms. Jennifer looked over her shoulder. Her slow, sweeping gaze studied the dark beneath the trees. She saw no movement but couldn't shake the sensation that someone watched her. An army could be moving through there, and she couldn't see them or hear them above the keening of the wind.

This wouldn't be a good place to spend the night.

Climbing back into the van for the shovel required more effort than it should have. She took a few seconds for a breather and then jumped down and moved around to the wheel. A couple of minutes later, she stood and puffed while she eyed the big cleats with approval. If the tires could get enough traction, they'd pull the van out of the hole.

Climbing into the cab again, she rummaged in the storage compartments under the two bench seats and found a jacket and two pairs of jeans. It wasn't much, but it would have to do. She saw a thermos and a fat, brown bag propped in a corner. Food? Maybe coffee? Her empty stomach rumbled. It had been a long time since breakfast. But first things first.

She carried the clothes outside and crunched her way around to the side of the van. Kneeling down, she crammed the jacket and jeans into the space in front of the wheel and then waded to the front of the van.

The wheels stood several inches off the ground. When the back tires bit into the clothes, the front end would drop and everything should be okay. The first try would have to do it. If she didn't do it right or the van slid back into the hole again, the loose snow would bury the clothes beyond her reach. She had nothing else for another try but her coat.

Jennifer looked behind her. Once again, she had the impression that unseen eyes watched her. Some bears came out of hibernation during the winter to forage for food and then went back to sleep. If it was a bear, could it smell the food in the paper bag?

Even worse, had it caught her scent?

Shivering again, she moved back to the rear door and stepped up into the cab. She had to get out of here as soon as possible. It took a few tries, but she finally closed the back door. As an afterthought, she locked the door before moving up to the front of the cab.

She bent over Stuart, took off her glove, and checked his neck for a pulse. Strong and steady. She started the engine and looked again at the heat control. He needed warmth. If she guessed wrong and something awful happened to the van, it would probably happen so fast she'd never know anything about it.

The thought didn't help her to relax.

She murmured, "Here goes," pushed the lever, and smiled when a warm flow of air hit her face.

Things definitely looked brighter.

She dropped into the driver's seat, strapped her belt, and took a deep breath. Without giving herself time to think too long about it, she engaged the gear and jabbed the accelerator.

The van leapt forward and shot into the gap between the trees. Jennifer carefully applied the brakes. She had to be close to the road Stuart had mentioned. It would be easy to miss it in this blowing snow. Equally worrisome, she noted that the track between the trees now had a downhill slant. Hopefully, that meant she was close to the highway.

She rounded a sharp turn to the left and saw something sticking up at the right side of the road. The base lay buried in snow, but she saw part of a yellow arrow, pointing left. In the distance, she saw a faint circle of yellow light. She bent closer to the glass and saw the light elevated above ground level.

An access road for the expressway.

Her delighted smile faded when she saw a large, black car standing at the top of the ramp. Garizon and his men. How had they known where Stuart's van would come out of the trees? There must be other access roads in the vicinity.

How they knew where to wait didn't matter. They were here. What was more important, the big car sat at the top of the entrance to the interstate. No doubt, Garizon felt confident that he'd soon have Stuart in his custody once more.

Garizon had told her stories, put doubts in her head, and she'd let him get away with it. Worse than that, he'd come to this country for the express purpose of forcibly abducting an American citizen. And he had the nerve to tell her that the American authorities would willingly extradite Stuart to Panama to stand trial.

From somewhere deep inside her, anger built to a boil. Garizon and his thugs had kidnapped her, threatened her, and injured Stuart, and still they weren't satisfied. They meant to kill him. And they'd have to kill her, too, because she could identify them.

She hunched over and tightened her grip on the wheel. Stuart had risked his life to save her. Now she planned to return the favor. Her pulse lurched. She gritted her teeth and stomped on the accelerator.

The van shot up the ramp. She saw the surprised faces of the two men standing on the road a moment before they jumped out of the way. She aimed the van toward a section of the railing to the left of the big car and heard a series of scraping noises along the left side of Stuart's vehicle. Jennifer dodged away when pieces of wood flew past the windshield. She heard a thump and more scrapes on the right side as the van sideswiped Garizon's car.

Sometimes, you got lucky.

★ ★ ★ ★ ★

Stuart felt warm air blowing in his face. Was he back in South America? Or worse, Garizon's prisoner?

He moved his arms and legs. No ropes. A sudden jar shifted his body. He heard the sounds of something breaking. What was going on? The pain wasn't so severe now, but his head felt strange, like it might be stuffed with cotton.

Something moved rapidly within his range of vision, like the wild swaying of a tree in a high wind. But no tree moved like that. He blinked again and focused on a rapidly moving windshield wiper. He heard what sounded like the whine of bees and looked across at Jennifer.

She sat bent over the wheel, her eyes wide and staring. Her head whipped around when he sat up. "Oh, Stuart!" Relief set a wide smile on her face. "I was ready to sing, yell in your ear, anything! I'm glad you're awake."

He put a hand to his forehead. "As I said once before, that makes one of us." The wheels skidded, and he lifted a hand to point. "Keep your eyes on the road."

She reached down by her left foot, retrieved her purse, and tossed it to him. "Take some aspirin. We're on the expressway. Garizon and his friends were waiting at the top of the access ramp. They shot at us."

So those were the noises he'd heard. Stuart shook a couple of pills onto his palm and tossed them into his mouth. "The windows and sides of the van are bullet proof."

The face she turned toward him held more than a little reproach. "Now you tell me."

"Better late than never."

She laughed. "I think I like you better when you're asleep."

"That's only because you're tired."

"I'm also cold and hungry."

"Some people are never satisfied." He nodded toward the

194

console. "It's too hot in here."

Jennifer moved the blower back to minimum force. "You worried me for a while back there. Which reminds me." She nodded over her right shoulder. "Does that bag in the storage area have food in it?"

"Cheese sandwiches, chips and pickles, but I doubt that Garizon will wait while we pull over to the side and have a picnic."

Jennifer glanced his way. "You said he couldn't follow us."

"I said he wouldn't try the road through the trees. He obviously used the main road."

"I wonder how he knew where to wait for us to come out of the trees?"

Stuart said nothing.

She checked the rear view mirror. "I don't see them behind us." She thought about it for a moment. "Do you think they'll turn around and follow us?"

"No. We have too much of a head start." His gaze lowered from her face. "Why are your clothes wet?" The look she threw at him made him wish he'd kept the question to himself.

"To use one of your phrases, Stuart, you don't want to know."

Automatically reaching out for the wheel to correct the van's sudden slide to the right, his eyes widened in surprise when she slapped his hand.

"*I'm* driving."

Something had transformed her from a gentle, rather shy girl into a confident, no-nonsense woman. He murmured, "Yes, ma'am," and watched to see if she smiled.

She did.

"Just follow this road, Jen."

She smiled again. "I think I've heard those words before." She leaned forward and looked up.

Stuart's gaze followed hers in time to see a large green sign at the side of the road. "Now you know where you are."

Jennifer nodded. "We're heading south on Interstate 270."

"Right. You'll hit the 495 in a couple of miles. Follow it to MacArthur Boulevard. Take that to Massachusetts Avenue, then to Dupont Circle. I'll direct you from there."

"I thought we were going home."

The comment came out so naturally that he stared at her for several seconds. "You are. I have something to do."

When he didn't explain, she said, "You might as well tell me. After the day I've spent, nothing could shock me now."

He shook his head. "It doesn't involve you."

"I've been involved all day. What do you think would have happened to you if I hadn't been here?"

"I don't know."

"Garizon meant to kill you."

Stuart silently conceded the truth. Aloud, he said, "He has tried to kill me many times."

"Today he would have succeeded." She looked at him. "You passed out almost as soon as we got into the van." She paused and then added, "I saved your life."

"Yes, you did."

"Have I finally earned my spurs?"

He frowned. "Where did you learn all these quaint phrases?"

"Don't try to put me off."

He looked into her frank gaze. "What are you saying, Jen?"

"Where you go, I go."

If ever he saw a woman with the bit between her teeth, here was one. Nothing he said would change her mind, but he had to try. "I appreciate what you did for me."

"Prove it."

He said, "How?" and knew what she was going to say.

"Let me be in on the finish."

"You don't know what you're asking, Jen."

"I'm not good enough?"

"It isn't a question of good or bad."

"You don't think I'm tough enough to do what's required?"

He said, "No, I don't," and waited for a stream of insults or arguments. Again, she surprised him.

"Until today, I would have agreed with you. I grew up with a sour, spiteful woman who devoted herself to convincing me that I was ugly and useless."

"Obviously, she didn't succeed."

"Oh, she succeeded better than she knew. The only place I ever really felt competent was in the hospital. I worked alongside some brilliant doctors and surgeons and felt equal to the task . . ." Jennifer paused. "My private life was another story."

"You mean Frank?"

"He wasn't the only man who ever found me attractive."

"I didn't mean to imply that he was."

She gave a soft laugh. "If you're worried about my feelings toward him, don't be." She glanced aside. "By the way, I haven't seen him again."

"I don't think you will." Stuart hesitated. "Jen, there's something I want to tell you."

"First, I want to tell you something. Things happened to me today, Stuart, but now I know I can do whatever I have to do. I couldn't have said that yesterday." She turned toward him. "Because of you, I'm a different person."

The beautiful smile she gave him wiped away any lingering doubts as to the depth of his feelings for her. If another man told him that he could fall in love with a woman after knowing her such a short time, Stuart would have said he didn't trust the feeling. True love only happened when two people got to really know each other. And that took a long time to develop.

Or so he always believed.

Now he knew what it was to love a woman with every fiber, every bone, and every sinew of his body.

"That's why I'm telling you, Stuart. I can handle whatever happens."

"You don't know what you're saying, Jen."

"Don't shut me out. Let me help you."

She was sweet, spunky and lovable. He hadn't thought her capable of dealing with the events of this day, but she did as well as any trained agent could have done. She also had untapped resources for handling pressure and personal danger.

He drew in a deep breath and averted his gaze from her animated features. She didn't realize it yet, but she wouldn't have much trouble convincing him to do anything she asked. He couldn't allow her to face Garizon again. She might not be so lucky next time.

"This doesn't concern you, Jen. I appreciate your offer of help, but it isn't necessary. When we get to where we're going, I'll have someone take you home."

From the corner of his eye, he saw her glance his way. He kept his gaze fixed upon the windshield. If she smiled at him again, he might do something stupid, like tell her how much he loved her.

He settled back and closed his eyes. He'd done the right thing to discourage her before either of them became involved beyond the point of no return. A sour smile curled the corners of his mouth. For him, there had been no going back from the moment he first saw her.

"Stuart! I see a black car coming up behind us. It looks like the one that tried to block the top of that ramp."

Stuart opened one eye and scanned the road ahead. "Tell me if it exits at the next off-ramp." He closed his eye again.

A short time later, Jennifer said, "I guess I was wrong. The car turned off at the exit."

Stuart sat up. "No, you were right, Jen. They wanted to make sure this is the right van, but they didn't want to draw attention to themselves on this road." He pointed toward the traffic passing them in the opposite lanes. "Too many people watching. They'll wait for us somewhere else." He settled back in the seat. "And now, I think I'll close my eyes and let the aspirin work."

CHAPTER FOURTEEN

Jennifer alternated glances between the snow-covered road ahead and the rearview mirror. Stuart hadn't said a word for several miles. She saw his eyes open and cleared her throat. "If I see someone else coming after us, what should I do?"

"Nothing. Keep driving."

"They've been trying to catch us for hours," she pointed out. "Why would they stop now?"

"I doubt that Garizon is in that car."

That surprised her. "Where else would he be?"

"He probably went ahead to make arrangements."

"What kind of arrangements?"

"Garizon didn't come to this country just to get me, Jen."

"What else does he want?"

Stuart looked at her but said nothing.

"Don't turn into a clam. I have a right to know." When Stuart got up from his seat and moved toward the back of the van, she glanced over her shoulder. "What are you doing? Are you going to get weapons to help us fight back?"

He came back carrying the paper bag and the thermos. "You read too many books."

"How do I know what you might have back there? You could have all sorts of gadgets that I wouldn't recognize as weapons."

He opened the bag and took out a wrapped package. "At the moment, all that interests me is getting on the outside of one of these sandwiches."

Her stomach rumbled. She opened her mouth to protest that it wasn't fair for him to eat while she had to drive. Before she could say the words, he broke off a corner of the sandwich, reached across, and put it into her mouth.

Several minutes passed while he ate, fed her bites, and shared the coffee.

"This is the craziest picnic I've ever had, Stuart." When he didn't answer, she glanced toward him.

He held what looked like a small cellular telephone. After punching in some numbers, he held it to his ear and said, "Mama is safe. We're on the way." He turned off his phone.

She waited for him to explain. When he didn't, she said, "Okay, don't tell me who or what 'mama' is. And I'm not going to ask you, because if I do, you'll just say that I see too many movies."

He sighed. "I liked you better before you found your independence."

"I believe you like me better now." She turned her head toward him again.

"Watch where you're going, Jen."

She obediently turned around to correct the weaving path of the van. Stuart could say whatever he wished, but she believed he felt more for her than he wanted to admit. Overcoming the truckload of guilt he carried wouldn't be easy. He blamed himself for Martha's death. It wasn't difficult to follow his line of reasoning. Allowing a woman to become close to him put her in danger.

Jennifer had to admit that recent events added weight to his arguments. The difference was that she had coped well with the situation. She had protected him at a time when he couldn't protect himself. What she accomplished today counted in her favor, but she needed to do a lot more to convince him that she wouldn't collapse like a wilted flower if the going got really rough.

And the situation could get a lot rougher.

All she had to do was to remember the injuries to Stuart's back. If she fell into the hands of someone other than Garizon, she might suffer worse physical abuse than Stuart had endured.

She could understand Stuart's reluctance to place the woman he cared for in jeopardy, but that wasn't the only fact to consider. His chosen line of work involved high-risk situations. Since jeopardy formed a large part of his life, she had to share it with him or have nothing at all.

The prospect of a future without him loomed too bleak to consider. She turned to look at him. She had to be ready to counter whatever arguments he put forth and convince him that they had a future together.

Stuart saw Jen looking at him, but now wasn't the time to talk. She must be getting tired, but it wouldn't be for much longer. She steered the van as he indicated, going left or right as he told her. It had been almost an hour since she'd last spoken to him.

He turned, but before he could speak, she said, "A van pulled in behind us about three blocks back. It looks like one I've seen before, like that one Garizon had." She pointed a gloved finger toward the rearview mirror. "It has that funny looking bird painted on the hood. Remember?"

Stuart said, "Yes."

"Isn't that a strange coincidence?"

"It's no coincidence."

She sent a worried look in his direction. "But how could they know where we are?"

"That's a good question." He pointed to his right. "Turn here. We're going to try to lose them."

She looked at him then. "You mean it is the same van?"

"Yes."

"But that's impossible."

At his direction, Jennifer spent the next half hour driving down alleys and back streets, with the van close behind. Going down the wrong way on a one-way street, she looked back and saw a large truck blocking the entrance.

"We got a lucky break back there," she said.

"Luck had nothing to do with it."

She opened her mouth and then decided not to ask.

He signaled for her to pull onto a parking lot. When she turned off the engine, he said, "Empty out your purse."

"What?"

"Empty your purse."

She retrieved her bag from under her feet and obediently dumped the contents onto her lap.

He leaned toward her. "Put everything back one at a time."

She picked up her wallet, a ring of keys, a checkbook, and a pack of tissue and put them away.

Among her remaining items, Stuart noted a slim, metallic object about the half the size of a cigarette case.

She picked it up. "I don't know what this is."

"I do."

He held out a hand.

She gingerly dropped the case into his palm. "It isn't some kind of bomb, is it?"

"No. It's a tracking device."

Jennifer stared back at him for a few seconds. "Louise put a blindfold on me before they took me into that warehouse." She paused and then added, "Garizon looked through my purse."

Stuart held up the object. "And put this inside."

Now she understood. "They've been tracking us all this time. That's why the car didn't follow us on the expressway."

"We'll give them another trail to follow, Jen." He opened the door and stepped down. "Come with me."

She followed close behind him. She wasn't about to let him go anywhere without her. They passed the deserted booth where the man who watched the lot usually sat. "I guess he's having an early breakfast," she commented.

Stuart walked to the sidewalk and looked both ways. When he said, "There's one," she turned and followed the direction of his gaze. "One what?" she asked.

"A cab."

She saw a man come out of a shop with a steaming cup of coffee and head for the taxi. "Are we going to leave the van on that lot?"

"No. Wait here where I can see you."

"Where are you going?"

He didn't answer. She watched him jog down the sidewalk and stop by the taxi. To her amazement, he opened the back door and slipped inside. A few seconds later, he stood up on the pavement again, turned, and headed back in her direction. He linked an arm in hers and turned her back into the parking lot.

"What was that all about, Stuart?"

"I asked the man if he could drive me to Charlottesville, Virginia. He said no."

"I'm not surprised." She thought about it for a moment. "Why did you do that?"

"While I asked him that question, I stuffed the tracking device down behind the cushion in the back seat."

"Cabs travel all over town. It'll drive Garizon's men crazy." Jennifer gave a soft laugh. "I never would have thought of doing something like that."

Ten minutes later, she pulled into a side street near Dupont Circle.

"There's a restaurant nearby, Jen, called The Monocle."

She turned to look at him. "At a time like this you're going to have something to eat?"

He took a breath and blew it out before he said, "I learned about The Monocle from a friend in the Canadian Embassy. It's a basement restaurant."

"Why the strange name?"

"There are pictures of Sidney Greenstreet all over the walls."

"That's interesting."

"It's one of the places I meet my contacts."

Why was he telling her? He'd never before shared that kind of information with her.

While she thought about that, a pickup truck, painted a bright cherry red color, moved out of a nearby alley and pulled across in front of her. She stepped on the brakes to avoid hitting him. To her surprise, the driver waved to her. She glanced toward Stuart and saw him tilt his chin to acknowledge the man's greeting.

"Friend of yours?" she asked.

"I have friends everywhere." He pointed to the alley behind the truck. "Pull in there."

She drove the van through the narrow opening. In the rear-view mirror, she saw the truck back up to block the alley.

Stuart reached up to the roof of the van and touched a switch. A door opened in the side of the building ahead of them. "Pull in there, Jen, and park against the wall."

She parked where he indicated and turned off the engine. "This looks like an abandoned store of some kind."

"It is. We'll be here for a while."

"About your friend back there," she commented. "I hate to point this out, Stuart, but we could have used his help or the help of some of your other friends during the past couple of hours."

"They were never far away."

She turned to look at him. "I should be past all surprises by now."

"My friends always know where I am." Stuart pointed to the dashboard. "That defroster knob you wanted to turn is a built-in homing and tracking device. It's also two-way communication."

"So you could have called for help at any time." She smiled. "Provided, of course, that you were conscious."

"Jen, there's no use trying to—"

"I'm not trying to do anything, Stuart. I'm pointing out that your devices work only when you're physically able to use them." Her smile widened. "And you couldn't use them at that airport."

After a moment, he said, "What's your point?"

She couldn't suppress a laugh. When she saw his frown, Jennifer laughed again. "Is it so painful for you to admit that a woman can be of some practical use?"

A grudging smile lifted one corner of his mouth. "Now that you mention it, I did feel a twinge." He jerked a thumb toward the back of the van. "Go and lie down. You look a little tired."

She was a lot more than a little tired, but she wasn't about to tell him that. "Where will you be?"

"Right here."

She slid off the seat and headed back into the van.

"Jen?"

When she turned around, he pointed to a small door in the warehouse wall directly ahead of the van. "There's a restroom over there. It's crude, but it works."

"Thanks."

Jennifer awoke and stared up at a metal ceiling. She blinked, looked around, and saw that she lay on a long, padded bench. Some sort of a soft, fluffy blanket covered her from shoulders to feet. A smile curled her lips. Stuart must have covered her.

She sat up. Where was he?

As though in answer to her question, he said, "I'm here, Jen."

"What time is it?"

"A little past one."

She indulged in a stretch and got to her feet. "I'm starving."

"There's a sandwich and coffee on that other bench seat."

She shifted to the other side of the van, sat down, and scooped up the wrapped package. A moment later she removed the covering and found a delicious looking roast beef sandwich. The coffee steamed when she removed the cap off the paper cup.

The day definitely looked brighter.

Jennifer barely had time to finish her lunch before she heard a loud thump. She jumped up and hurried the few steps to the front of the van.

Stuart twisted around, flipped the lock, and Julio opened the door. "You are well, my friend?"

"More or less." Stuart waved a hand toward Jennifer. "Ask Mitch to take her home in the other truck."

She stiffened. "Why?"

"What I have to do now doesn't concern you, Jen."

"I've been part of what you had to do for a long time. Or have you forgotten?"

"I'm grateful for your help."

"But you don't need me any more. Is that it?"

"That's it."

Without waiting for her to comment, he slid off the seat and walked away.

Julio motioned to Jennifer to move forward.

She sat down on Stuart's vacant seat. Julio helped her down to the cement floor of the garage. "Did you leave Johnny alone?"

"No. A lady he knows is with him." Julio stared down at Jennifer for a moment. "Something is wrong?"

"Yes, something is wrong. I offered my help to Stuart and he refused."

"I tell him you are a smart woman. Now I am not sure."

"What does that mean?"

"He has much to do. He can do it better if he does not worry about you."

"I understand that, Julio, but Stuart has the idea that getting close to any woman puts her at risk."

"It is true."

"Doesn't that depend upon the woman?"

Julio put a hand under her arm. They walked outside and started down the sidewalk. "You think like a female."

"Of course." She studied the big man's stern profile. "What happened to Stuart's wife?"

"If he wants you to know, he will tell you."

"That's just it," she argued. "He won't tell me. I think it would help me to understand him if I knew the whole story about Martha."

"Stuart is my friend."

"Would you feel disloyal to him if you told me about his wife?"

"I would never be disloyal to Stuart. I have been his friend since the night he helped me to bury my family."

"Oh, Julio, I'm . . . I'm sorry."

"My wife felt as you do. She wanted to be with me. I knew it was not wise." Julio said nothing for a few seconds. "Enemy agents surrounded our camp in the jungle. They tied me up and left me to die while they took her and my children away."

"How awful for you."

"Stuart found me the next day. I was weak with fever. At times he carried me on his back while we followed the trail of the raiders. He gave me his last bite of food and his last drink of water. When we found my family, he helped me to bury them."

The bleak look Julio sent her way chilled her as much as the cold air whipping around her body.

"If you care for Stuart, stay away from him."

Putting his hands near his face, Stuart blew warm breath on his fingers while he stood in the doorway and watched Jen's retreating figure. Her slumped shoulders told him all he needed to know. She had courage, no doubt about that, but he couldn't risk her safety. She meant too much to him.

He drew in a deep breath and let it out in a long sigh. If Garizon got hold of her, the game was over. He'd have the ultimate weapon against *Sombra*.

Stuart moved back inside and checked the garage in all directions. His gaze swept over the parked cars again before he got out his phone.

After a single ring, an impersonal voice said, "The number you have called is out of order."

"This is *Sombra*."

"Hold on. I'll get Uncle."

Moments later, another voice said, "Glad you're safe."

"It was a near thing, but I'm okay."

"And Mama?"

"She's fine."

"But?"

"I couldn't have made it without her," he admitted.

"I'm glad you and Mama are back. That's good."

"No, not so good."

"A lover's quarrel?" the voice asked.

"That isn't funny."

"Stay close. You'll receive orders within the hour."

Jennifer shivered against the cold bite of the wind. "Are you angry with me, Julio?"

"It is useless to be angry with a woman."

"Why do you say that?"

"A woman cannot control her emotions." He shrugged. "Only a foolish man argues with her."

She marveled at his simple answer to an age-old problem. "Can men always control their emotions?"

"No." He paused. "Sometimes a man must leave his woman for a while."

Was that what Stuart had just done? Gone elsewhere because he loved her more than he wanted to admit? "Tell me about Stuart, Julio."

"He is an honorable man."

"I know that." She tried again. "What did they do to him?"

"You have seen his back."

"I'm not talking about that."

Julio said, softly, "I am almost an old man, and still I do not understand women. They always want to know what will hurt them the most."

What was that supposed to mean?

A moment later, he shoved her away from him. "Run, Jennifer."

She looked ahead and saw a familiar dark car pulled across the road. "But, Julio—"

"Run!"

She slithered between two parked cars. She heard the sound of running feet, someone yelled her name, but she didn't look back. She saw a bus pulling away from the curb and waved her arms at the driver.

He stopped and popped the door open. "That's dangerous, lady. You shouldn't run into the street."

A hand grasped her elbow from behind. "Come along, my dear."

She gasped and whirled around.

Garizon smiled and put his other arm around her. "You should not run out like that. I worry about you."

She looked at the driver. "Help me! These men are trying to kidnap me."

"Do not make a scene, my darling."

Jennifer tried to twist out of his grasp. "Let go of me!"

The bus driver got out of his seat. "Now, wait a minute."

Another man moved forward. He was about Garizon's size with dark hair and eyes. He took a stethoscope out of his pocket and dangled it for the driver to see. "I am a doctor." To Jennifer, he said, "You are safe now, Mrs. Hernandez."

She sent a desperate look toward the driver. "They're trying to kill me."

He frowned and took a step closer to the door, but the new arrival waved him back. "This lady is my patient. A nervous breakdown. I will be responsible for her."

Jennifer twisted harder but couldn't break Garizon's hold. "They want to kill me. You must help me. Tell the police."

The man with the stethoscope produced a small case, opened it, and took out a hypodermic. "You are much too excited, Mrs. Hernandez. I did not wish to do this, but I will have to sedate you."

"Don't let him touch me," she pleaded with the driver.

"Be quiet, my darling," Garizon soothed.

"Now, wait a minute," the bus driver said.

Jennifer felt a prick on her arm. She gave a violent twist and the needle popped out, spilling its pale contents over the fabric of her storm coat. Her arm hurt, but at least she hadn't gotten the entire drug.

"Wait until I call a policeman," the bus driver suggested.

"I regret I cannot do that," Garizon replied. "I must get my wife back to the hotel. She is not well."

"Which hotel?" the driver wanted to know.

"We are staying at the Hyatt Regency," Garizon answered. "I am Miguel Hernandez, and this is my wife."

"That isn't his name," Jennifer began.

His companion slung the stethoscope around his neck and moved around to support her on the other side. She turned to send another silent plea for help over her shoulder.

The bus driver gave her a nod.

Jennifer saw the people on the bus standing at the windows. They looked fuzzy.

Garizon turned her around and began walking her away from the bus. "Did she get enough of the drug?" he asked his companion.

"I do not know."

If they thought she was in worse shape than she actually was, they might get careless and give her a chance to get away. Jennifer allowed her feet to trip over each other. She pretended to try to speak around a thick tongue. "Where . . . where are you taking me?"

"We must get her off the street," Garizon said, "before we attract any more attention."

Jennifer stumbled along with them.

"I said she would be my means of capturing Kendall."

The other man said, in a soft whisper, "Why did you tell that man where we are staying?"

"That is where Kendall will come looking for her." Garizon laughed. "When he does, we will be waiting."

Jennifer couldn't prevent a gasp of alarm. She gathered her strength to make one last attempt to jerk free.

At that moment, two men reeled out of the door of a bar on the corner. They began laughing and supporting each other while they sang a popular Christmas song. They paused to wish "Merry Christmas!" to people passing on the sidewalk.

The men wove their way through the crowd, laughing and

singing. When Jennifer and her escorts came closer, the two drunks staggered over and put their arms around the shoulders of Garizon and the doctor, who tried to shrug the singers away without success. Garizon and the doctor finally released Jennifer to try and free themselves from the smothering embrace of the two drunks.

She slipped sideways. A moment later, she pushed by some people passing on the sidewalk and edged farther away. Then she started running.

Garizon yelled her name, but she didn't look back. Her head felt peculiar. The sidewalk tilted at a funny angle, making it difficult to pick up any speed. She slowed to a rapid walk and began looking for a place to hide.

Stuart checked his watch. Julio should be back by now. Mitch's truck sat no more than fifty feet from the door of the garage.

That strange tingle started in the back of Stuart's neck. He strode to the doorway and stepped outside. Halfway down the block, he saw a bus pulled against the curb. Incredibly, Julio stood at the door and talked to someone inside.

Stuart ran toward them and came to a stop by the big man's side. "Is Jen with Mitch?"

"No," Julio answered. "This man—" he pointed at the driver "—says two men took her away."

Stuart swung around and stared up at the uniformed man framed in the doorway of the bus. "What did they look like?"

"Dark hair and eyes, foreign looking, spoke with an accent," the bus driver explained. "I didn't like the look of it, mister. One of the men said the lady was his wife, but she kept saying they were trying to kill her and that I should call the police. The other guy said he was a doctor and tried to give her a shot of something. She jerked away, but I guess she got some of it because she staggered when they walked her away from the bus."

"Do you know which way they went?" Stuart asked.

"Better than that. I asked where they were staying and one of them told me his name was Hernandez. They're staying at the Hyatt Regency."

"Thank you," Stuart said. "We'll take it from here."

"Don't you want me to make the call?"

"The lady's a friend of mine. I'll take care of it."

Stuart didn't speak until he and Julio entered the garage. "How did it happen?"

"Five men got out of a car. I told Jennifer to run. Garizon and another man ran after her. I could not assist her. The other three attacked me."

"Only three? Hardly enough to work up a sweat."

Julio gave him a questioning look before he said, "I broke one man's arm and some ribs of another. Then they all ran away."

"I'm glad you're on our side."

Julio gave him that same look again. "I know you for many years. You joke most when you are most upset." He put a hand on Stuart's shoulder. "You care for Jennifer."

Stuart took a long breath and let it out slowly. "You know me too well, old friend."

"We will rescue her, Stuart." After a moment, he added, "If Garizon told the truth about where he is staying."

"He did. He wants me to try and rescue Jen."

"Then he will be waiting for you."

"Garizon issued an invitation to me, Julio." Stuart took the pistol out of his jacket and checked his ammunition. "It would be rude not to accept."

Jennifer awoke with her head pounding. Her mouth felt parched.

She needed a drink of water. Putting her hand to her forehead she felt dampness. How could she sweat when she felt so cold?

And why was it so dark?

She held up her arm but couldn't see the dial of her watch. She blinked, looked around, and saw slats covered by cardboard. Her shelter looked like some kind of crate big enough to hold a large refrigerator.

She brushed the cement around her body and breathed a sigh of relief when she found her purse. Her dry mouth made swallowing the aspirin difficult, but she managed to get the pills down.

The time had been about one-thirty when she'd left the warehouse with Julio. A few hours must have passed since she had found this abandoned crate and crawled inside. She reached over to feel her right arm and found a sore spot. Yes. Now she remembered. Fortunately, she'd only gotten part of the dosage the doctor intended to give her.

If he was a doctor.

Pushing up on her elbow, she slid close enough to the edge of the crate to look out. The light from a window above cast a pale rectangle around several, bulging garbage cans about twenty feet from where she lay. The area beyond was too dark to see what might be there.

The sound of voices made her jump. Two men arguing about something. From the rattle and clank of metal against metal, they must be looking in the garbage cans as they passed by.

Jennifer checked behind her head. The crate lay with one end propped against a wall. Maybe they wouldn't check her hiding place, but she didn't want to be here if they did.

She slid backward and out of the crate on the side away from the men and continued to move away from them until her back hit a hard surface. She couldn't prevent a gasp of surprise and saw one of the men turn to look in her direction.

"You hear that?" one of them said.

"Probably a rat," the other one replied.

"I guess so."

When the first man turned away, Jennifer looked behind her. The alley ended in a brick wall. She craned her neck, looked up, and estimated the height of the bricks at about ten feet.

Fear stabbed through her as the men moved toward her former hiding place. From their weaving gait, they'd had a few drinks to celebrate the season. One of them bent over the crate and upended it. She clenched her teeth at the thought of what might have happened to her if she hadn't awakened when she did.

One of the men suddenly turned and pointed in Jennifer's direction. "Hey, George. I told you I heard something." He laughed. "You see what I see?"

"Santa left us a present," the man named George replied.

"Come here, sweetheart," the first man said. "You look cold. We'll warm you up." He dug the other man in the ribs with his elbow. "Right, George?"

"Right."

They headed in her direction.

Jennifer looked at the boxes and cans against the wall and hoped they were sturdy enough to bear her weight. Jumping up onto the lowest one, she began climbing.

"Hey, sweetie, don't leave yet!"

A large hand grabbed hold of her ankle.

She jerked her foot from his grasp and kicked back as hard as she could. He yelped and clapped both hands over his nose.

Jennifer scrambled onto the other boxes, threw a leg over the wall, and dropped down on the other side. One ankle twisted under her, but it bore her weight when she pushed upright and leaned against the wall.

The streetlights at the end of the alley traveled in a lazy circle.

With one hand on the side wall, she walked to the end of the alley and looked out. The snow had stopped. A few people walked past, but they wore mufflers for protection from the high wind and didn't look her way. She checked the nearby cars and didn't see the black limousine. A smile curved her lips when she saw a taxi on the other side of the street.

Jennifer sprinted out of the alley and waved to the driver. Seconds later, safe in the back seat, she relaxed back against the upholstery. Her body ached in various places and she was dizzy and nauseous from the drug, but she was safe.

"I'm going to Alexandria, driver." She gave him the address.

Stuart was right. She didn't have an aptitude for this line of work.

CHAPTER FIFTEEN

"This is not a safe place, Stuart."

"We know that Garizon hasn't left the Hyatt. He must still be here with Jen." Stuart scooped a light-colored wig from the bag at his feet and pulled it on. "Since I'm going to take the place of one of the waiters, this locker room off the kitchen is the best place to wait."

"Why will you be a waiter?"

"When I'm ready, Julio, I'll go out into the kitchen and carry one of the trays upstairs."

"What if no one wants a meal?"

"You don't have to worry about that. Americans love room service."

Stuart put on a pair of steel-rimmed glasses and dipped in the bag to retrieve a small, wrapped package. It took only a few seconds to remove the vial of special glue from the wrapping, apply it to the area above his upper lip, and add a small mustache that matched the wig.

He adjusted his uniform and then looked toward the closed locker where the owner of the uniform lay tied and gagged. Then Stuart headed for the door.

Julio said, softly, "You should not do this, my friend."

Stuart paused with his hand on the doorknob. "Garizon wanted me to know where he was taking Jen. That's why he told the bus driver about the Hyatt."

"You are not well enough."

Stuart slipped the pistol into the back of his waistband and buttoned the uniform's jacket. "I'm okay."

"The coat is too small for you."

"I'll just crouch over a bit."

Julio put a large hand on Stuart's shoulder. "If Garizon captures you this time, he will kill you."

"I'll be careful."

Stuart opened the door just enough to look out into the kitchen. Uniformed personnel moved hurriedly back and forth. No one glanced in his direction.

He waved Julio forward and opened the door a little wider for the big man to look out. "The waiters taking meals to the upstairs rooms wear the same outfit I'm wearing. See the lighted numbers over there?" Stuart pointed to the opposite wall. "All of those people requested meals."

"Garizon will recognize you, Stuart, even in this disguise."

"By the time he sees me, it'll be too late for him to do anything about it."

Stuart eased the door open, stepped outside, and moved forward to join a group of waiters. One by one, they received meals to carry to patrons. Finally, the man in charge waved Stuart forward.

"Room ten-twelve. And hurry."

He accepted the tray but halted when the man put a hand on his arm. "I don't know you."

"One of your guys didn't report for work," Stuart explained. "I'm filling in for him."

The man frowned. "That must be George. He's probably loaded to the gills again." The man jerked a thumb toward the door. "Take it on up. And come right back."

"Yes, sir."

Stuart moved to the door leading out of the kitchen area. Once outside, he followed another waiter, precariously balancing two loaded trays. "Let me help you," Stuart said and punched the elevator call button.

"Thanks."

"No problem."

When they stepped inside the car, the man said, "Eighth floor."

Stuart punched that button and then the one for ten.

"I heard Barney tell you to take that up to ten-twelve." The man grinned. "I took something up there a little while ago. Several guys in there, with accents. I got a fifty dollar tip from one of them."

"Big spender," Stuart commented.

The waiter gave him a knowing wink. "They have a good looking woman in there, a brunette with a great body."

"Only one woman?"

"They're expecting another one. A redhead." He gave Stuart a dig with his elbow. "She must be something special, judging by the remarks I overheard."

Stuart's grip tightened on his tray. "Sounds interesting."

"The brunette wanted to leave without her, but the tall guy, the one who gave me the money, said they wouldn't go without this new girl." The waiter chuckled. "I guess she must be a real looker." The waiter stepped out when the doors swished open. "See you, pal."

"Right."

The doors closed behind him.

Stuart heard the ring of his phone and set the tray down. Taking the compact instrument out of his pocket, he tapped the button and said, *"Sombra."*

"Mama is home. Repeat, Mama is home."

Stuart ended the connection. He reached up, pushed the elevator button for the basement, and then tapped in some numbers. When a voice answered, he said, "Mama is home. The time for assistance is here. The Hyatt Regency, Room ten-twelve. Notify the appropriate people."

"Will do, *Sombra.*"

He ended that call and punched in another set of numbers. "Change of plans. Mama is home. I'll be right down."

He heard Julio's voice say, "Understood."

Refreshed by a hot shower, Jennifer changed into her favorite green silk dress and headed for the nursery. She glanced toward the closed door at the other end of the hall. According to Roberts, the Wilsons had stayed in their part of the house all day long.

Jennifer turned the corner for the nursery and saw a middle-aged woman standing outside the door. "My name is Anna, ma'am. Mr. Kendall asked me to stay with his son."

"Hi, Anna. I'm Jennifer." She shook hands with the lady. "Have you had your dinner?"

"Not yet."

"I'll stay with Johnny. Go have it now."

"Thank you, ma'am."

Jennifer shoved the door open to the nursery and gasped in surprise when she saw Johnny climbing the shelves filled with toys. He saw her, gave her an impudent grin, and put his foot on the next highest shelf.

The shelf collapsed, dropping him to the floor.

"Don't try to move," she called as she ran forward.

He had a cut on his forehead, oozing blood. His face began to turn red. Whether it was pain or temper, she couldn't tell. She checked his arms and legs for any broken bones and lifted him into a sitting position.

Johnny's mouth opened but no sound came out.

"You can't catch your breath?"

He nodded. His eyes widened in fear.

Jennifer scooped him up into her arms and hurried to the bathroom. She quickly turned on the cold water, grabbed a glass from the cabinet, and pushed it under the running stream. Giving him no sign of what she meant to do, she tossed the water into his face. He caught his breath in a gasp and began to cry.

She grabbed a towel from the rack and carried him to a chair by the table. He welcomed her touch. She wiped the water from his face and hair, dabbed the small cut until it stopped bleeding, and then wrapped her arms around him.

She rocked him gently back and forth. When his arms slipped around her waist, a remarkable feeling of contentment spread through her body. She cuddled him closer and began talking about Christmas and asking him what he wanted from Santa.

Jennifer didn't protest when he twisted off her lap. Keeping her one-sided conversation going, she stood up and reached a hand out to him. "How about some hot chocolate?"

He put his hand into hers.

Half an hour later, she helped him put on pajamas and a robe. "Anna will be back soon to give you your dinner."

"Will you stay with me for always, Jennifer?"

She waited a few seconds, until she could trust her voice not to wobble. "I'll stay for as long as you want me to."

"My mommy didn't love me."

She took his hand in one of hers. "I think she loved you a lot, but she didn't know how to show it." Jennifer gave his hand a gentle squeeze. "Sometimes grownups find it hard to tell other people how they really feel."

"Do you like little boys, Jennifer?"

She smiled. "Yes. I like little boys."

His arms lifted. "I love you."

Happiness burst inside her when she stooped down to allow him to give her a hug. Unbelievably, he kissed her cheek. "Do you know me long enough to love me, Jennifer?"

She scooped him up in her arms. "Yes, Johnny. I love you very much."

"I drew a picture of you."

She set him down. He ran to his small table, grabbed up a sheet of paper, and brought it to her. Jennifer looked at a drawing of a red-haired angel with large wings.

"Do you like it?"

She bent to kiss his forehead. "It's beautiful."

"Can Santa find me here?"

"Of course." The door opened and Anna entered, carrying a tray. Jennifer smiled at her and then said to Johnny, "I'll see you before you go to sleep."

Jennifer entered the drawing room and sat down in a chair by the fireplace. Johnny loved her. He had actually hugged her and given her a kiss. And this time it wasn't because his father urged him to do it.

That made it all the sweeter.

"Lost your last friend, Jen?"

She twisted around to see Barbara standing in the doorway. The tall blonde wore a loose fitting purple dress, sprinkled with sequins. The short garment flowed around her slender body as she moved forward.

Barbara halted a yard or so from Jennifer's chair. "We haven't seen much of you lately."

The young woman's words sounded slurred. Her cheeks held a flush that Jennifer suspected wasn't due to rouge. She caught the odor of whiskey or some other strong drink.

"You have my father worried."

"I beg your pardon?"

"Good little Jen, begging my pardon." Barbara leaned closer in the manner of someone imparting a confidence. "I'll tell you a secret. When you're polite, nobody notices you."

"I don't think you have to be rude to be noticed, Barbara."

"I agree. Being rich would do the job nicely."

Barbara staggered to the chair across from Jennifer, sat down, and crossed her shapely legs. She opened her evening bag, took a cigarette out of a long, leather pouch, and lighted it. "You know about being rich, don't you, Jen?"

"What do you mean?"

Jennifer watched the young woman's red nails carving furrows in the chair's upholstery. Why was Barbara so edgy? Her pale eyes held a glitter that had nothing to do with the firelight. Her gaze darted here and there, focusing on nothing in particular, while she continued to drag her nails back and forth on the arm of the chair.

"Are you feeling okay?" Jennifer asked.

"I never felt better."

Barbara pushed off the chair, walked to the fireplace, and threw her cigarette into the flames. "Life can be strange sometimes, Jen."

Unsure what that meant, Jennifer said, "I suppose so."

"People pretend to care for you. And all the time, they're waiting their chance to destroy you."

"What makes you say that, Barbara?"

A harsh laugh greeted her comment. The girl looked up at the nearly life-size painting over the fireplace. "That's my great-grandfather William. What do you think of him? He looks forbidding, doesn't he?"

Jennifer studied the portly man dressed in what was probably the height of fashion a hundred years ago. "I think he has a happy twinkle in his eyes."

"Twinkle? That's an angry glint." Barbara twisted around and stalked away from the fireplace. "I need a drink."

"I'll ring for some coffee."

Barbara looked back over her shoulder. "I've never seen you take a drink, except for wine." A moment later, she added, "Perhaps you never had a good enough reason to drink."

"And you do?"

"That's clever, Jen. Now you'll pretend to be my friend so I'll tell you."

"Tell me what?"

Barbara waved a finger. "Oh, no."

"What are you talking about?"

"You know exactly what I mean."

"I'll ask Roberts to bring some coffee." Jennifer stood up.

Barbara rushed forward and grabbed one of Jennifer's arms. "You're not so clever."

The girl's long nails dug into her skin, but Jennifer twisted free and stepped back.

"Miss Goody-Goody." Barbara swayed on her high heels. "Maybe you'll soon have a reason to drink." Her features twisted into a sneer. "You act like you're better than the rest of us, but we know what's going on upstairs."

Jennifer turned away. She didn't want to get into a cat fight with Barbara.

"How do you do it, Jen?"

Curiosity turned her around. "Do what?"

The girl's assessing gaze swept from the top of Jennifer's upswept hair to her shoes. "You're nothing out of the ordinary." She frowned. "Frank is handsome. And I hear you also have a bearded friend. Quiet little Jen gets all the men she wants."

Barbara began to laugh. Her laughter grew shriller and more uncontrolled. Tears ran through her mascara, leaving dark tracks in their wake. Her eyes held a wild look that Jennifer had seen before. She stepped forward and slapped Barbara's cheek.

The wild laughter abruptly stopped.

"I'm sorry," Jennifer explained. "You were getting hysterical."

The girl's nails dug convulsively into the soft fabric of her evening bag. Her mouth trembled. Tears slid down her cheeks.

"Leave her alone!"

Jennifer spun around.

Harold and Phil crossed the room to Barbara's side. Harold slipped an arm around his daughter's shoulders and gently fingered the red marks on her cheek. "Did Jen do that?"

Barbara nodded.

His angry glance stabbed at Jennifer. "Why?"

"She was hysterical."

"She doesn't look hysterical to me," Harold said.

"Nor to me," Phil put in.

"She started laughing," Jennifer explained to Harold, "and couldn't stop. I've seen it before."

"Are you implying my daughter is loony?"

"Of course not, but she does have a drinking problem."

He pointed an accusing finger at Jennifer. "You hit her for no reason. Now you're trying to excuse your action by saying that Barbara is an alcoholic."

Jennifer said, "Look at her. She has the shakes because she needs another drink. You should get her some professional help."

"Don't presume to advise me about my daughter." His mouth curled with distaste. "A woman like you."

"Pardon me, ma'am." Roberts paused on the threshold. "Did you summon the authorities?"

Jennifer frowned. "What?"

The butler moved aside and two men stepped into the drawing room. One of them wore the uniform of a police sergeant.

Harold walked over to them, turned, and pointed a finger at Jennifer. "There she is, gentlemen. Arrest her!"

"Where are we going, Stuart? Do you not wish to talk with Jennifer?"

Stuart turned the truck's windshield wipers to a faster speed to cope with the steady snowfall. "I have another stop to make first."

"Do you not wonder how Jennifer got away from Garizon? That is something many men can not do."

"She's resourceful, Julio, and she doesn't panic in a dangerous situation."

"She wants to share your danger, Stuart."

"I can't allow her to do that."

"I understand."

Stuart looked at his friend. "You're a smart man."

"No," Julio replied, "just a man." He stared back at Stuart. "Jennifer also wants to know about your wife. Will you tell her?"

"Yes, Julio. I'll tell her. Jen has to know why I can't let her be a part of my life."

"I regret this, Jen, I truly do." Harold came toward her with the officers but remained a little behind them. "I gave you every opportunity to return the stolen items, but you refused."

"What stolen items?"

"Barbara's diamond necklace, for one."

"You think I took it?"

"You coveted it the moment you saw it," Harold replied. "You told Barbara that if she didn't take good care of it, someone would steal it. Do you deny saying that?"

"No. I said it because—"

"Of course you can't deny it," Harold cut in. "You wanted the necklace, so you took it, along with my wife's string of pearls."

"I've never stolen anything."

"Poor child," Harold murmured. "You couldn't afford such luxury items on a nurse's salary, but you wanted them. So you took them."

"This is ridiculous, Harold."

The sergeant cleared his throat. "I'm sorry, miss, but we have a court order to arrest you."

"But I didn't steal anything," Jennifer protested.

The man wearing ordinary clothes with a heavy top coat said, "You'll have every chance to prove that, miss."

"I'm sorry for you, Jen," Harold said. "Truly sorry."

Barbara began laughing, at first softly and nearly normal, but then her laughter erupted into a high-pitched screech.

As Jennifer had done earlier, Harold stepped forward and slapped his daughter with the flat of his hand. She collapsed into the chair and sat moaning and nursing her cheek in her hand.

"Is something wrong with that girl?" the sergeant asked. "Is she ill?"

"The man she loves jilted her," Harold explained.

The officer nodded. "I've seen this kind of thing before."

"What kind of thing?" Harold's heightened color showed his resentment. "My daughter is a sensitive young girl. She loves this man very much and he married another woman this afternoon. That's the reason for her upset." He swung his attention to Jennifer. "Now, gentlemen. I want this woman out of my home."

Jennifer straightened her back. "I am the legal mistress of this property. I'm not the one who's going to leave, Harold, you are. You and all of your family."

"You can't bluff me, Jen. In addition to grand theft, I intend to bring charges against you proving that you're not suitable to have the custody of a young child." A satisfied smile parted Harold's lips. "Remember the bearded man? There's also Julio. And Frank. What do you think will happen when a judge hears about your activities with all these men?"

The younger policeman stepped forward. "Will you come

with us peacefully, miss?" He cleared his throat and held out his set of handcuffs. "I don't want to put these on you."

Jennifer felt as though she'd fallen from a great height and hit the ground with a thud. This couldn't be happening. What should she do? Who could help her? Banning . . . she'd call Banning. Arrested people could make one telephone call, couldn't they?

But it was three days before Christmas. Banning could be out of town or even out of the country for all she knew. Without his help, what else could she do?

She'd tell Stuart. Her momentary elation quickly drained away. The only way she could contact him was at that restaurant he mentioned, The Monocle. And she couldn't get there, not with these policemen waiting to take her into custody.

Besides, Stuart had his own problems. He had apparently slipped quietly into the United States and probably intended to leave just as quietly. She couldn't involve him in her problems.

This had all happened because she'd underestimated Harold. She hadn't believed he'd carry out his threats, but she should have known better. With a fortune at stake, he'd do anything to get control of Johnny's inheritance.

The man in plain clothes stepped forward. "I'm Detective Crawford, of the District Police Department."

Harold smiled. "Do your duty, Crawford."

The detective waved a hand toward the hall. "May I speak with you alone, Miss Denton?"

"Of course."

"Now, wait a minute," Harold began.

"We'll return shortly, Mr. Wilson." Crawford put a hand under Jennifer's elbow. "The rest of you remain where you are."

When they stepped out into the hall, Crawford indicated a nearby door. "Shall we use this room?"

Jennifer nodded. When he opened one of the double doors,

she preceded him into the library. Uneasiness slid down her spine when he closed the heavy partition and leaned back against the smooth panels.

As though he understood her unspoken concern, he stepped forward and presented his identification.

"How do I know that's genuine?" she countered.

"Ah, you're an astute, young lady. When I asked to speak privately with you, it had nothing to do with the . . . uh, unfortunate happening out there." He paused and studied her for a moment. "We're looking for Stuart Kendall and we need your help."

Whatever she said could be the wrong thing, so she said nothing.

"We want to ask Kendall some questions."

"All I can tell you, Mr. Crawford, is that I have the care of his son."

"Yes, of course, but there are facts I feel you should know about him . . ." He paused. "What I have to say may upset you."

"I'm a nurse, Mr. Caldwell. I don't upset easily."

"Stuart Kendall is a dangerous man."

She'd heard that before.

"A man whom we recently captured identified Kendall as a member of a group of mercenaries whose prime purpose is the overthrow of our government."

She hadn't heard that.

"The man may have lied, but you understand that we must investigate Kendall's activities. With your permission, we'll put a tap on your phone."

"No."

His eyebrows climbed at her abrupt refusal. "Since you have the care of his son, it's logical to assume that Kendall will call you at some point and arrange to see the boy. Once he does that, we can make preparations to take him into custody."

"A tap is an invasion of my privacy."

"I appreciate that, Miss Denton, but we have to be ready to move quickly."

"I don't want a tap on my telephone."

"Very well." After a pause, the man said, "Then we must depend upon you telling us when Mr. Kendall contacts you." He paused again. "Shall we rejoin the others?"

Back in the drawing room, everyone turned to look when Jennifer and Crawford stepped over the threshold.

"All right, Crawford, do your duty," Harold instructed.

"I know very well what my duties are, Mr. Wilson."

Harold's complexion reddened. "Of course. I didn't mean to offend you. I just want to end this unfortunate affair." He waved a hand toward Jennifer. "Take her away."

"Problems, Jen?"

The familiar, deep voice made her heart skip a beat. She spun around toward the door and saw Stuart and Julio on the threshold.

Banning stood behind them.

CHAPTER SIXTEEN

Stuart walked to Jennifer's side and put an arm around her. "Why didn't you wait for me?"

Surprise made her blink. "Well . . . I didn't . . ."

He bent and gave her a gentle kiss. "It doesn't matter. I'm here now."

Banning stepped toward the officers. "If you'll come with me, gentlemen, we'll settle this matter."

"Who are you, sir?" the sergeant asked.

"Walter Banning, attorney at law." He retrieved an envelope from an inner pocket. "I have a release order for Miss Denton, signed by Judge Saunders."

Harold jumped forward. "What nonsense is this, Banning?"

"Exactly what I said, Mr. Wilson. The judge of the state supreme court hereby remands Miss Denton to my custody."

"You won't get away with this!" Harold blustered.

"I'm not the one who's trying to get away with something, Mr. Wilson." Banning turned to the officers. "Come with me, gentlemen. I have other documents to show you that I think you'll find interesting."

"Wait!" Harold pointed toward Stuart. "That man is Stuart Kendall."

Crawford turned toward Stuart. "Is that true?"

"Yes."

"In that case, I must take you into custody."

"Not so hasty, officer," Banning put in. "I also have a court order from the judge regarding Mr. Kendall."

Crawford held out a hand for the document. A short time later, he nodded to Stuart and then accompanied Banning and the sergeant from the drawing room.

Julio followed them.

Harold swung around toward Stuart. "I should have realized who you were when Phil described the bearded man." His gaze stabbed Jennifer. "Have you no shame?"

Stuart turned to look at Harold. "That's an interesting question, coming from you."

"What was I to believe? I saw men coming in here at odd hours and staying upstairs with Jennifer." Harold straightened. "This household has always stood for morality and decency."

"Not since you moved in," Stuart commented.

A dull red crept into the older man's cheeks. "You would say anything to protect her, but it won't stop me from pursuing my legal right."

"You have no legal rights where Jen is concerned."

"How about battery?" Harold pointed to the marks on Barbara's cheek. "She struck my daughter."

Stuart nodded. "Good cure for hysteria."

"Barbara has never been hysterical in her life."

"I've seen it before, Harold," Jennifer said. "I'm a nurse, remember?"

Harold gazed angrily at Jennifer. "You're not fit to raise the Wilson heir. I don't know how you got around the charges of theft, but I intend to start proceedings to become Johnny's guardian."

"He's my son," Stuart corrected.

"What kind of a father are you? Gone all the time, associating with the scum of the earth. And now you're conducting a sordid affair in a dwelling where your son resides, and with the person charged with his care." Harold snorted. "When a proper court hears my testimony, Jennifer won't be able to get a job scrubbing floors."

Stuart stared at him until Harold's gaze slid away. "You're a spineless old man, but that won't keep me from breaking your neck."

Harold took an involuntary step backward. "You dare touch me and I'll have you arrested."

"If you're able to summon help."

"You're my witness, Phil," Harold said.

One look from Stuart and Phil slunk back behind his father. "He carries a gun, Dad. I saw it."

"I don't think your son wants his neck broken, either," Stuart said.

"You can't come in here and threaten us," Harold pointed to the hall. "The police are right out there."

"You have five seconds to apologize to Jen."

The underlying steel in Stuart's voice made Jennifer shiver. She glanced toward Harold. He looked pale and sick.

"Four seconds."

Barbara began to moan.

"Three seconds."

Phil grabbed his father's arm. "He means it!"

"Two seconds."

"Sorry . . . Jen." Harold licked his lips and reached up with trembling fingers to loosen his tie. "Sorry."

Stuart reached into his jacket and pulled out an envelope. "Let's talk about Simon Blount."

Jennifer didn't think it possible for Harold's face to turn any paler, but it did.

"Too late now . . . can't . . . do anything . . . about it," he stammered.

"What is it, Stuart?" she asked.

"Papers leveling a charge against you for having a less than exemplary character." Stuart waved the envelope in Harold's direction. "You instructed Blount to institute charges against Jen, but he had second thoughts and surrendered the papers to Banning." Stuart smiled. "At this moment, Blount is on a plane to Paris."

The older man's mouth worked, but no words came out.

Stuart stepped back and slipped an arm around Jennifer's shoulders. "You're through, Harold. Find somewhere else for your family to live."

"It isn't fair." Barbara shrugged free of her father's arm. "Little Miss Nothing wins again."

"Shut up, Barb," her brother warned.

"Don't tell me to shut up." She pointed a finger at her father. "You're worse than your son."

"Now, now, my dear," Harold soothed. "You're overwrought."

She made a face. "Where did you dig that one up?"

"Come upstairs, Barbara."

"No." Her slender body trembled with anger. She swung around to face Jennifer. "This is your doing. It's your fault. Since the first day, you worked against us."

"That isn't true."

"All those months, spying on us." Harold put a hand on his daughter's shoulder, but she jerked away. "Roger would have married me, but he found out we didn't get the money."

Harold sent a look toward his son.

Phil stepped forward. "Come on, Barb. Let's go upstairs."

Barbara scowled at Jennifer. "Hate you . . . make you pay."

Phil took hold of her arm. "Come on, Sis."

She whipped her other arm around and dug her nails into her brother's face leaving long scratches. He yelped in pain. His hand lashed out and hit her cheek.

Barbara's features contorted with fury. She drew back her arm, slapped her brother, and then stared down at him from her superior height until Phil's gaze slid away from hers. Her lips curled with contempt. "You spineless weakling!"

"That's enough from both of you."

Harold grabbed an arm of each of his children and hustled them out of the drawing room. At the door, Barbara turned and sent a malevolent look at Jennifer, before her father pulled her away.

"That girl is close to certifiable," Stuart murmured.

"I had no idea Barbara hated me so much."

"She hates everything, most of all herself." He looked down at Jennifer. "What's wrong?"

He had always dodged her questions. As he himself said, he was an accomplished liar. Evasion was his specialty, but the time for that was over. One way or another, once and for all time, she had to know the truth.

"That detective told me the police suspect you of belonging to a band of mercenaries trying to overthrow the government."

Stuart hesitated, as though trying to decide how much to tell her. He pointed to the chairs by the fireplace. "Let's sit."

She sat down opposite him and waited for him to speak.

"My duties take me from the jungles of Africa to the Arctic Circle. The special nature of my assignments made it necessary to create a background for these activities."

"You allow people to believe you're a traitor?"

"Yes."

The implications of his words made her frown. "Then I did the wrong thing when I refused to allow the telephone tap. I made him suspicious."

"Probably. There's something you have to face, Jen. Wherever you go, you'll never be safe. Eventually, Garizon or one of his men will be after you again."

Fear skittered down her back. "You're scaring me."

"I'm scaring myself, as well."

Realization was slow in coming. When it did, she gave a shocked gasp. "I made your job more difficult, didn't I?"

"Ah . . . now you begin to see."

"This job you have," she asked, "why do you do it?"

"Someone has to."

"That's no answer."

"Did you ever think what life would be like in this country if there were no people like me?"

"Until I met you, I was happily ignorant about your kind of work, but now there's something I have to know. Have you killed?"

"No one chooses to kill, Jen."

"Scruples?"

"Practicality. A live agent can tell you things. A dead one can't."

She shivered. "It sounds so bloodthirsty."

"Killing is usually the last resort, for both sides."

"You'd rather have someone to torture?"

His mouth thinned. "I've never tortured anyone."

"I'm sorry. I didn't mean that the way it sounded . . ." She paused. "If I ask you a question, will you answer it?"

"If I can."

Jennifer frowned. "You won't answer honestly?"

"I'll tell you what I can."

"You still don't trust me, do you?"

"This isn't a matter of trust, Jen."

"It is to me. I've proven you can trust me."

"What is it you want to know?"

"Garizon said you killed his brother. Is that why he's after you?"

"That's part of it, but I didn't kill his brother."

"But he was so sure you did."

"His own men did it, Jen. I overheard them talking back at

the warehouse."

She nodded. "You said that was part of it. What's the rest?"

"Garizon is second in command of a drug cartel. He came to the United States to set up a distribution and money laundering operation. He's a wanted man in Panama."

"How does that involve you?"

"There are loyal Panamanians who want to get rid of Garizon and his boss, and I know who they are."

She said, barely above a whisper, "That's why he . . . he worked on your back, to make you tell him their names."

"Yes." Stuart took a long breath and then said, "There's something else I have to tell you."

A discreet cough made her jump. Roberts stood in the doorway. "Excuse me, ma'am. Dinner is served."

A reprieve and no more, but Jennifer accepted it eagerly. "Will you have dinner with me, Stuart?" Fearful he'd say something she didn't want to hear, she arose from the chair. "Please?"

Her smile willed him to play the game, to wait until after their meal.

He stood and stepped to her side. "My pleasure."

She looked toward the butler. "We'll eat now."

"Very good, ma'am." Robert bowed and turned away.

"Give me five minutes, Jen. I want to make a call."

"Okay."

"I'll be right back."

Stuart stepped into the empty library and got out his phone. After two rings, a voice said, "Office hours are eight until five."

"This is *Sombra*. Anything to report?"

"The next feature starts in half an hour."

Stuart said, "Understood."

"We'll call you as soon as we have the answers."

Stuart ended the call. If all went according to plan, Garizon would soon be in custody.

In the dining room, Stuart seated Jennifer on his right and then sat down in the chair she indicated. Roberts waved the servers forward before walking to the serving cart for a bottle of wine. He presented the bottle to Stuart for inspection and then poured a small amount into a glass.

Stuart took a sip. "Where did you get this wine?"

"One of the best suppliers, sir," the butler replied.

"The bouquet's all wrong."

Roberts smiled politely. "Perhaps you're not familiar with French wines, sir."

The butler's eyebrows formed two, amazed arcs when Stuart began speaking French. Jennifer spoke rudimentary French, but it sounded to her as though Stuart had nearly perfect command of the language.

Roberts bowed. "I'll get another bottle."

Through the rest of the meal, Stuart continued to surprise her. The confusing array of silverware posed no problem for him. He was at ease and comfortable, despite his casual clothes. While they waited for the serving of the dessert, she said, "I wouldn't be surprised if you told me that you know the Queen of England."

"I've been to Buckingham Palace a few times."

Jennifer's burst of laughter dwindled when he didn't join her. "You aren't joking. Who *are* you, Stuart?"

"Does it matter?"

She took another drink of her coffee. "Most of us live such quiet lives that we can't grasp what it's like to live as you must, always on the move, always on the cutting edge."

He considered that for a moment. "I never thought about my job like that until I talked with some agents, men who've been at it for a long time. They said that, in the work we do, we live one step away from the hereafter. They called it 'the edge of forever.'"

She poured coffee for both of them and gave him a smile.

He stared at her for a moment. "We have to talk."

Jennifer cleared her throat. "Whatever you want to say isn't going to make me happy, is it?"

For the first time since she'd known him, he looked uncomfortable. "I told you how I met and married Martha." He drew in a long breath. "Now I'll tell you the rest."

His voice held a bitter edge she hadn't heard before. Though his anger wasn't directed at her, his grim expression told her that she'd pushed him into telling her something he would have preferred not to divulge.

Apprehension tied knots in her stomach. The next few minutes could spell success or failure for her hopes to be a part of his life.

"After our marriage, Martha's emotional problems became worse. She grew afraid of other people and clung to me like I was the only raft in the middle of the ocean."

Stuart's grim expression said a lot more than his words. Jennifer sympathized with what he had endured.

He stared past her, as though gathering his thoughts. "Perhaps, if I had loved her enough to break down the fence she had built around her emotions, I might have given her the confidence she lacked."

Jennifer felt pity for the woman who'd had so much within her grasp but couldn't take advantage of it. "Good intentions can bind you to a person, Stuart, but they don't generate love."

"I found that out."

He sat for a time studying his coffee, as though the words he wanted to say might lie beneath its creamy surface. "You probably wondered why Johnny was so hostile to you when he first came here."

"Yes, I did think about it. I get along well with children as a rule."

"I'm sure you do." Stuart took a drink of his coffee. "Martha rejected him from the day he was born."

"But Maria said—"

"That Martha was the perfect mother?"

Jennifer nodded.

"The first time I picked Johnny up and held him, I knew I'd made a mistake. Martha wouldn't touch the baby again." His mouth tightened. "I didn't believe a woman could be jealous of her own child."

"A woman can be jealous of anything that diverts the attention of the man she loves."

A thoughtful frown wrinkled Stuart's brow. "Any woman?"

"Any woman," Jennifer replied. "Many new mothers feel vulnerable and depressed after the birth of their child, especially a first child. They expect their husbands to praise their accomplishment and tell them how pretty they are. They don't want to take second place to something they carried inside them for so many months."

Stuart nodded. "I never thought about it that way."

"On his first visit after the birth, a smart man won't notice the baby until his wife calls his attention to it."

"Interesting," Stuart murmured.

"I've always felt sorry for myself because I lost my mother when I was so young. But I have my memories. I can't imagine what it would be like to never know a mother's love."

"Johnny doesn't lack for love."

Stuart's quiet words held no censure, but Jennifer wished she hadn't said those words. "Anyone who sees the two of you together knows that Johnny feels secure in your love."

"When he was learning to walk, he occasionally wandered

close to Martha. She always screamed at him to stay away. He learned to avoid her and cling to Maria." Stuart sipped his coffee and set the cup down. "Neither Martha nor I enjoyed our years together."

"You did what you could to help her."

The dark look flitted across his face again. "You might as well know it all."

Jennifer reached out to put a hand over his. "Tell me."

"Martha got worse during storms. On that last day, I heard the strain in her voice over the telephone, so I left the embassy early. We had a meal, but she didn't eat much. She sat in the chair, looking up at the ceiling and jumping at every rumble of thunder."

"I've had patients who did that," Jennifer commented.

"After dinner I had to leave for an assignment. Martha pleaded to go with me. She said she wanted to help me in some way. I told her I couldn't take her along. About that time, someone knocked on the door, a man who brought me information from time to time. He told me that Garizon's people had planted mines around my house. When I asked for more information, he ran away."

"What did you do?"

"It wasn't the first time I'd heard about mines around the house. I headed for my study to get some papers I needed to take with me. Martha called out that she knew how to help me. Then I heard the front door slam."

"She ran out of the house?"

"Yes. I ran after her, but I had to wait for a flash of lightning to see which way she went. I saw her running toward the river and started after her. She was about fifty feet ahead of me when she stepped on a mine."

Jennifer's fingers tightened upon his.

"I was the one they wanted to kill." He expelled his breath.

"Because of me, Martha's dead."

Jennifer put her other hand over his. "It isn't your fault, Stuart. Martha had problems. You can't blame yourself because she ran out into the night."

He shook his head. "Words, Jen."

"Johnny didn't see anything, did he?"

"No." Stuart studied her face. "Well, now you know. I have enemies who will stop at nothing to get what they want."

"It must have been terrible for you."

"Once will suffice."

She stared back at him while a suspicion grew to certainty. "What are you saying?"

"Martha died because of me."

"You can't believe that."

"I swore when I buried her that I'd never be the cause of another woman's death."

Stuart set down his cup and walked to the door.

"Where are you going?"

He said, over his shoulder, "To see what Johnny wants for Christmas."

Stuart adjusted the covers over his son and sat down on the edge of the bed. "How are you doing, Johnny? Are you happy with Jennifer and Mrs. Ashton?"

"Yes, Daddy." He stared up at his father. "Will they always look after me?"

"No." Stuart thought about that for a moment. "Nothing lasts for always."

"I'm afraid, Daddy." Johnny's eyes grew bright with unshed tears. "When you go away again, will Jennifer also go away and leave me?"

Stuart leaned down and scooped the boy into his arms. "Don't worry, son." He smoothed back an errant lock of hair from Johnny's forehead. "Jennifer will be around for a while."

"I want her to stay. I love her."

"I'm glad to hear that."

Johnny leaned back to look up at his father's face. "Do you love her too?"

Stuart said simply, "Yes, Johnny. I do."

"Will you marry her?"

"I have things to do, son. I must finish my work before I think of anything else." Stuart heard his phone ringing, dug it out of his pocket, and tapped the appropriate place. "This is *Sombra.*"

"We're batting one thousand."

He released his held breath in a gush. "That's good news."

"All accounted for, *Sombra.* Repeat. All accounted for."

"Understood." He turned off his phone and put it back in his pocket.

"Do you have to go away, Daddy?"

"No, son. This was my last job." Stuart gave the small boy a hug. "I won't be leaving you anymore. From now on, I'm going to be a regular dad."

Jennifer sat at the table. Stuart had told her goodbye, and he meant it. He wouldn't put her safety in jeopardy, but she had to make him understand.

"I love you, Stuart, and I'm going to be your wife," she whispered.

She pushed back her chair and left the dining room.

Jennifer entered the bedroom of the Rose Suite and headed for a cabinet against the wall. She took down a roll of Christmas paper, cut a suitable length, and fastened it around her waist with sticky tape. Taking a large red bow out of a drawer, she stuck it at her waist and turned to look at herself in the mirror. She looked like a Christmas present.

Smiling with pleasure, she headed for the nursery.

When she entered the nursery, Stuart turned around and held a finger up to his lips. "Johnny's asleep." He stared at her for a moment and then murmured, "How did you know what I wanted for Christmas?"

That sounded promising, but Jennifer meant to make her feelings plain. "You might as well accept it, Stuart. I'm part of your life now. I love you and I intend to be your wife and Johnny's mother."

He moved forward and gathered her into his arms.

His kiss was everything she'd ever dreamed a kiss could be. She smiled up at him. "Don't tell me any of that nonsense about not wanting to put me in danger. Whatever you have to do, Stuart, go and do it. Then you can quit. The three of us have all of our lives ahead of us."

"Where did you learn so much about people, Miss Denton?"

"Chapter Two of the nurse's manual."

That called for another marvelous kiss.

"I'm not Martha. Whatever comes our way, I can handle it. You can trust me, Stuart."

His green eyes glowed with tenderness. "Don't you think I know that?" He bent and gave her a gentle kiss. "I'd trust you with my life."

Jennifer leaned her head against his chest and slipped her arms around his waist. "Julio told me about his family."

"To my knowledge, he never told anyone else." After a moment Stuart added, "I don't think Garizon meant to harm them."

"You almost sound as though you're defending him."

"I am, in a way."

"But he tried to kill you."

"Yes, I know." Stuart bent to kiss the edge of her mouth. "I had a call a few minutes ago. Federal authorities raided a secret meeting of Garizon's drug distributors and took them into custody. More of his men arrived tonight. They were arrested as soon as they stepped off the plane."

"What does that mean?"

"It means the word will go out, discreetly, that I'm no longer a double agent."

Joy widened her smile "It's over?"

"Yes. Garizon is in custody. This was my last assignment."

"You can tell me all about it later." She reached up to put her arms around his neck. "Right now, Mr. Kendall, I want you to attend to more important matters."

His arms tightened around her ribs. "Yes, ma'am."

ABOUT THE AUTHOR

Nancy Kelley draws upon her rich background as a mathematics teacher and as a computer systems consultant for the Department of Defense to portray people in complex and stressful situations. Nancy is a graduate of West Virginia University and is currently working on her sixth novel, *A Perilous Bargain*.